THE COLDEST CASE

Tessa Wegert

SEVERN HOUSE

First world edition published in Great Britain and the USA in 2024
by Severn House, an imprint of Canongate Books Ltd,
14 High Street, Edinburgh EH1 1TE.

severnhouse.com

Copyright © Tessa Wegert, 2024

All rights reserved including the right of
reproduction in whole or in part in any form.
The right of Tessa Wegert to be identified
as the author of this work has been asserted
in accordance with the Copyright,
Designs & Patents Act 1988.

British Library Cataloguing-in-Publication Data
A CIP catalogue record for this title is available from the British Library.

ISBN-13: 978-1-4483-1423-2 (cased)
ISBN-13: 978-1-4483-1424-9 (e-book)

This is a work of fiction. Names, characters, places and incidents are either the product of the author's imagination or are used fictitiously. Except where actual historical events and characters are being described for the storyline of this novel, all situations in this publication are fictitious and any resemblance to actual persons, living or dead, business establishments, events or locales is purely coincidental.

All Severn House titles are printed on acid-free paper.

Typeset by Palimpsest Book Production Ltd.,
Falkirk, Stirlingshire, Scotland.
Printed and bound in Great Britain by TJ Books,
Padstow, Cornwall.

THE COLDEST CASE

Also by Tessa Wegert

The Shana Merchant novels

DEATH IN THE FAMILY
THE DEAD SEASON
DEAD WIND *
THE KIND TO KILL *
DEVILS AT THE DOOR *
THE COLDEST CASE *

* *available from Severn House*

Praise for the Shana Merchant novels

"Both a satisfying stand-alone and a compelling continuation of [Shana Merchant's] deeply absorbing journey. Ice-pick sharp and superbly sneaky"
SUSAN WALTER, bestselling author of *Good as Dead*

"Tense. Sharp. Gripping. Tessa Wegert [is] one of the foremost crime writers of our time"
JULIA BARTZ, *New York Times* bestselling author of *The Writing Retreat*

"No one today is writing locked room mysteries like Tessa Wegert – claustrophobic, heart-stopping, twisting like the frozen surface of the St. Lawrence"
JULIA SPENCER-FLEMING, *New York Times* bestselling author of *Hid From Our Eyes*

"Another exhilarating installment in the Shana Merchant series that treats readers to the kind of riveting, deeply felt narrative found in the very finest thriller fiction"
E.G. SCOTT, international bestselling author of *The Rule of Three*

"A chilling and propulsive addition to one of the most bingeable detective series going"
VANESSA LILLIE, bestselling author of *Blood Sisters*

"A compelling, unique mystery with twists I never saw coming. I couldn't put it down"
SAMANTHA DOWNING, bestselling author of *My Lovely Wife*, on *Devils at the Door*

"Stellar . . . Rich characterization, and a compelling circle of suspects"
SARAH STEWART TAYLOR, author of the Maggie D'arcy mysteries, on *Devils at the Door*

"An extremely well-written crime novel"
Booklist on *Devils at the Door*

"[Wegert has] rightly earned the badge as one of the finest talents of the past three years"
The Strand Magazine on *The Kind to Kill*

"[A] standout crime thriller . . . Fans of DENISE MINA's Alex Morrow will be pleased"
Publishers Weekly Starred Review of *Dead Wind*

About the author

Tessa Wegert is the author of the Shana Merchant series of mysteries. A former freelance journalist, Tessa has contributed to such publications as *Forbes*, *The Huffington Post*, *Adweek*, *The Economist*, and *The Globe and Mail*. Tessa grew up in Quebec and now lives with her husband and children in Connecticut, where she studies martial arts and is currently at work on her next novel.

tessawegert.com
Facebook: TessaWegertBooks
Twitter/X: TessaWegert
Instagram: TessaWegert

For you, dear reader

I hope you enjoy the ride

PROLOGUE

East Village, New York City

Four Years Ago

The dead woman was smiling, mouth tipped in a way that made her look friendly. Tender. Good. *Guesswork*, I thought, but the full-color sketch was strong, the forensic artist going beyond bones to animate the victim. Breathe life into what little remained. She would never smile that way again, reduced now to a bloated corpse. This woman from the water.

The body had been fished from the East River, found by a man walking his Bichon Frisé. I was on the catching schedule for homicides, which meant that for the next two weeks, I'd be focused on nothing but the new case. With no ID, she'd become a Jane Doe, but I was hopeful the disappearance of a woman her age, in that neighborhood, hadn't gone unreported. Of course, there were no guarantees. Violent crime was still up in Alphabet City. The area was gentrified, all craft cocktail lounges and 'upper bohemians' now, but I couldn't rule out the possibility that Jane had been living hard. Either way, she'd been abandoned. Swallowed by the river like a baptism gone wrong.

The medical examiner's report was on my desk, and something in it didn't translate to the sketch on the screen. MEs always included key details on differentiating characteristics: tattoos, piercings, disfigurements worthy of note. Jane Doe, whoever she was, possessed a facial wound. I was told the cut had been made postmortem. My fingers drifted to my own face as I read.

Jane bore a violent gash on her cheek that mimicked a seam come undone.

Squint, and she looked a little like me.

ONE

Alexandria Bay, New York

Now

'No! Let go!' She screamed it, her voice shrill and rough. Her heel had connected with the man's foot, the knock strong enough to fold him at the waist, but it was what came next that mattered most. Only when the girl braced her hands, shoved him backward, and took off at a sprint did my shoulders ease up. Her technique was getting better, response time on the uptick too, but the message we wanted to leave her with was this: if given the chance, always turn and run.

'That makes no sense,' the student, a freshman dusted with orange freckles, said. 'What's the point of teaching us self-defense if all we do is run away?'

'The point,' I replied, 'is that you don't always get the *chance* to run. The skills we're teaching you create that opportunity. Provide an escape hatch. Out there' – I gestured at the walls of the gym, toward the wider world outside – 'physical combat has consequences. Trust us, you don't want a fight. Not even with decades of training.'

'Not even you guys?' She widened her eyes at me and Sam.

'Not even us,' said my sensei, smiling as he puffed out his chest.

Sam finished the class the same way he did when I came to his dojo in Watertown, asking the students to bow first to him, then to each other. And like always, several kids hung back, elbows jabbing ribs until someone found the courage to speak up. The freshmen kept their distance from the dark stuff; their queries were about when I'd be getting my black belt, or how long it took to become a detective. I always answered honestly and kept my tone light. They were children, after all, barely out of middle school, and I was the woman whose name they'd heard spoken in urgent tones by parents, barbers, shop clerks in the context of violent crime close at hand. I wondered if they remembered what was said in the early days, when I first got to Alexandria Bay. If they did, they were polite enough to hide it.

No, freshmen never stressed me out. The juniors and seniors were another story. Every now and then they'd ask about my niece, now a junior herself. Henrietta had moved back to Vermont over Christmas break to finish the school year in Burlington, but she'd left an impression on the student population in A-Bay. On me, too. When Sam and I taught kids on the verge of adulthood, I got the odd question about murder. What was it like to arrest someone you knew had taken a life? *Satisfying*, I'd reply, and sometimes that was enough. But I knew what they were really asking.

What's it like to be related to one of the worst killers of all?

One day, someone would muster the mettle to ask it. And when they did, I had no idea what I would say.

As the freshmen dispersed and Sam packed up the kick pads he'd used to demo strikes, I spotted Courtney waving from the gym door. 'You're doing a wonderful job, both of you,' Tim's stepmother said, sleek blonde hair hanging down to her waist. 'The administration is so happy with this program, I can't even tell you. We've had positive feedback from parents, too.'

'I'm just window dressing. It's all him.' I'd been attending Sensei Sam's karate classes on and off since moving to the area, and his teaching style was the best I'd seen. 'But thanks,' I said, 'That's great to hear.'

I'd asked Courtney, who worked as school secretary, to let me know how the program was being received. It had been my idea to propose it, though Sam was on board from day one. Martial arts had been part of my routine for years and had become a life raft, the techniques I'd learned from Sam and others fundamental to my survival. Karate kept me afloat, and spending almost four months with Hen and her friends had reminded me how important self-defense was for teens. The school, I'd been told, had featured me in their parent newsletter: *As a Senior Investigator with the New York State Police's Bureau of Criminal Investigation, Shana Merchant says she wants to 'give back to the community by teaching students to defend themselves against the real-world dangers beyond A-Bay.'* In truth, I'd seen Hen and her friends try to fend off threats like those right here in town. No amount of training was enough. But this was a start.

'You're doing well, hon?' Courtney's eyes got serious, her round, ruddy face cinching like a pouch. 'We think about you constantly, Dori and me. Are you taking good care of yourself?'

I reached for the woman's arm, gave it a squeeze. 'With Tim for a husband, is there any other way?'

'You do have a point. Whoops, I see that you're needed.' Courtney's gaze skimmed past me to the young girl waiting down the hall and I caught a flash of rainbow braces.

'See you Friday?' I asked Courtney. 'Sam and I are tackling wrist grabs with the juniors.'

'Then I'll see you twice! You're still coming for dinner that night, right?'

I hugged her and said, 'We'll be there.'

My sneakers squeaked on the linoleum tiles, conspicuous. By the time I'd made my way to the girl, she had crossed her arms.

'So?' she said. 'Have you got it?'

'What, you mean this?' I reached into my backpack and pulled out a brown bag. 'If I didn't know better, I'd say you were using me for my baked goods.'

Bobby grinned and shrugged but didn't answer, her mouth already full of the chocolate muffin Tim had baked the previous night. In a way, I was using Bobby too. I hadn't expected to miss Hen as much as I did once she went back to my brother's place in Vermont, but the house I shared with Tim felt punched through with silence. Surrounding myself with adolescent verve was an effective distraction, and like the five-week mini-course on self-defense we were teaching at the school, my time with my new investigator's daughter helped fill a void. Like that chocolate muffin, Bobby Ott had become my fix.

There was another reason why I'd offered to drive Bobby home a few times a week. It wasn't long ago that A-Bay parents would have taken up arms to keep me away from their kids. Every passing day put more distance between the locals and Blake Bram, but small towns have long memories. I hoped my volunteer work would scrub away the tarnish that had blackened my name. I might not have a sparkling-clean reputation, but I'd take whatever absolution I could get.

Some offenses could never be forgiven in full.

The North Country was a chameleon, adopting a new skin each season, and over the last month the brittle, twig-brown of fall had been replaced with winter white. Acres of pristine fields unfurled like down blankets, but the roads had gone grimy with use, ice melt bespangling everyone's cars with slush that would stick around until spring. I could hear its splatter as I drove, a wet, uninterrupted drone beneath the tires of my SUV.

It was after three by the time I dropped off Bobby at Val's place and made it to the barracks. I wasn't there to punch a clock – only Tim and Val were on duty today – but despite its dry heat and salt-stained floors, the State Police station kept calling me back.

'How was class?' Tim asked as I clicked the door shut behind me. The weather had been brutal, two straight weeks of bone-numbing cold the likes of which the area hadn't seen in years, but indoors, I found myself overheating. Tim watched with amusement as I wrested off my winter coat, shedding the season's confining second skin.

Despite the familiar setting, or maybe because of it, seeing Tim lit up my chest like a flare. Two months we'd been married, our red and white midwinter wedding at the Sackets Harbor Ballroom still a freshly cut bloom, and even in the most mundane of moments, it astounded me that he was mine.

'Class,' I said, 'is as exhausting as everything else these days, but man, do I love it. Every kid should learn self-defense. That's my new mantra, the hill I'll die on.' The fact that I hadn't thought to implement the program in the fall pained me. Maybe if my niece and her friends had known how to defend themselves, things would have played out differently. 'Where's Val?' I asked, scanning the room for our colleague as I dropped into a desk chair. 'Bobby's home safe and sound.'

'Break room. Cup of decaf?'

'I'm good. Courtney says hi, by the way,' I told Tim. 'We've got that dinner on Friday.'

His eyebrows quirked. 'Will there be French onion dip?' It was his moms' new go-to recipe for guests, the caramelized onion spread served with salt-and-pepper ripple chips, and Tim was obsessed.

I opened my mouth to tell him I was sure dip could be arranged, but something stopped me short. A mechanical whir in the distance, tinny and muffler-gruff, coming from the main road. It wasn't the snowmobile that alarmed me – they roamed the area in herds, crisscrossing icy farmland until the crisp, bluish powder looked like scratched glass. What curbed my reply and brought us both to the front window was the shouting.

The shouting was also what told me the figure now stumbling across the parking lot was a woman. Given the insulated snowmobile suit and helmet, it would have been impossible to gauge gender by sight, but her pitch and resonance spoke volumes. The State Police barracks on Route 12 had a small lobby, and by the time Tim and I got up front she was in it, pummeling the on-duty trooper with a chain of harried words.

'We need help. Out on Running Pine.' The woman was nearly breathless. She flipped up her tinted shield to reveal teal eyes outlined in black liner and glittering with apprehension.

'Afternoon, ma'am. I'm Tim Wellington, and this is Shana Merchant. We're investigators with the State Police.' Tim extended his hand and held the stranger's just long enough to convey a promise of the security she seemed desperate to find, though she must have noticed the lines of concern etched into his face. They'd deepened in the three years since I'd met him. I tried not to take that personally. 'Did you say you came from Running Pine?'

'Yes. I'm Jane. Jane Budd.'

'You a year-rounder out there?'

Her helmet bobbed. 'That's right.'

I said, 'Tell us what's going on, Jane.'

She pulled in a juddering breath. 'My neighbor – Cary Caufield – he's missing. We think he may have fallen through the ice.'

'When?' asked Tim.

'This morning. Sometime between ten and noon.'

I felt the hot intensity of Tim's gaze, and did my best not to meet it. February in the Thousand Islands, and it was one of the coldest on record. It was also after two p.m. If there had been an accident on the frozen St Lawrence hours ago, then Cary Caufield was almost certainly already dead.

I had yet to set foot on Running Pine, but what I knew about the island made my anxiety spike. More than five thousand acres of thick woods and farmland, it was one of the few islands in the area where people overwintered, the only one with a multi-family community of year-round residents. For as long as anyone could remember, a handful of cabin owners chose to stay on rather than head back to shore with the summer people who took their families back to Rochester, Boston, New York when leaves turned gold and temperatures fell. I'd heard the stories – legends, really – about the hardy souls who made do with what they had on a land mass with no bridge or ferry. I knew Running Pine was sometimes inaccessible for days, even weeks, at a time. According to Jane, there were just eight people overwintering this year. Eight people, one of whom had gone fishing at dawn and still hadn't returned.

There's a difference between missing and presumed dead. A sudden, unexplained absence doesn't always end with a coroner, but it always, always begins with questions. Where was the individual last seen? Who were they with? Could they be in danger? It took little effort to determine that Cary Caufield was at risk.

Tim said, 'And you came here by snowmobile? All the way from Running Pine? That must have taken an hour.' As he said it, I noticed that Jane was shaking despite the jumpsuit and electric heat.

I said, 'Do you not have cell service out there?' The State Police had access to an ice boat – an airboat, to be specific – that was used to traverse the river in the winter months. If Jane had called us from the island when she first learned her neighbor was missing, we'd have a rescue team there by now. A recovery team, if nothing else. Why had the islanders waited so long to report this?

'We do,' Jane said. 'We all have phones. His girlfriend, Sylvie, didn't want to call 911.'

'Why not?'

'She didn't know who she'd get. She only wants to talk to you.'

Jane was looking at me as she said it.

I dropped my hands to my stomach.

Things had changed over the last month. The bump was visible now, straining against my sky-blue button-down. I was in that awkward stage when my belly looked like a prosthetic, its concentrated roundness making the rest of my body appear too thin. There was no hiding that I was pregnant anymore, not from the troopers Tim and I worked with daily, or the students at the high school, or even the barista at the Bean-In coffee shop. When Jane's gaze followed the trajectory of my arms, her eyes got a little wider.

'She wants to talk to Shana?' That was Tim, thinking ahead. Concerned already, about me and the baby out there on the ice. There wasn't much field work to be done in A-Bay this time of year, but I hadn't put myself on desk duty yet, either. If a case came up, I intended to work it. Tim had a different attitude about my current state. Once or twice, he'd caught me tripping over my own feet, an uncharacteristic clumsiness that would be less entertaining three miles from town with a subzero river as the only access route.

Jeremy Solomon, a long-time investigator in my troop, once described something called frazil, a type of ice intent on making winter boating even more deadly. *A snowstorm in the water*, Sol had called it, which didn't sound good at all. Weak spots and ice jams were a concern too, and the wind chill was even worse in the open. Ice cover wasn't always a given, fluctuating water temps being what they were, but this year could hardly have been colder.

Tim and I had a view of the St Lawrence from our antique Victorian on Otter Creek. We spent a lot of time at the table by the window, doing puzzles and playing cards while a fire hissed and spit in the hearth. Insulated from the snow-draped world outside. The river was a polar desert now, dotted with fishing shanties and the occasional coywolf. The local paper had reported that packs of the coyote-wolf hybrid were being observed across the county, but all I'd ever witnessed was a lone hunter, slush-gray against glittering white. As light as that coywolf was on its feet, seeing it alone on the ice always tightened my chest. A swift current beneath the surface was all it would take to cause a crack that freed frigid water, and when that happened the river, so pleasantly fresh in summer, would rear up to swallow that solitary creature in one hungry gulp.

Jane's uneasy gaze bounced around the room, only landing on my face when I asked her why. Why me, when we had Tim and Sol and Valerie Ott, brand new to Troop D but a skilled investigator all the same.

'There's a whole team here,' Tim added. 'We'll get you the help you need.'

'No. I'm sorry.' Jane's heavy helmet swung back and forth. 'It has to be her. Sylvie specifically asked – *begged* – me to bring back Shana Merchant.'

If history had taught me anything, it was to move quickly. There would be time for more questions down the line, but every second spent here at the barracks might be another second ticking off Cary Caufield's life.

I knew Tim was thinking the same thing. This was all feeling familiar: the urgent call to investigate an accident on an island, the missing man. Three years ago, when I first moved to A-Bay, I'd sat at my desk and listened to Tim say we'd need to take a boat ride to Tern Island, violent weather be damned. I'd rushed out there with him, not so much as a thought for my own welfare, or even for his.

So much had changed since then. Now, it was Val who was new to the troop, a fledgling A-Bayer ripe for initiation. There were other less senior plainclothes detectives champing at the bit to take my place.

What was more, the situation made me queasy. Though spending time at the high school always served as a reminder of my notoriety, this woman's request didn't feel like admiration. Instead, it smacked of some creepy obsession with true crime. With *me*. I didn't think it likely that Sylvie, whoever she was, had simulated a criminal act just to get me to the island, but Jane's insistence that I make the trip didn't sit right. A man was missing. We were wasting time.

'I'll call Clayton,' said Tim. 'With any luck, the airboat's already on the river.'

'And I'll get Val,' I said, turning back toward the door.

Jane's gaze pinged between us. 'Oh no, please don't go. I left her with Emmeline, but Sylvie's frantic. You have to help. We have to *hurry*.'

'You're in good hands,' I told Jane. 'We have an experienced team. They'll find your friend.'

'But—'

'They can handle this,' I assured her. 'I promise.'

Jane's uncertainty was writ large, her features scrunched, but the wheels were already in motion. Tim would summon Val, and place a call to the Clayton Fire Company. As I waited with Jane, though, I knew how helpless she felt.

Out there on the river, a community no bigger than my own extended family was making a life for themselves under some of the harshest conditions imaginable. It was the ultimate exercise in survival. I wanted to understand their situation.

I wanted to know how one of these island residents had been separated from the pack.

TWO

I wasn't afraid of the cold. Growing up in Northern Vermont, not far from the Quebec border, the skills required to defend against frostbite were a birthright, numb toes and ice-encrusted nose hairs as familiar as the crack of an axe on a log. In that respect, adjusting to life in Upstate New York had been easy.

The chill rolling across the frozen river was like nothing I'd ever known. As I stood at the dock in Clayton, squinting at the dark smear on the horizon that was Running Pine, my eyes were frozen marbles, unblinking in the stark winter light while the wind threatened to lash the skin right off my face.

I'd seen this part of the river in recent weeks, when Tim and I came to Clayton for dinner – he liked the poutine at the bar near Frink Park – but it was even more striking in daylight. On the ice, a row of pine trees stood like fenceposts, stretching from the mainland all the way to the island. Eight residents weren't a lot, but they needed to make supply runs. That's where the trees came in. Tim had explained it all over gravy-soaked, cheese-curd-studded fries: Every January, a couple of the islanders collected discarded Christmas trees in Clayton, augered holes, and planted them to mark the safest path from shore to shore. *The good ice*, they called it, these people for whom the desolate island was home. Upon every visit to Dillon's Pub in town, they'd collect empty beer cans to decorate the trees. Those cans would catch the light from the highbeams of their snowmobiles, should they need to make the three-mile journey at night. When I first heard about it, the rough and ready tradition had seemed like a novelty. Some holdover from a bygone century that endured due to nostalgia more than anything else. Now, that makeshift highway was about to help keep Val, a team of first responders, and my husband alive. My gratitude for these mysterious islanders ran deep.

'You know what I'm going to tell you,' my mother had said on the phone a week prior. 'It's one thing to put yourself in harm's way – which, as you know, I don't enjoy one bit – but you have the baby to think of now. Let Tim and Val take the lead for a change.'

'Oh, I intend to,' I'd replied. 'For once, I'm happy to watch from the cheap seats. And you can hold me to that.'

So far, I'd managed to keep my promise. I was hanging back while my team took the risks. The problem, of course, was that Tim's life meant as much to me as my own. He was my partner in every way, about to become a father, while Val was raising a tween whose dad was miles south in Verona. A case on an island in winter was a danger to everyone involved, so while I was safely planted on shore, watching the airboat pull away, the pact I'd made with my mother offered little comfort. As I stood on that dock, I was blitzed by images of the black trench of water below the ice. North America's third largest river, sucking everything I loved into its silty depths.

Damn, that wind was cold.

I hadn't told my mothers-in-law about the case, knowing Dori and Courtney would worry. I didn't have the information yet to answer the questions that were sure to follow. This trip might be a one and only, or the search might stretch like maple sap on snow, twisting and hardening into a shapeless mass. What I knew: That morning, twenty-seven-year-old Cary Caufield had accompanied two local men ice fishing on Buckhead Bay. Both islanders – one of whom was Jane's husband – had deep roots on the island. After Sylvie reported her boyfriend MIA, the men had searched the fishing site to no avail. It was then that she sent Jane to get help.

Jane had told me all this in the lobby, shivering as much from adrenaline by then as the cold, while Tim and Val mobilized the team. Cary Caufield and Sylvie Lavoy were new to Running Pine, having moved to the island in August. The cabin they lived in had belonged to Sylvie's father, who died the previous summer. She'd visited Running Pine as a kid, but for his part, Cary grew up in Ottawa in a family that didn't spend much time outdoors. Jane was quite sure he'd never even been camping. The island's only two other men, both twice Cary's age, had set up the outing at Cary's request. The morning had been cold but sunny, the ice plenty thick, and when they had enough for the day, Cary insisted on staying.

No one had seen the man since.

Why me? I'd asked, confounded all over again by the time we'd lost to Jane's needless mission.

I don't know, Jane said. *But she insisted.*

Only now, Sylvie Lavoy was getting Tim and Val instead.

Whatever reason she had for wanting me on the island, she was going to have to come to terms with my absence.

As the airboat carrying my team shrunk on the horizon, I hoped I could do the same.

'Lots of activity over on Running Pine.'

The man who sat beside me at the diner counter had thinning hair parted like a tattered curtain, a riotous beard, and the build of a bowling ball. He used one hand to fork chicken parmesan into his mouth while the other sopped up marinara sauce with a hunk of oily bread.

Local interest in the traffic to and from the island was the least of my concerns, but I knew there would be chatter. It wasn't every day you saw an airboat on the ice, and emergency vessels always spawned rumors. Cary Caufield's disappearance hadn't yet made the news, but the man beside me was likely one of many Clayton residents who'd noticed Tim and the crew loading into the boat.

Tim had pledged to keep me updated on the search, and had already texted once to let me know he was OK. Even so, I remained on edge. The Clayton Fire Company's summer boat was called *Last Chance*, but the one Tim had taken was known as *sNO Chance*, which did little to allay my nerves. I'd been told the New York State Police used to have an airboat of our own, but with the craft's high center of gravity and tendency to tip if you hit a pressure ridge, it had proven too treacherous for the uninitiated. Now the fire team in Clayton loaned us theirs, complete with an expert operator, a young man known to everyone as Steady Teddy, who Tim had assured me was as good as they come. That day we'd been in Clayton eating poutine, though, he had also told me something else. Traveling by airboat is like riding a hockey puck. It's only smooth until you hit something, and then it all goes sideways.

'You're that woman with the State Police. Merchant, innit?' The man beside me sucked his teeth and nodded at my bump. 'Looks like you got a bun in the oven that's just about cooked. That why you ain't out there too?'

I'd seen this man before. He had the familiarity of a delivery guy; his face sparked recognition, but I couldn't be sure we'd ever talked, or that I'd learned his name. Wherever I knew him from, one thing that felt new to me was his smell. The stench coming off the guy was astounding.

I was almost finished with my linguine alfredo, so I twirled my noodles faster as he studied me. The diner visit had been an attempt to get my mind off Tim and Val, but it wasn't working – and now I faced unwanted conversation with a man who reeked of rotting fish. I could have asked for the check and split, but I had a feeling that would lead to rumors of police evasion. Better to slap on a smile and clean my plate as fast as I could.

'It's nice to meet you, mister . . .'

'Bloom.'

'Mr Bloom. I'm afraid I can't tell you what's going on, but it's nothing you should be concerned about.'

There was a red smear of sauce at the corner of his mouth and crumbs caught in his beard. I set down my fork, reached for my water glass, and sucked up a cube of ice. I hadn't noticed any weird food cravings over the course of my pregnancy to date, but every now and then I got a hankering to chew on ice. After consulting Doctor Google, Tim had insisted I ask my OB whether the obsession might mean I was deficient in iron, but my levels were found to be fine, so he kept me in cubes now. He even went so far as to flavor them, though I liked the plain ones best.

Bloom said, 'Sure. Fine. I guess you don't remember me.'

'I meet a lot of people in my line of work.'

'Oh, we never met,' he told me. 'Just figured you'd know my name.'

Bloom. *Bloom*. A memory glittered on the outskirts of my vision, silvery bright and just out of reach. I started to apologize, but he waved the attempt away as he used the knob of bread to soak up the last of his dinner. The crumbs in his beard reminded me of someone too – but who?

'I just hope it's not that woman.' The sight of half-chewed chicken cutlet in his open mouth nearly made me gag. 'I met her, you know,' he said. 'She was sittin' right where you are now. The pretty little thing who moved out to that island.'

This was something else I'd gotten used to: the townsfolk needing to let me in on their secrets. What they chose to share rarely proved useful; the currency I dealt in was more likely to be socked away. This time, though, in spite of the smell and the food in his beard, I found myself paying attention.

'She's a social media star, you know,' he said, unprompted. 'The girlfriend. She told me that herself. Plans to live out there for a whole year.'

'I'm sorry – a what?'

'She's famous. Like you. She involved in this at all?'

It was possible this man was drunk. Though he smelled more like dead fish than liquor, he was stumbling over his words, slurring some together while others were washed away mid-sentence like loose grains of sand. A social media star? Was he talking about Sylvie?

'I'm sorry,' I said. 'I really can't discuss it.'

Bloom said, 'Bet she is' before hiking his swollen body up off the stool. 'The pretty ones are always trouble.'

As he turned to go, his eyes lingered on my scar.

'Need a refill?'

It was a moment before I registered the new voice, unwilling as I was to turn away until the man was gone. When I spun my stool back around, I was looking at the waitress with frizzled hair and strong cheekbones who'd served me dinner. Her smile was yellowed but sincere.

'Sorry if he was bugging you,' she said. 'He's a talker, but he's harmless. Sprouts from that same stool two or three times a week and waits like a trap for a fly.'

'What's his story?' I asked.

'Billy Bloom? He does something with bait I think, but he's more interested in gossip.'

My jaw unhinged. What Bloom did with bait was use it to trap mink holed up in people's boathouses. I'd never met the man, that was true, but he'd been right. I knew his name. Three years ago, on my first big case with the Bureau of Criminal Investigation, Billy Bloom had been a suspect in the disappearance of Jasper Sinclair. The Sinclair family's caretaker had hired Bloom, ostensibly to rid the boathouse of the pests. It hadn't taken Tim long to dismiss the trapper, having confirmed the man had an alibi. The night Jasper disappeared, Bloom had been drinking at The Riverboat Pub.

It was a crime I thought of often, because of all the cases I'd worked in the Thousand Islands so far, it was the one that truly could have ended me. For more reasons than I could count, I shouldn't have been working it at all – but work it I did, and the outcome had been close to catastrophic. I liked to imagine the investigator who'd gone to that island and come face-to-face with a monster was somebody else, but it was me out there, handing my demons the reins and sitting back while they wreaked havoc. Much as I tried to push those memories away, they never failed to surface like a swollen corpse.

'I thought the name sounded familiar. Pregnancy brain,' I said through an awkward smile. 'You said Bloom likes to gossip. Did he tell you anything about the people on Running Pine?'

Refilling my water glass, she said, 'Not that I recall, but if you want my opinion, they're crazy. My parents used to overwinter on Grenell, before they wised up and moved to Tampa.'

'Grenell. How many houses on that island?'

'About seventy I think, but most years it was only my folks there all winter. They once went a month without seeing another human being.'

'Now that's the test of a relationship.'

She laughed. 'Sure is. It scared the crap out of me, though. Every time they did the crossing, Dad would stand on the dock and ask himself if it was worth it. Do I really need to do this? Can it wait?' She rubbed the cleft in her chin as she spoke, a matching crease between her eyes. 'If the answer wasn't convincing, he'd go back inside, make a fire, and thank his lucky stars he was alive. Every crossing has the potential to be deadly. Every single one.'

I thanked her weakly, settled my bill, and grappled with my coat on my way out the door. All of a sudden, I couldn't wait to get home.

If anything, the wind outside had gotten fiercer. Icy fingers down my neck and over my earlobes turned my skin to gooseflesh. As I walked to my SUV, I had a sensation of being seasick, but it wasn't because of the rich meal or even the smell of Billy Bloom.

Something else my mother had told me while insisting that I keep myself safe was to listen to my instincts. 'When I was hugely pregnant with Doug,' she'd said, 'I almost ate bad shrimp. It was at a friend's place, a party, and I didn't want to offend her. Everyone told me the shrimp was great. She had grilled it. Lots of cilantro and lime. But I had a feeling. An instinct. All the guests got deathly ill that night, and my friend ended up in the hospital. Trust your gut, Shay,' Della had said. 'Now more than ever, it *knows*.'

Bring them back, I thought on the drive home, staring at the snow-caked road. I'd seen the night's low on TV at the diner, the minus sign glowing bright white. Until Tim and Val returned, all I could do was pray the ice stayed intact.

I could only think of one other time that I'd needed my mother so badly, and that was four years prior in New York. Tonight, I was safe. I was free.

But I'd never felt more alone.

THREE

A young man, anvil-jawed and unseasonably tan, stands before the kind of rustic old barn that modern farmhouse designers mine for reclaimed wood. Dressed in jeans, a thick Fair Isle sweater, and shearling slippers that can't possibly have any grip, he smirks at something, or someone, off camera while a Golden Retriever grins at his side. There's a mug in his fist, hand-painted with the American flag, but it isn't steaming. His other hand hoists an open bottle of Dom Perignon. At his wrist, a heavy-looking watch glints in the bright winter sun, which sparks off the snow all around him. He's a cover-ready lumbersexual, the embodiment of outdoor chic, and in the foreground there's a snowman – button eyes, carrot nose, the works.

There was something off about the photo, posted just that morning, and it provoked a niggling feeling as I stared down at my phone. I'd found the social media account easily enough, searching Instagram for 'Running Pine.' Cary Caufield and Sylvie Lavoy had called their endeavor Running Wild, and the pictures they'd posted were artfully composed, featuring the couple in various sharp outfits against a backdrop of island scenery. But this one of Cary nagged at me, and in a flash of comprehension, I understood why. With the temps we'd been having, the snow was dust, about as sticky as desert sand. The snowman was a fake, the image doctored to perfection. Colors heightened, impact maximized, imperfections buffed away. Every picture on the Running Wild Instagram feed was as vibrant as a jar of jelly beans, Cary and Sylvie's life flawless and enviably glossy.

Sweet enough to rot your teeth.

If I dreamed at all that evening, the memories crumbled like leaves over flame. I'd done my best to keep watch for Tim by the window, a modern-day whaling wife, but sometime around ten I'd curled up on the couch and succumbed to a rerun on HGTV. Now that our house renovation was behind us, all those seemingly endless months of stripping and scraping and living in a ghost world of plastic tarps and footprints in the dust, I could finally turn on the home improvement network without breaking out in hives.

Since my second trimester I'd been sleeping more soundly than I had in years, so exhausted that I could finally ignore the creaks and nightmares that always jolted me to consciousness. When I dozed off while waiting for Tim, though, the soft clack of his key in the lock woke me up like a cold-handed slap.

'Thank God,' I said when I saw him, unsurprised to find my voice rough with emotion.

'Aw, hon, don't tell me you waited up.' It wasn't much of a rebuke. By the door, where he was unlacing his boots, Tim looked spent but delighted to see me.

'Tell me everything while I make you some tea.'

He gave a heavy nod and went straight to the sofa, drawn to the warm spot I'd created like a cat with a patch of sunlight. His face was more haggard than I'd seen it in months, deep mauve gullies under both eyes and his hair downy and slightly flat from his hat. 'It's good to be home,' he groaned, and the words were a salve for my heart.

The team had been on Running Pine for a full eight hours. No doubt Tim oozed optimism all the while, encouraging everyone to stay both vigilant and hopeful. Most knew as well as he did that the odds weren't in their favor, but a missing man deserved more than a perfunctory search. Eventually, the darkness had halted their work, that highway of trees a godsend on the ride back when the river turned to black ice under a cloud-covered moon.

'It's a tough one.' Tim accepted the mug of caffeine-free tea with both hands. 'I was hoping he'd turn up. We all were. It's like the guy just vanished.'

The story Tim had brought home with him was alarming. Accompanied by Val, Teddy the airboat driver, and a search crew, he'd been led by locals Rich Samson and Ewan Fowler into the wilderness of ice. Buckhead Bay was beautiful in summer, a horseshoe carved into the island's rocky flank rimmed with lush trees that were skeletal now, stripped and shivering. It had snowed a little that morning, a bit more throughout the day, but Ewan had managed to retrace the route the three fishermen had taken before dawn.

The men had traveled by snowmobile, pulling their gear onto the bay with a metal dog sled and drilling test holes as they went. For safety, Ewan had explained, reminding Tim that river ice was

15 percent thinner than ice on a lake or a pond. He pointed out how cautious fishermen had to be, because you never knew where a current or creek that emptied into the river might create a weak spot. When he drilled, Ewan always looked for six inches. 'He drills, then measures, then walks ten more feet and drills and measures again. This morning, the ice was solid,' Tim told me. 'Seven inches where they stopped.'

Ewan had led the team to the two fishing rods Cary left behind, which Tim and Val had examined and photographed. Even the fishing holes beside them, along with all the test holes Ewan said he'd drilled, had already sealed themselves up. They'd found the aluminum lawn chair Cary had sat in while waiting for a bite. It had tipped over in the wind, snow drifts settling against its frame. No fresh footprints of any kind.

Solemnly, Tim said that was the last place they saw him. 'The men, Ewan and Rich, searched for two hours after they realized Cary hadn't come home. They found no sign of him either.'

Tim had finished his tea already. I took the mug from his hands. 'You must be famished,' I said. 'Please tell me you found something to eat out there.'

It was then that he told me about the soup.

'You wouldn't believe it. The minute the islanders realized he was missing, even before our team arrived, the women of Running Pine started cooking a bottomless pot of soup. It's tradition, apparently. People do go missing now and then. Hunters and such. Anyway,' he went on, 'the soup started at Emmeline's, and once it was ready, Jane strapped it to the back of her snowmobile and brought it out to where we were searching. Ladled it into mugs to keep us all warm. When we moved to a new area, the soup moved with us – and when it ran low, Jane took the pot back to Emmeline, who added whatever ingredients she could find.'

'That's brilliant,' I told him, feeling a rush of warmth at the thought of strangers, these battle-ready island women, working so hard to keep Tim and our crew fed. 'You're no good to the missing if you're weak and freezing.'

'Honestly, it saved us. The terrain wasn't easy to navigate – we're talking acres of frozen woods and farmland. Snow up to my thighs. It felt like we were in a freaking episode of *Game of Thrones*, in the Land of Always Winter beyond the Wall.'

'And they left Cary out on the ice alone? Even though he was a newbie?' It was hard, being on this side of things. Knowing how much I'd missed by staying on the mainland, eating diner pasta with stinking Billy Bloom and nodding off on the couch. I was desperate to help, to get a handle on the scene. My next questions for Tim came like fast balls. 'I thought Jane said the couple's only been on Running Pine since August?'

Tim said, 'That's right. It's their first time overwintering. But yeah, Ewan and Rich left the site just after ten this morning. Ewan says there was no reason to think he wouldn't make it home just fine. It's just a quarter-mile trip from where they were on the bay to Cary and Sylvie's cabin, and he was dressed for the weather – in a bright red jacket, we're told, though that hasn't helped us yet. The men did suggest he leave with them, but Cary hadn't caught anything and it was making him look bad.'

'Look bad to *who*?' It was an island of eight people. Who was there to impress?

'His followers. That's the craziest part of all this.' Tim was talking fast now too, revived by the fire and hot drink. 'It's the whole reason Cary Caufield and Sylvie Lavoy moved out there. They're a big deal on social media. They have an Instagram account called Running Wild.'

'I've seen it.' I'd spent more than an hour scrolling through the feed in awe of Cary waterskiing with a jack-o-lantern on his head and a bikini-clad Sylvie playing in the snow, but it hadn't occurred to me that Cary would document the fishing excursion for fans. Since launching the account, though, the couple had amassed more than fifty thousand followers. Links in their profile had led me to interviews with *Outdoor Life* and *Backcountry* that legitimized their brand. There was, it seemed, a whole subculture devoted to 'untracked experiences' and living 'out of bounds,' and Sylvie and Cary were doing a bang-up job of cashing in.

'Who knew we had real live social media stars living in the Thousand Islands,' I said.

'Yeah. Ewan Fowler says they started the account last summer, right after moving in. The plan was to spend a year on Running Pine and document it all online. I get the sense that Ewan's not impressed by the gimmicky angle, but the couple has plenty of supporters. Sponsors and everything. Rich Samson – he's the one married to Jane – delivers the mail out here, and he says they get free products all the time, more stuff than they could possibly use. They take photos of it for their feed.'

I still had more questions, about how Rich Samson could deliver mail when access to the island was hit or miss, and about the nature of those free products, but I filed them away for later and coiled myself next to Tim by the hearth. Though he was the one who'd been walking all day, he took my socked feet in his lap and started kneading while I burrowed deeper into the couch, listening to the crackle of the fire.

'So Cary went out on the ice to get content for Instagram?'

'Pictures, videos, you name it. He told the men he wouldn't be long, but at noon, Sylvie called Ewan's wife, Miranda, in a panic to say he hadn't come back. There's some speculation that he went farther on to the bay.' Tim dug his thumb into the sole of my foot and worked the ligament there, the feeling akin to heaven. 'There's a spot where a creek flows out from the mainland. A place where the ice is notoriously soft. Cary was told about it, what to avoid in order to stay safe, but it's possible he forgot or wasn't paying attention.'

I was putting it together now. When Hen lived with us, she used to joke about 'doing it for the gram,' but there were countless examples of people who'd taken real risks for the sake of a photo, falling in front of trains and off cliffs. Sacrificing their lives for those coveted likes. It sounded to me like Cary might have done something similar, pushing the envelope for the perfect post. Pushing too far. If he didn't know the ice, the dangers of walking on the frozen river, how fast hypothermia could kick in, he wouldn't have understood the importance of staying where his neighbors had put him.

'Late twenties, with little experience in the great outdoors . . . they're both green as they come,' said Tim. 'That's according to Ewan Fowler. All five of the other adults have been educating Cary and Sylvie best they could. Again, that's coming from Ewan.'

I did some quick math. 'Five? I thought there were eight people out there this year?'

'There are,' said Tim. 'The eighth islander is a child.'

My chest tightened like a drum. 'There's a kid on the island?'

'Imogen. She's five. Ewan said – and I quote – "I mean no disrespect, but my daughter's better prepared for this life than Sylvie and Cary by a mile."'

I didn't know whether that was true or not, but my hand had once again found my belly. Was it responsible, bringing a kid to overwinter on an island in the frozen north? Her parents may have believed she could handle the dangers of island life, but being raised in an environment like that, with no other children around for miles? I had my doubts about how well-adjusted the girl would be once grown. This wasn't my first winter in the North Country. I'd seen what it could muster. Living on an island year-round was not for the faint of heart.

'Talk to me about Sylvie,' I said. 'The girlfriend.'

'She wasn't much help, unfortunately. Emmeline – she's the oldest on the island, a widow – stayed with her during the search. Gave Sylvie some brandy to calm her nerves, and kept it coming.'

That made me wince. Booze wasn't the best prescription for a desperate, frightened woman, and what Tim said next confirmed my suspicions that the brandy had only made things worse.

'I got about ten minutes with her before she threw up on the rug and had to be put to bed. She confirmed Ewan's account, though. Three men went fishing, two came back.'

'So all that talk about wanting me out there,' I said, 'what was that about?'

Tim shrugged. 'She didn't bring it up, probably because she was blotto. Just as well you didn't make the trip. We'll get back out there first thing tomorrow, but I think at this point we should call in the Huey.'

'Tomorrow.' I felt my stomach drop. Having Tim safely back at home was like a miracle, and now I had to gird myself for another river crossing.

There was something close to pity in his eyes when he reached for my hand. 'Even with the helicopter, we'll need boots on the ground.' He opted not to add the words we were both thinking: *you know that, Shana. You know how this works.* 'With eyes in the sky and that red jacket, I'm hoping we'll get lucky. We'll be fine, hon. Really.'

Reluctantly, I gave a nod. 'That poor man – and woman,' I said, thinking of Sylvie Lavoy alone in her cabin tonight. 'Any family in the area for either of them?'

'I did wheedle some information out of Sylvie about that. Cary's an only child, but he's got a mother up in Ottawa. She has some mobility issues, so she's staying put for now. Sylvie grew up in Cape Vincent with an American mom and Canadian dad. The mom died when she was young, and her father never remarried. He dated a woman on and off for years, and Sylvie's got a half-brother in Ontario, but he lives way north now, working as some kind of tour guide. He's a lot younger than Sylvie, so they aren't close. And you already know about her father. Died just last summer. He's the one who left her the cabin.'

'I'm glad she's got a community out there, then. Sounds like the islanders are pretty close.'

'Seems that way. This'll be hard on her, though. She and Cary have been together for a year.'

'Only a year? Wow. Living out there's a hell of a relationship barometer.'

'I'll say. The sweet old woman, Emmeline, said she'd stay with her tonight.'

We both fell silent then, listening to the tinkle of snow blowing against the window panes and thinking of the missing man. Fighting off a yawn, Tim picked up the remote and clicked off the TV – but not before I caught sight of the weather report. *Brutal arctic blast sweeps the North Country.*

As I felt my eyes grow heavy again, my gaze trailed away from the screen to the window. Beyond the glass the river glowed in the moonlight, and I thought I saw a dark spot on the ice.

The lone coywolf, hunting for its dinner.

FOUR

'What are you up to today?' Tim asked the next morning, taking one last slug of coffee to fortify himself before heading back to the Clayton dock.

At the front door, I held his mug for him while he yanked wool socks over the cuffs of his pants. Day two of the search and the team would be ready, doubling up on thermal underwear and donning insulated helmets that would make their scalps sweat. I'd forced Tim to eat enough breakfast for two and packed him a substantial lunch. I'd also made him promise to text. No telling how long he'd be on the island, or what the day would bring.

'Actually,' I said, 'I was thinking of reconnecting with an old friend.'

As Tim's eyebrows hovered, I forced a smile. Whatever my husband was envisioning, he didn't expect what was coming next. Like him, I'd gone to bed thinking about a missing man.

But I'd awoken thinking of a woman.

'It reminds me of something,' I explained as I handed him his headgear. 'This case.'

'Tern Island.' Tim gave a solemn nod. 'Jasper Sinclair, right? Me too.'

'Not just that. It's this murder I worked years ago. Back in New York.'

It was a combination of things, really: the river, the woman named Jane, even Bloom with the crumbs in his beard at the diner. Together, they'd raised a memory from the dead, a time I hadn't thought about in a long while. 'Did I ever tell you about the homicide I caught right before getting pulled into Bram's orbit?' When Tim shook his dark head – he'd gone short again, said he was sick of ski hats messing up his hair – I said, 'It was a Jane Doe. Someone spotted her floating in the East River. She'd been sexually assaulted and strangled. Dead for days.'

'Jesus.'

'Yeah. You know how there are some cases that elude you, no matter how hard you work to get a solve? Jane Doe was like that.

We came at her from all angles, me and this borough detective, but there were aspects of her death that never made sense to me.' *One in particular*, I thought, feeling a tingle zip along my jaw. 'It was just a few weeks later that three other women turned up dead, and the Seventh Precinct made the link to Blake Bram.' I didn't need to explain the rest to Tim; he'd heard this story before. Investigators learned that Bram was from Swanton, Vermont just like me. It was full steam ahead after that. 'I abandoned her, Tim,' I said. 'Moved on to those stabbings, and never looked back.'

'You couldn't.' Tim's face softened as he took my chin in his gloved hand. 'Shana, you worked those serials for, what, a week before—'

'Before Bram got me too.' I said it so he didn't have to. 'I still have contacts in the city,' I added before Tim had a chance to speak again. 'I was thinking about asking someone to check the file. See if anyone picked it up after me.' I didn't mention Adam Starkweather, whom I hoped to reconnect with too. In some ways, he'd been just as involved with Jane Doe as I was.

'Where is this coming from?' Tim looked confused, which meant he looked adorable, his wide, dense eyebrows quirked above smoke-blue eyes. 'Is this some kind of pregnancy thing? Like the police equivalent of nesting?'

'Very funny,' I said with a roll of my eyes. 'And you've gotten off easy, my friend. Did I tell you Josie sends Doug out for Froot Loops in the middle of the night?' My sister-in-law was due to have a baby boy in a few weeks, and we'd been comparing notes. My yearning for ice cubes was nothing compared with Josie's demands.

'I'll have you know I spend all my free time on eBay, actively bidding on a vintage Snoopy Snow Cone Machine.'

I gave him a playful shove, though the snow cone machine did make my mouth water. 'This isn't some *pregnancy thing*. More like a loose end that needs tying. It could be a good distraction,' I said. 'Something to keep me busy while you're on Running Pine.' *Keep my mind off the crossing.*

'I guess,' Tim said, though he looked uneasy. 'What is it you're not telling me?'

Again I thought of Adam, but the image was quickly replaced with an autopsy photo, Jane Doe's face sizzling on my visual cortex like a brand. 'The victim,' I said. 'She had a cut on her cheek.'

'A cut.' He didn't ask what kind, or why that upset me. One look at my face was all it took for Tim to understand. The comma-shaped scar that marred my own cheek had come from my cousin. The boy from Swanton, Vermont, who'd grown up to be a killer.

The one who'd become Blake Bram.

Back then, when I was assigned to Jane Doe's case, I hadn't known what I knew now: that the kid who'd been raised by my aunt in a house we both feared and run away at sixteen had settled in New York. That Abraham Skilton, who'd left his mark on me when we were young, had reinvented himself as Bram and forced his way back into my life. Tim was right; I shouldn't blame myself for failing to revisit the Jane Doe file. After Abe barreled into my world as Bram, toying with me like a cat with a mole until I realized we were linked by blood, there was no way I could have gone back to my job with the NYPD. I'd almost lost my life in an apartment block basement. Of the four women he'd taken that summer, I alone had survived.

All of that was of little comfort to Jane Doe's family, who'd lost their daughter to murder.

It was of little comfort to me.

Tim took a step forward. Snaked an arm around me and the baby, and pulled us both close. 'The task force is still active, right? The FBI's on the lookout for other possible victims of Bram's?'

'Technically. But it's been close to two years since his death. The threat has been neutralized, and they've already linked him to more than a dozen cold cases. My sense is that they think they found them all – his past victims, the women he hurt. But what if they missed someone, Tim? What if they're wrong?'

'Jane Doe. You said she was assaulted and strangled?'

'Yeah,' I said, reading his mind. Nearly all of the victims linked to Bram had been stabbed, and not one had shown signs of sexual assault. 'But that cut—'

Tim stopped my words with a kiss. 'This happens to me sometimes too,' he said when he'd pulled back. 'I work a case, and it gets me remembering another. It's like reading a book that makes you think of a whole other story – and it doesn't even have to be exactly the same. It's more of a hunch, right? That they have something in common?'

'You're saying I should leave the cold case alone.'

Tim sighed. 'I guess I thought your pregnancy project would be something a little less dark. Like baking, maybe.'

'There's only one baker in this house, and you can't deprive Bobby of her muffins.'

'Fair enough. Look, I do get it. You're stuck on the sidelines, and you're not used to that. You like to be productive. If calling that detective in the city keeps you from tearing your hair out, I'm all for it.'

'That,' I said, 'is why I love you. You always let me get my way.'

'You wish.' When Tim kissed me again, his warm lips lingered on mine. 'I'll be back soon. I'll check in often. The airboat driver knows what he's doing – Steady Teddy, remember? It only takes thirty minutes to cross the ice.'

'Only?'

'We'll be fine,' Tim said. 'I'll be back soon. I promise.'

I nodded as he opened the door. A woman had lost her boyfriend, and Tim had to help. Under any other circumstances, I'd be helping too. As I watched him go, though, past the snow drifts on the porch we'd given up on sweeping and into the car on which he'd already started to melt the windshield frost, I couldn't stop hearing the waitress's voice in my head. *Every crossing has the potential to be deadly*, she'd said, and here was Tim, heading back on to the ice.

He'd promised he would be back soon.

I had to wonder if Cary Caufield had told Sylvie Lavoy the same thing.

FIVE

I hadn't talked to Dave Johansson in years, and that fact flooded me with guilt. It wasn't as if we were old friends or even longtime partners, but at a pivotal moment in my life, he'd been the person I'd spoken with the most. No one else could claim to be the one I sipped coffee with each morning. For a couple of weeks one scorching August, Dave had been my ride or die.

I hoped he'd remember that when I phoned him to ask for a favor.

I thought about calling his office, but all those years ago I'd saved his cell number in my phone, and reaching out that way felt more personal. When I got a voicemail greeting, I stammered out a hello. 'It's Shana. Shana Merchant? Long time.' My laugh sounded forced. 'I hope you and' – *oh God, the wife, what was her name?* – 'that you and your family are doing well. Listen, I know this is out of left field, but I was hoping we could talk. Give me a ring? I'd love to catch up.'

It was only after ending the message that I realized the catch-up would only go one way. Dave Johansson didn't need me to tell him what I'd been doing since leaving New York. I had to assume he'd heard the staggering reports coming from upstate, the most shocking of which had made the national news. I'd managed to hide my connection to Bram for a long time, but the truth was out now, my identity as the detective he'd taken captive forever linked to a brutal criminal. Even hundreds of miles south in Manhattan there was a strong chance Dave knew Bram was my cousin, and that my cousin had followed me here, and that my cousin was dead.

Dave had visited me in the hospital after my rescue from that apartment building basement, where for eight days I'd been the prisoner of the killer I'd been searching for. My partner's cheeks had been damp with tears he refused to acknowledge even as he clutched a bouquet of limp street vendor flowers in a trembling hand. *Maybe he won't bring it up*, I thought now, but the notion lacked conviction. If Dave called me back – *if* – I'd have to face his questions head-on.

If anyone deserved to know the truth about what had happened to me, it was him.

I had a routine for my days off, and it started with cleaning the house. I'd wrestle my kinked hair into a ponytail, turn on the TV for background noise, and start scrubbing. The distraction worked – right up until I went back downstairs to hear the voices of the CNN morning anchors. Cary Caufield wasn't an A-list celebrity. Not a prominent political figure or a pop star. With a fan base of fifty thousand, though, he was high-profile enough that he would make the news. It didn't take much to nudge out the types of reports we got in A-Bay, reminding citizens to check their smoke detectors or sharing winter activities at the senior center, and soon enough, Cary's dire situation would be the talk of the town. I didn't see much of my state-appointed therapist anymore, but Gil Gasko had told me that humans are attracted to suffering. We consume stories that make us sad so we can feel better about our own lives. Though I hoped Cary's story wouldn't end badly, I felt the weight of every hour that passed without a triumphant message from Tim.

Hitting the mute button, I threw another log onto the fire. Daytime burns weren't a luxury reserved for winter bed and breakfasts; I'd feed the flames all day, until Tim came back and we resumed our routine of cuddling on the couch with a bowl of something hot to eat. *Chicken chili*, I thought, feeling my stomach twitch. Not too spicy. I'd make a run to the Price Chopper, have it ready when Tim came home. In the meantime, maybe I'd crack open one of his novels. It had been a while since I'd done some reading. I'd show him I knew how to relax.

The trill of my cell phone lodged a shard of panic in my chest. It was Dave's name, not Tim's, on the screen.

'Shana.' The way he said it triggered a rush of memories. 'Wow. It's good to hear your voice.'

'Yours too.' I dropped the dust rag on the table and lowered myself to the couch. We were awkward in the way of old friends who've grown apart. No rift to speak of, just a sink hole that opened between us, slowly widening with every passing month until it obliterated the entire road. We asked about each other's lives, both of us skirting the details. *It's good, I'm good, no complaints.*

'Gotta admit,' he said, 'I was surprised by your call.'

'I get that. It's been a long time, and this is out of the blue. I was a little worried you'd hung up your badge.'

Prior to police academy, I'd thought it strange that so many detectives retired in their fifties. That was before I understood the job felt like drinking from a fire hose with a broken nozzle.

After a pause, Dave said, 'The old dog's still at it.'

'Your wife must be thrilled.' My tone was dry. Based on his near-constant string of complaints, I'd assumed Dave's wife would have loved nothing more than a retirement ceremony and overdue trip to Cabo.

'Ah, no. Angela and I split.'

'I'm sorry,' I told him.

'Yeah, thanks. Our kid's doing great, though. Would you believe she's engaged to be married?'

'Weird, since you're only thirty yourself.'

'I knew I liked you. Heard you moved north,' Dave said. 'Scored a gig with the State Police?'

'That's right. But it's not why I called. Do you remember the case we worked before—' I paused, not yet ready to bring up Bram. 'The last case we worked together? That Jane Doe recovered from the river?'

Dave said, 'Haven't thought about her in years.'

'Then you're probably wondering why I'm asking. My husband was, too.' I tried to laugh, but the sound came out strangled.

'No, I know why. At least, I think I do. That woman,' said Dave. 'She had a cut just like your scar.'

I nodded to myself. 'Yeah. That's been bothering me. Always has.'

There was a long break before he said, 'I guess you heard about Starkweather.'

'What about him?' Unlike with Dave, I'd reconnected with Adam a couple of years ago, swallowing my pride and embarrassment to call for advice after discovering Bram had come north. Though I hadn't been ready to confess then that we were linked by blood, Adam's insight helped me understand Bram's frightening behavior.

'Shit. I'm sorry to be the one to tell you. He passed,' said Dave. 'Just a few weeks ago.'

The news was a gut punch. Adam Starkweather, gone. 'Christ. What happened?'

'I don't know for sure, but I heard it was a heart thing. Real sudden.'

Vincent. The name rushed in unbidden. I'd never even met Adam's son, but I knew he and his dad were close. Vincent would be about fourteen by now. Fatherless. My head felt like a balloon leaching air. This death, the image of Adam's grieving son – it was too much.

There was another call coming in, a name on the screen. Val, phoning from the island. 'I'm sorry,' I stammered. 'There's – I need – I have to go. Can we talk again?'

'Still as popular as ever, I see.' Dave's words were sour, curdled by bitterness and chased by a sigh of regret. 'Forget I said that. Of course we can talk again. Anytime.'

I prattled off a few words of thanks and quickly switched lines.

'We have a situation out here,' said Val.

When I first met Valerie Ott, I'd been impressed – and a little intimidated – by her no-nonsense manner. She'd been brought upstate from Oneida to help with a homicide case I couldn't work due to a conflict of interest. Pint-sized Val pulled no punches during that investigation, and as nervous as her competence had made me when I feared someone I cared about might be facing a criminal charge, it had since become invaluable to our troop. It worried me, though, that she was calling now. Val, not Tim, who was out there too.

It took seconds for her to explain what was going on. Sylvie Lavoy claimed she knew something that might lead us to her missing boyfriend. Upon the team's arrival this morning, just an hour prior, she'd insisted she had critical information.

Problem was, she wouldn't tell Tim and Val what it was.

'She only wants to talk to you.' Val was outside; I could tell by the whistle of wind on the line, the mere sound of which roused a shiver. My newest investigator sounded pissed.

'You're kidding,' I said. 'She knows something about the guy's whereabouts and she's refusing to talk?'

'Is that not fucked up? Tim's in there now, trying to reason with her, but this woman is stubborn as hell. Her live-in boyfriend's out in this cold, possibly injured or dying. She has intel that might help us find him before the man freezes to death, but she'll *only talk to Shana Merchant*. I volunteered to call you and got out of there before I lost my cool. No pun intended.'

What was it Jane Budd had said about Sylvie when she arrived at the barracks?

She asked me. Begged me.

It has to be you.

My notoriety had caused problems in the past, both for the troop and my family. Now, that dark curiosity was a risk to someone's life. 'I don't understand,' I told Val. 'Why'd she sit on this until now? You've been searching for hours. There's a whole rescue team on the case, plus the Huey. Every minute this man is out in the elements is a minute he's closer to death. Why didn't she tell you this yesterday?'

'Yesterday, she was drunk. We barely got a chance to question her before she hurled and passed out.'

I remembered that part of Tim's account now. The woman had been impossible to interview, and the elderly islander – Emmeline – had put her to bed. Nearly twenty-four hours had passed since Jane Budd pulled up to the barracks on her snowmobile, calling for help. Calling for *me*. In my head, that wasted time tolled like a death knell.

'Can you put her on the phone?' I asked. 'Right now?' The sooner I could find out what Sylvie thought she knew, the faster the team would find Cary Caufield.

'You don't understand. She wants to talk to you *in person*.'

'Her boyfriend is missing,' I said, aghast. 'Right now, that island's one of the most dangerous places in America. What possible reason could she have for needing to talk to me face-to-face?'

'I don't know,' Val said. 'But Shana, she's not budging.'

I didn't remember getting to my feet, had no recollection of pacing, but somehow I'd come to stand by the window where cold air seeped through the glazing like lethal gas. There was no way it made sense for me to go out to that island. I wasn't bedridden, or so pregnant I could hardly move, but it was impossible not to notice all the ways my once-reliable body was starting to betray me. The lack of confidence I had in my balance and coordination was as real as the hot flashes and swollen feet, which had already puffed up to look like Shrek's – pigs-in-a-blanket toes and all. I wasn't in fighting shape, not even close.

'What does Tim say?' I couldn't imagine him being on board with the idea of me journeying to the island.

Val said, 'He doesn't know what to do. He told me to get your advice. He's been trying – you know how good he is with witnesses – but the woman won't say a word.'

Tim was leaving it up to me, then. If he'd asked Val to call, it could only mean he'd tried every avenue and come up against brick walls.

I could stay right where I was. Let Tim have another go at Sylvie.

Cary had been missing for a full day and night; if Sylvie cared about him, then surely she'd crack. Tim's insistence that Val call me didn't augur well, though, because Tim *was* good with witnesses. And still, this one couldn't be swayed.

Teddy was new to Clayton's fire department as of last summer, but by all accounts, he was the best airboat operator in Jefferson County. No doubt he'd treat me with kid gloves; get me there safely, and back in one piece. If it took thirty minutes to cross the river, though, and I'd still need to get home, I was looking at an hour skidding puck-luck across unpredictable ice.

You have a baby to think of now. My mother's words rang in my ears.

Every crossing has the potential to be deadly.

'Can I talk to Tim?'

Silence on the line. A moment later I heard Val crunch across the snow as she made her way back to Sylvie's cabin. There was some chatter I couldn't make out, the rustle of a winter jacket overlaid by a string of quiet curses, and then, finally, Tim's voice. A beam of sunshine through dark clouds.

The light didn't last.

'This lady is out of her goddamn mind.' Tim was walking too now, breathing heavily as he paced with enough hot rage to melt a path in the snow.

'Val says you tried to reason with her?'

'I've been trying for more than an hour, but the silly, stupid woman won't budge.'

I didn't like it, the way he was talking. Tim wasn't immune to losing his shit, but even his most livid moments had nothing on this. 'You're not doing it, obviously,' he said. 'I won't allow her to take control of this investigation. I'm not having it.'

'I don't get it,' I replied. 'This doesn't make sense.'

It felt like a ruse. Like we were being played. Could this woman, this Sylvie Lavoy, have made it all up just to get me out there? She had a platform, after all – a presence on social media. Did she plan to use me to drum up views? Generate more likes and follows? I'd seen stranger things . . . but the other islanders had confirmed it. A man was missing in this arctic cold.

'She's keeping us from doing our jobs. Impeding the investigation. We're trying to save this guy's life, and every minute we waste is a minute too long.'

'I know,' I said, my mind cycling through options. Tim seemed adamant that I stay put. And yet, he'd sent Val out to call me. He sucked a hard breath through his nose.

'What the hell? What the hell are we going to do?'

This time, I didn't answer.

I knew what Sylvie Lavoy wanted. Tim did, too. She wanted access to the woman with a killer for a cousin, who'd brought violent crime to sleepy A-Bay. A front-row seat to see the freak who'd cheated death in Manhattan and scarcely escaped it upstate. Sylvie, a celebrity of sorts herself, was using her boyfriend as leverage to get an audience with me. It was ludicrous. Sickening.

It left us with no choice.

'How's the ice?' I asked it slowly.

Silence. Then, 'It could be worse.'

Thirty minutes each way, on ice that could be worse. An hour of dread in exchange for a life.

'Keep searching. Tell the air crew to hustle now that the light's good.' Fighting through the tightness in my chest, I said, 'And tell Teddy I'll meet him at the dock in Clayton.'

Tim was quiet, a searing meteor of fury. Doing everything he could not to storm back inside and shake some sense into Sylvie Lavoy.

She may have been willing to risk Cary's rescue.

Me, I'd seen too much death already to give up on the living, and I wasn't about to start now.

SIX

New York City

Four Years Ago

The search for Jane Doe's killer began on a Tuesday, on an entirely different island.

Back then, I spent most of my time in a state-of-the-art eight-story station house on 5th Street. The Depression-era building that had once stood in its place was long gone by the time I moved to Manhattan, the original Ninth Precinct replaced with a structure more suited to modern police work. Not a morning went by that I didn't marvel at its lobby, fashioned from white brick and chrome with locked gates separating us from the public, every foot of the too-bright space monitored with cameras. It was a place that made me feel secure despite the nature of the job, which was probably the point.

That day, it was where I hoped to solve a murder.

You never knew who you were going to get paired with from the borough squad. The detectives from Manhattan Homicide existed to support investigators like me and reduce the draw on precinct resources. But blind partnerships weren't always a good match. I'd been sent my share of the old guard just looking to make overtime, men with all the verve and will of a trampled cockroach. I didn't get a dud this time, though. Instead, I got Dave. I'd worked with him twice before, and had a feeling he'd requested the case. We made a good team, he and I, and both of us knew it.

'So. The cut,' Dave Johansson said that afternoon. 'You think there's something to that, huh?' He tapped his fingers on the arm of an office chair as he spoke, drumming to a tune only he could hear. In his early fifties, Dave had the sloped shoulders and squinty eyes of a mole, but any perceived weakness conveyed by his looks was made up for by his impressive record of solves. Dave had two decades of experience on me, and while he didn't always flaunt it, I got the distinct sense that he saw me as, well, *young*. It wasn't the first time I'd brought up the mark on Jane Doe's face, or even the second. The detail had stuck in my throat like a fish bone, and apparently – *finally* – Dave was ready to give it some thought.

Twelve hours since we found the woman in the river, and we were still struggling to get an ID. Dave and I had sifted through dozens of missing persons reports about females her same age, race, weight. We'd tried to trace her fingerprints. So far, the victim remained a ghost.

'It's the fact that it's postmortem,' I told him, twisting my hair into a low bun. It was longer than I liked to keep it, perpetually frizzy in the August heat, but self-care wasn't something I prioritized. 'Why disfigure her after she's dead? It feels personal.'

'Crime of passion?' Dave ventured.

'Could be. But if it's personal, wouldn't he *want* her to suffer?'

'Who knows what goes through these maniacs' heads. Wasn't there a guy in Texas who removed his victims' eyes and pocketed them as souvenirs?' Dave's shoulders shuddered, and I mirrored his response. There was a bag of green grapes in my desk I'd been looking forward to eating. I made a mental note to offer them to patrol.

'I wish I was joking. Look it up,' he went on. 'That was done postmortem too. The guy was obsessed with eyes. Background in taxidermy, I think.'

'So there was a reason for it, however sick and twisted. What was the reason for this?'

'It's never that easy. Too bad we don't have an Adam.'

He said it absently while thumbing his chin. When he clocked my confusion, Dave whistled low and shook his head. 'I'm disappointed in you, Merchant. Adam Starkweather's a fucking legend. I took a class with the guy at the police academy back in the day. Best course of my life, best criminal profiler I know.'

The reproach, however good-humored, brought a flush to my cheeks. I'd taken courses of my own while training in Albany, everything from criminology to forensic psychology. I liked to consider myself well-versed in criminal behavior. Starkweather had gone deeper, Dave said, requiring his students to revisit both famed and little-known cases to analyze victim and offender profiles, situational elements, characteristics of the crime. He expected his students, students like Dave, to understand serial murder through a biopsychosocial model that explored the connection between biology, psychology, society, and culture. It was the only way they stood a chance of knowing where to look for a perp. That was Starkweather's theory, anyway.

I tried not to look too rapt as Dave spoke, but the truth was that I was intrigued. Starkweather was one of the few criminal profilers in the city who'd been trained by the FBI, and founder of the NYPD's Criminal Assessment and Profiling Unit. He'd just published a book that had become a bestseller. When Dave described the way he could create order from chaos, I pictured a man cupping clues like fireflies, coercing them to flash in unison in the safety of his strong hand.

'Could he help us?' Ours was a single homicide, one unidentified woman in a sea of the missing that swelled around Manhattan like the ocean itself, but Dave had piqued my interest. I had to ask.

'Not likely,' he replied, dashing my hopes with two hasty words. 'Starkweather's a big shot in real high demand, and this crime doesn't look like a serial.'

Once again, I felt the blood rush my cheeks. 'Let's leave the cut for the moment,' I said, 'and focus on the ID. I'm thinking Crime Stoppers. We could put in for a reward.'

We'd need approval, which meant a trip to the Civic Center in the morning, but we already had a forensic sketch, and with any luck the Deputy Commissioner for Public Information would agree to disseminate details about our victim to the press.

That cut meant something. I was certain.

And I had to know what it was.

SEVEN

'Don't worry,' said the man at the controls. 'I get it. Precious cargo. Trust me, you're in good hands.'

Teddy was young, far younger than I'd been expecting, with flowing brown hair pinned down by a North Face beanie. The confidence with which he handled the airboat was reassuring, yes, but I was crossing the river in February, on ice that couldn't be trusted, in a boat that – even in capable hands – was prone to flipping. If it meant our team had a shot at saving Cary Caufield, the risk was a necessary one. My nerves were frayed and jangly all the same.

A jolt, and we were airborne. I pictured my mother's face as the airboat's aluminum hull glanced off a chunk of ice and my body hovered above my seat. 'Hang on,' shouted Teddy, a moment too late. There was a metallic clang when we came back down, a force so great I felt it in my bones.

If I squinted through the clear plastic sheeting that doubled as windows, I could see the island. We were making good time. It had taken some effort for me to gear up and get myself to Clayton, but Teddy was waiting when I arrived, well aware – thanks to Tim – of the time crunch. I'd half expected to see my husband on board as my personal escort, but Teddy told me he'd stayed behind to continue with the search. Fuming, no doubt, over Sylvie's insistence that I come to Running Pine.

As we rode, Teddy briefed me on the situation. Anytime the fire department, of which Teddy was a member, got a call, they needed details on the location before making a plan of attack. Island searches posed unique challenges, but the crew was managing. Though the airboat was designed for four, Teddy could handle more if the ice was good, no danger of the boat punching through. With a six-hundred horse power V8 engine, it had the muscle to move some serious weight. He'd flushed solid crimson when he told me that, yanking his eyes from my swollen body.

Apart from Tim and Val and the team we had in the air, the search party consisted of Teddy and five others, all of them well-versed in rescue work. Ewan Fowler, along with Rich Samson and Jane Budd, had offered to help as well, while Emmeline stayed with Sylvie and Miranda Fowler cared for her young daughter.

The team had already searched the ice and area around Buckhead Bay, combing drifts along the shoreline on foot. Using the islanders' snowmobiles to hunt farther afield, and following roads that forked north and south. Ewan, Rich, and Jane had checked all the homes in a two-mile radius, just in case Cary got turned around and had to take shelter. Apart from those belonging to Running Pine's eight winter residents, all were empty now, closed for the season with doors and windows sealed tight.

If Cary had wandered into the woods, even if he'd stuck to a road, he would have exhausted himself quickly. None of the residents' snowmobiles were MIA, so the team knew he was on foot. I didn't need Teddy to tell me that snow slowed a person down, the deep stuff especially. That wasn't even accounting for the panic. If Cary realized he was lost, that could have set in quickly. Would the man, new to the island and accustomed to city life, have known to find a creek that he could follow to the river? Hang a brightly colored scrap of clothing to a tree as a signal for the rescue crew? Make a fire? Or would he let the horror of his dilemma overcome him, stop moving, succumb to hypothermia, give up hope? More than five thousand acres. Seven miles end to end. Three miles wide. Running Pine was a bit like northern Siberia, only it had fewer people and, at the moment, an even more pitiless cold.

As we neared the shore, several cabins dotting the lip of the bay came into view. Three of them sent up a stripe of white woodsmoke, a scene that took me home – to Swanton, yes, but also to the steam vents of New York, and from there straight back to the East River. It hadn't frozen solid in over a century, but snaps of extreme cold did create the odd floe, packing the span with thick plates of jagged gray ice that I'd seen only once before fleeing the city and wasn't likely to witness again.

'That's Emmeline's place.' Teddy pointed at the cabin nearest to the public dock. 'Those other two farther up the road belong to Rich, Jane, and the Fowlers. You know Jane?'

'We met when she came to the barracks.'

'Oh, no,' Teddy said, 'I meant do you know what she does. She wrote a bunch of books about life on the river. They sell them at the bookstore in Clayton. People around here love Jane.'

'I'll check them out.' There was a dark spot in the sky over the island. Our State Police helicopter, still circling. 'So they all live pretty close together. What about Sylvie and Cary?'

'Their place is inland a bit, not on the water like the others. Emmeline's their closest neighbor, about five minutes up the road. Nearly there.' He whispered now, and though his back was to me I could read the tension in his frame as the boat approached the shore. When at last we reached the island, he released the breath trapped in his chest and dragged a glove across his shining brow.

We made landfall by the public dock, on the south side of the bay straight across the river from Clayton. Teddy had promised Tim he'd get me to Sylvie's, and explained that Ewan Fowler was bringing down his snowmobile. That was welcome news. I felt fine, good even, but that wouldn't be the case if I had to spend the next fifteen hours on my feet.

Together, Teddy and I disembarked to trudge through snow already trampled by my team. That was one nice thing about a search in winter: barring another heavy snowfall, and provided we could work out where he'd gone, we might actually be able to follow Cary's tracks.

There was sound in the distance already, a motorized grumble I knew well. I hadn't given a thought to how the islanders kept their roads accessible, and Teddy must have registered the surprise in my eyes, the only part of me exposed to the cold. Up ahead, just past the bay, the road looked like a bobsled run with drifts on either side as tall as I was.

'They have a plow,' he told me. 'A truck they use in winter. They keep it at the Fowler place. No gas station here, so fueling up can't be easy. Sounds like they don't use it much for that reason.'

'How much of the island do they clear?'

'There aren't a lot of roads to begin with, but they go on for miles. They've been plowing just enough so they can get to each other's houses. That, and the river. The rest stays untouched until the spring melt. I did see snowmobile tracks farther out, and west too,' he said, 'while we were searching. They probably go off-roading for fun. Not a lot else to do around here.'

I was inclined to agree. Overwintering might have been a badge of honor, but it wasn't an easy life.

The snowmobile materialized from between the trees and lurched to a stop. Like Jane the previous day, the figure who dismounted wore a snowmobile suit, but this time I was sure about gender. Ewan Fowler cut a masculine figure, imposing in his black helmet and winter gear.

As he introduced himself, he flipped his visor to reveal the face of a man in his early fifties. Downturned eyes, a knife-edge nose, a small mouth overcrowded with teeth. Ewan hadn't shaved in days, and I wondered if his patchy black stubble was for warmth or because he couldn't be bothered. 'I still can't believe this is happening,' he said after we'd shaken hands. 'I saw Cary just yesterday morning. Me and Rich both.'

'I'm told you helped with the search. Thanks for that.'

'Of course. It's not our first time. Rare,' Ewan said, 'but this kind of thing does happen. Just last year there was a hunter who got turned around after dark. We found him pretty quickly, though. We've got a system.'

'Best I've ever seen,' said Teddy. 'And I've done a lot of searches.'

'How's that?' I asked. If these islanders knew a better way for tracking down missing people than I did, I wanted to hear about it.

Teddy and Ewan traded a look, and Teddy's face split into a grin. 'It's all about the soup.'

I almost had to laugh. Tim had been impressed by the soup, too. 'How long have you all lived out here, exactly?' Tim and Val were sure to have gathered those details already, but I was new to the investigation, still getting my sea legs.

'Rich Samson and Jane Budd are our longest winter residents. What is it now . . . ten years, I think.' Jane Budd – she'd retained her maiden name, Ewan explained – came from a family of fishermen. Her great-grandfather had brought a fishing party to Brockville in search of northern pike, and liked the area enough to buy land on Running Pine. He built a farmhouse not far inland and, later, a cabin by the bay. The couple now lived there year-round. Ewan said, 'As for Rich, he grew up in Clayton, but he'll tell you he prefers it out here. He winterized the cabin himself.'

'That must have been tough.' I was thinking of Tim's cottage on Goose Bay. He still owned the place, his one shot at selling having fallen through last year, but before it became a tourist attraction for crime-obsessed teens, Tim had renovated and insulated every inch by hand.

'Tough, and expensive,' Ewan confirmed. 'Everything had to be brought here by barge – tools, materials, furniture. Still does. But now, the job of transporting supplies falls to Rich.'

'Like the mail?' Rich delivered the post. Tim had mentioned that.

'Mail, firewood, food, you name it. We'd be lost without Rich. Mail delivery's covered by the county, of course – he's doing the bare minimum right now so he can be around to help search – but we pay him to handle the rest.'

'Sylvie and Cary too?'

'Oh yeah. They need him more than anyone. Few of us have the skill to make regular trips across the ice. Rich knows the river like no one else. Even so, he takes his life in his hands every time he makes a crossing.'

'He told me yesterday that he broke through once,' Teddy said.

My eyes widened while Ewan's went dark. 'That's true. Rich and his snowmobile both went in the river. Even with his gear on, he was hypothermic. If the marine unit had been any slower, he would have died that day. We pitched in to get him and Jane a new machine – a three-seater. He's out searching with it now. I'll come back for you, yeah?' he said to Teddy. 'Once I drop her at Sylvie's?'

Teddy told Ewan that was fine; he'd start walking toward Emmeline Plum's. 'Emmeline told the detectives they could use her place to warm up anytime,' Ewan said as he gestured for me to mount the machine.

'That's kind of her,' I said. 'What about you?' I asked as he started the engine. 'How did you and your wife come to live here?'

'Miranda's been here all her life. Left for university – in Maine, where we met – but she missed it so much she came back. The Plum family's had people here for three generations.'

'Plum,' I repeated. 'As in Emmeline?'

Ewan had flipped down his visor. When he turned his head again, it wasn't his face I saw but my own round eyes reflected in the tinted shield. 'Emmeline is Miranda's aunt by marriage. Em's husband, Oscar, was her uncle. He was born and raised here, too. Jane and Miranda have been best friends since they were kids. They're third cousins, actually, both from two of the island's first families. The Budds and the Plums.'

I hadn't expected that. I'd assumed the islanders were close, but their connection both to the land and each other was far deeper than I'd realized.

Ewan didn't take the road he'd come down on. Instead, we headed west. 'If you don't mind my asking,' I shouted over the machine's roar as a stand of pines next to the road cast streaky shadows across our path, 'what do *you* do here all winter long?' Eight minutes on the island and already I felt itchy, the wide band of white river between us and the mainland hemming me in.

It was a few seconds before Ewan answered, and he let off the gas a bit when he did so he didn't have to yell. 'I'm a psychologist by trade. Psychosociology, to be exact.'

'Huh.' I knew a bit about that. It factored into the study of how criminals were raised, and whether that impacted their behavior as adults. It was the field Adam Starkweather specialized in, and it had always fascinated me. 'Is this a sabbatical, then?' I asked. Psychosociology had to do with studying people, and there were very few of those on Running Pine.

'More like a research project. I've been studying the effect of silence and isolation, actually. Looking at how they impact us. Seems like a timely subject, given modern society's assaulted by noise.'

When he hit the gas again, the snowmobile's tracks kicking up chips of snow, I felt pretty battered by noise myself. I leaned in close to hear what Ewan had to say.

'Silence is linked to everything from psychological development to physiology, neurobiology, even spirituality. There are countless benefits to exposing ourselves to complete and utter quiet. But it can be hard to get used to.'

'Silence and isolation,' I repeated. 'You have a child, is that right?' The memory prompted me to check in with my own kid, who seemed to be faring the trip well so far.

Ewan's helmet bobbed as we edged up against a snowbank, the move tipping me sideways. 'We had Imogen – that's our daughter – later in life. She just turned five, but she was hooked on the iPad by two. We wanted to put some distance between her and screens. Miranda's a trained teacher, her family owned property here, so we figured, why not? Next year she'll be in kindergarten, but until then it's back to basics. No TV, no internet, not even kids' shows on YouTube. Those things are engineered to hook children.' He spoke loudly now, enunciating every word. 'They exploit weakness in young people's psychology and encourage impulsive behavior. We've seen a positive change in Imogen already.'

My mind made a beeline for Cary and Sylvie. If that was Ewan's attitude toward social media, how did he feel about sharing the island with Instagram stars? What I said was, 'You have something in common with your new neighbors.'

'How's that?' Ewan asked.

'Back to basics?' I raised my voice, unsure whether he had heard me. 'Isn't that what Running Wild's all about?'

'Right,' he said quickly. 'Yes. We're here.'

Had I come on foot, I would have known the cabin by the snowmobile tracks that zigzagged everywhere; in the past twenty-four hours, this place had seen a lot of action. The cabin itself was modest, no more than a thousand square feet with barn-red siding and canoe paddles mounted beside the front door. The path to that door had seen some action, too. Though it looked like it hadn't been shoveled in months, the snow was trampled flat.

We were a long way from the water. I'd expected Sylvie's home to be on the river like most of the houses built on the islands, but Teddy hadn't been kidding when he said it was inland. The few houses we'd passed along the way were shuttered for winter, kayaks covered in tarps and blinds closed against the cold. Like the homes I'd already seen by the bay, Sylvie's had a large picture window, but instead of overlooking the St Lawrence it faced a dense thicket of trees. This wasn't a summer home made for family time and grilling on the deck so much as a witch's cabin in the woods.

No sooner had Ewan driven away, back to get Teddy and rejoin the search, did I hear the hum of another machine approaching. It was Val, riding solo along the plowed road on a snowmobile painted black, white, and royal blue. Emmeline's snowmobile, I assumed. Another two-seater like Ewan's. She stopped beside a snowbank and hurried over, her face slicked with sweat. She looked double her normal size in the suit, the rigidity in her limbs imposing. Her posture spoke of trouble.

'You talk to Sylvie yet?' she asked. No time for niceties.

'I was about to go in. What is it?'

'I found blood,' Val said, deadpan. 'In the snow behind Rich and Jane's cabin.'

Rich and Jane. Hadn't Teddy said Rich and Jane were out searching? 'How much blood?'

Her lower lip disappeared, a row of small teeth appearing in its stead. I had my answer.

Mere feet away, Tim was inside the cabin with Sylvie, waiting for me to arrive so we could cajole what she knew out of her. Val's discovery was a whammy. Our ultimate goal was to find Cary Caufield, and blood in the snow was a sign of distress.

'Show me,' I said, following Val back to the machine.

EIGHT

We took the same road I had ridden with Ewan, back down to the water – only this time, we veered east. Val pointed out Emmeline's house as we went. Like Teddy had said, it was the closest occupied home to Sylvie and Cary's, positioned halfway around Buckhead Bay. The lights were on inside to combat the gloomy sky, warmth leaking through frosted windows, and I wondered if Emmeline had left Sylvie's for home. If maybe she was inside right now, stretching that pot of soup as far as it would go.

The Fowler home came next, and it had the markings of a summer place enhanced over time. There was a small room tacked on to the side like an afterthought. A sunroom, maybe, providing the family with a few more square feet. None of the homes I'd seen so far had looked bigger than a Manhattan apartment. Not a lot of space to hole up in when the outside world got brutally cold. As we passed it, a shadow darkened the window and a face appeared, giving me a start. Behind the glass the young girl's eyes narrowed, watching us as we drove by.

Rich and Jane's home was last on Val's impromptu tour. She cut the engine on the Ski-Doo, and I trailed her around the back.

'I checked when I saw it,' she told me. 'There's nobody home. They're both out helping with the search.' We walked a few steps farther, and there it was. Blood in the snow, a red so bright it was searing.

And smack at its center, like an arrow that had found its mark, stood a coywolf.

'Jesus Christ,' Val hissed as we darted behind the cabin.

'I'm guessing he wasn't here when you found it.' I didn't take my eyes off the creature as I spoke, didn't like that the coywolf hadn't bolted on our approach.

I didn't like how hungry it looked with its muzzle sunk into that bloody snow, either.

This was not a situation I was familiar with. In Vermont, we'd once discovered a black bear in our yard. The animal had climbed a tree, we'd stayed inside until it cleared out, and that had been the end of it. I'd been told by friends who liked to hike that encounters with wild creatures required a calculated response. Get loud. Back away slowly. Avoid eye contact. Did the same rules apply to this feral canine who, at a time of year when much of its prey was in hibernation, had a hankering for flesh? Val and I were so close I could hear the crunch of gore-splashed ice between the coywolf's teeth, and when I thought of my bowl of ice cubes at home, my stomach did a flip. I'd come here expecting to find dangerous cold and off-the-grid people who, if I was honest, already seemed a little strange. Being mauled by a coywolf wasn't on my bingo card.

In the trees beyond the outhouse a twig snapped, then another. Back in A-Bay, the coywolf I'd seen was alone, but didn't coyotes and wolves sometimes travel in packs? If this animal was hungry enough to feast on bloody snow, what might it do when its attention turned to us?

We had a policy against firing warning shots, which could lead to unintended injury. This wasn't the city, though, or even a small-town neighborhood. There was no one here but the animal and us, and so I communicated my plan to Val with a look, and watched as she withdrew her Glock.

A few feet away, the coywolf's gray-brown ear twitched. It turned its head, and locked us in its amber gaze.

The sound of the shot aimed at the sky was colossal, the creature gone before Val had a chance to re-holster her sidearm.

The silence that followed felt bigger than anything I'd known.

'Call Tim,' I said quickly. 'Let him know what's going on.' Val's shot would have echoed for miles.

'On it,' she told me, digging out her phone while I approached the evidence.

The problem with blood is that it looks the same whether it comes from a person or animal. There's no way to gauge the difference by sight; regardless of whose body it leaves, the effect is the same.

At the sight of it up close, the mess squarely between the cabin and an outhouse on the opposite end of the yard, I felt my stomach pitch once more, the sensation so abrupt that I teetered in my boots. I wasn't squeamish – I'd seen more gruesome things than this – but the violence of the scene made me want to run for the airboat, straight back to the comfort of home.

'You OK?' Val was at my side, the task of calling Tim forgotten.

'Pregnancy thing,' I assured her. 'Just woozy. I'll be fine. Nobody else mentioned this blood?'

'No one reported it to me. But someone knows about it.' She nodded at the boot prints in the snow, a single tread. As I studied the pattern, fistfuls of bloodied diamonds mashed into geometric shapes, I brought the back of my mittened hand to my mouth.

'Maybe the coywolf did this,' said Val. 'Attacked a small animal and gobbled up the remains.' That didn't explain the prints, though. She tried again. 'An islander could have cleaned up what it left behind.'

It was one theory.

But there were others.

'Are all of the islanders accounted for?'

Valerie said nothing.

I'd only just arrived on the island. Sylvie was with Tim at her cabin. It hadn't been long since I'd seen Teddy and Ewan, but a lot could happen in a handful of minutes out here. Ewan's daughter was in the Fowlers' house – but where exactly was her mother? And Rich and Jane, and Emmeline Plum?

My mouth filled with liquid as my stomach grew tight. When I looked at Val again, her lips were devoid of color.

I didn't want her visiting the cabins alone, not until we knew what we were dealing with. 'I'll take you to Teddy,' I said. It hadn't been long since he dropped me off; with any luck, he'd still have access to Ewan's snowmobile. 'Call and tell him you're coming his way, then go with him to check on the others. Make sure all the residents are safe, and inform them about the coywolf – but only that there was a sighting. Let's keep the blood to ourselves for now.'

'What about you?'

'I'm going to meet Sylvie. I'll fill in Tim at the same time.'

'You know how to drive that thing?'

I followed her gaze, and almost laughed. Though born in French Polynesia, Val had grown up in Munising, a Michigan Upper Peninsula town on the edge of Lake Superior that often got more than 200 inches of snow a year. But I was from Northern Vermont. When it came to snowmobiling, Val Ott had nothing on me.

'Stay sharp, OK?' I said as we mounted the machine once more. 'Keep your phone close.'

Val nodded as she dialed Teddy's number, I gave the Ski-Doo some gas, and we skidded back on to the snow-covered road.

Tim opened the door when I knocked, his expression thawing at the sight of me. 'Thank God,' he muttered, leaning in close. 'I heard gunfire.' He stepped aside to let me, along with a flurry of snow-flakes, inside.

Considering Sylvie had lured me out here by withholding information, he'd done a valiant job of calming down. Tim had wasted no time adopting the role of doting father-to-be, making sure I was always hydrated and well-fed. In a few hours it would be dark, though, and even with our floodlights and those reincarnated Christmas trees, the trip back could be thorny. I knew Tim had promised my mother he'd keep me safe. That my presence on Running Pine felt like a failure to him.

'We found blood,' I told him, my mouth near his ear. 'Behind Rich and Jane's place. A coywolf, too. Val scared it away and she's checking on the crew and islanders now.'

'A coywolf?' Frustration pulled at his features as his eyes flicked behind me. Tim thought for a moment, bit his bottom lip, and said, 'I'll go find her. I've done everything I can here, anyway. It's you she wants to see.'

'Be safe,' I whispered as Tim began the arduous task of suiting up for the cold.

Only then did I step beyond the door to face Sylvie Lavoy.

I'd seen photos of Sylvie online, but real life was unfiltered. There was a dull, brittle quality to the woman's unwashed hair, and her skin spoke of dry heat and too much canned food. Her lips were severely chapped, cherry red around the edges, and though she'd been gifted the dark, dramatic eyebrows modern girls yearn for, her eyes were widely spaced. With her hair pulled back it was a bovine innocence I saw now, not the sultry beauty she achieved online. Even through layers of clothing, a dove-white fisherman's sweater over a denim shirt and long corduroy skirt, I could tell she had the build of a person who, a few decades from now when her back bowed like a bentwood chair, would be child-sized. Tim had said she'd consumed enough brandy to fell a grown man, but maybe volume wasn't the problem so much as this bird-boned woman's low tolerance for alcohol.

Sylvie wasn't alone. There was a lady sitting by her side, and despite not having met her yet, I knew her at once. *Oldest on the island. A widow.* This was Emmeline Plum. Two islanders safe and sound. It was a start. On the other side of Sylvie was a dog, the same one I'd seen in photographs. Picture-perfect in a plaid bandana, smiling up at its master with lolling tongue and glistening teeth. Sylvie had a handful of the dog's fur in her hand, holding on as though it was a life rope.

'You came,' she said when she saw me.

'I came,' I replied, unsmiling. 'Where is he, Sylvie? Where's Cary?'

NINE

You *have to find him. He can't be gone. This can't be happening.* These were the pleas I'd grown accustomed to hearing from families of the missing. Most were hopeful, especially once help arrived. Surely the police, with our team of qualified experts, could get results. Spot prints and signs and scraps of evidence invisible to the untrained eye. It wasn't unheard of for us to magic clues from places where there appeared to be none, though we were not, in fact, magicians.

Try telling that to a woman whose boyfriend had done a vanishing act in the cold.

Sitting in Sylvie's cabin felt like hunkering down in a hobbit hole. Though the floor plan was open, the narrow house was packed with stuff, every wall bricked up with lidded storage bins that encroached on the limited living space. It was cozy, yes, especially after the chill of the crossing, but it bore an unsettling quality I couldn't put my finger on. At length, sundry objects coalesced to create an impression. The collection of vintage vases on the sideboard, the hodgepodge of mugs on the open kitchen shelves . . . there was nothing cohesive about it, no indication of effort at all. When I gave the storage bins a second look, I saw they were labeled with words like 'sundresses' and 'ribbon belts' and 'Valentine's.' Sylvie's house didn't feel like a home; it was a prop room, inharmonious and impersonal. Sentiment-free.

'The team's still searching,' I explained. 'We've got a helicopter over the river to get an aerial view. We'll keep looking until we find him, but if you know anything that might help us, it's vital that you tell me now.'

'It's OK, Bash. Shhh.' The Golden Retriever's bandana was hunter-green gingham, and I might have been surprised that Sylvie had taken the time to dress him were it not for Instagram. Her most recent post had gone live an hour before I'd woken up; while her boyfriend was still missing, she'd shared a photo of Bash sitting in the driver's seat of a luxury SUV. The car's interior was creamy butterscotch leather, the same tone as the dog's fur, and objects ranging from designer sunglasses to a vintage lunchbox and old-timey camera were strewn across the passenger seat. The SUV wasn't on Running Pine, and likely never had been, but the image was convincing. It was tagged as a #sponsoredpost, and Sylvie had directed her followers to the car manufacturer's website for details about *our favorite all-weather SUV ever*. Like all of the other photos on the feed, the colors were a mite too bright, the shadows hyper-dramatic. As if the island had been recreated on a movie set, a counterfeit place passing as real life.

Sylvie said, 'Do you have to report this to the press? The fact that he's missing?'

With cases like Cary's, we often relied on the media for help. A public plea – *Have you seen this man?* – could flush out a crucial eyewitness account. Before I could explain any of this, she added, 'I mean, could you not?'

'Not publicize the fact that your boyfriend is missing?'

'Just until we actually know something. Would that be OK?'

I towed in a breath through my nose. She was stalling, killing even more time though I was right in front of her now, all but begging for information. On top of that, it was a strange ask. If Tim played by the book, and he usually did, his next move would be to report the incident on Running Pine to Jefferson County's Public Information Officer. Larisa Ruthers would withhold Cary's identity if we asked her to. But how would that help our missing man?

Sylvie had the puppy-eye thing down. She looked like an emoji that had sprung to life. 'How old are you, Sylvie?' I asked now. I couldn't remember Tim mentioning her age.

'I'll be thirty in June,' she said. 'We were going to do a special post.'

Nearly thirty. I could scarcely believe it. 'We'll see what we can do,' I told her, leaning forward. 'But you have to work with us on this. Whatever information you have might help us bring him home.'

'It's not that simple,' Sylvie said.

Before I could answer, the older woman, Emmeline, put a hand on Sylvie's arm. She had to be in her late seventies, too fragile to be living this hard, uncomfortable life. Her white pixie cut was neatly combed, her clothing wrinkle-free, but the red around her eyes suggested it hadn't been a restful night. Every now and then, she pressed two fingers to the thin skin of her temple and held them there. Trying, perhaps, to keep dark thoughts at bay. This sweet old woman, who reminded me of Tim's mom, was most likely exhausted, yet she stayed, calming Sylvie's nerves by issuing soothing sounds not unlike the ones Sylvie whispered to Bash. 'Tell the detective what you know,' Emmeline said. 'For Cary's sake.'

Smoothing her straight brown hair behind both ears, Sylvie let her eyes drift to the window. 'There's nothing out here. Nothing at all.'

Beside her, Emmeline stiffened.

'I mean, we knew it would be remote. That was the whole point,' said Sylvie. 'We just didn't think being here would feel so . . . oppressive.'

'This is your family's cabin,' I said. 'Is that right?'

'Yeah. We used to come in summer. There are people here then.'

'There are people here *now*,' Emmeline muttered, getting to her feet. A moment later she was in the open kitchen, boiling water for tea on a little white stove.

Technically, she was right. The winter community was tiny though, and I could see that being an issue for a couple like Sylvie and Cary. I'd only just arrived on Running Pine, but between the dicey trip, the encounter with the coywolf, and the memory of that blood – spilled from a creature I had yet to identify – the island wasn't my scene either.

'This place,' Sylvie went on, her voice deepening. 'It got to him, it . . . got him.'

'It doesn't sound to me like you're the island's biggest fan. Can I ask why you and Cary stayed?'

Dipping her glossy, seal-like head, Sylvie said, 'We have nowhere else to go. Cary gave up his apartment in Kingston. I did too. We quit our jobs to come here. He's a graphic designer, and I did office management. We thought this was what we wanted.' They were government jobs, Sylvie explained, for the Ontario Ministry of Transportation, but the couple was tired of feeling like numbers. Sardines in a tin. 'We used to joke about going off the grid, but I never thought we'd actually do it. It was Cary's idea, moving here to start the account. Have you seen it?' A tilt of the head.

'Running Wild? I have. Beautiful photos.' Some of which must have required real risks to get.

'That's Cary,' said Sylvie. 'He has the best ideas for pics. People love them. We can't believe how big it's gotten in just a few months. People love it,' she repeated in a way that made me wonder why she felt the need to justify a life she'd just disparaged.

'It must be a lot of work, keeping the content coming.' I knew from watching my niece that maintaining a social media account could be taxing. If Cary had been overwhelmed by the relentless demands of his followers, the pressure to craft an irresistible endless scroll, was it possible he'd fled of his own accord?

'This was his first time ice fishing. Cary wanted to do a polar plunge, but Ewan and Rich talked him out of it. The fishing pics were supposed to be for tomorrow's post. I don't know what I'm going to do about that.'

By the sink in the kitchenette, Emmeline's head swiveled, her translucent blue eyes meeting mine. The mood in the room had been somber from the start, but Sylvie's words were a shock to the system. Cary was missing, and she was thinking about her next post. Emmeline looked as stunned as if she'd been smacked.

For my part, I resisted the urge to bury my head in my hands. That Cary had been unhappy on Running Pine was something we'd needed to know yesterday, ideally before we set foot on the island. It was key information. But it wasn't enough. There had to be something else here we could use. After the risk I'd taken to come, no way was I leaving the cabin empty-handed. I would probe, I decided, relentless in my pursuit of the facts: where Cary spent time, where he might be prone to go, anything that could help narrow the search. I would feed that intel to the team so they weren't combing the island blind. I'd get what I came for, even if it took all night.

But again, my thoughts wafted toward Jane Budd and Sylvie's plea that I make the trip. For some reason I had yet to discern, Sylvie Lavoy was playing me. Wasting time when time was what might save her boyfriend's life. And I was in no mood for games.

'Sylvie,' I said. 'What do you think happened to Cary that stopped him from coming home?'

Her teeth scraped a pink gully in the flesh of her lower lip. 'I think he's dead,' she said. 'I think being out here killed him.'

Shit. 'Why didn't you tell that to the others? Why wait for me?'

'I know who you are.' Her eyes looked heavy now. 'I knew you would help, no matter what.'

In recent years, I'd gained unwanted fame for finding missing people. Linking evidence and accounts until I had a solid chain that, with a little luck, led me straight to the lost. In almost every case I'd worked since leaving New York City for a life upstate, the search had morphed into a homicide investigation. In some ways, lost was lost.

'It's our job to help,' I explained. 'We've all trained for this. Everyone here has experience with missing people.'

Sylvie looked at me askance. 'You say that now, but they'll feel differently when they find out about my family.'

My spine snapped to attention. *I knew you'd help no matter what*, Sylvie had said. What was it about her family that she thought would drive others away? I recalled my conversation with Tim when he got home from searching the island. Sylvie's father had died the previous year, and she had a half-brother she wasn't close with. Tim hadn't mentioned anything unusual about the Lavoys.

Sylvie said, 'They have a reputation. The men in my family. My great-grandfather. My dad.'

'I'm not worried about that right now.' I couldn't imagine what her lineage had to do with finding her missing boyfriend, and as much as I pitied the woman, my patience was thinning as quickly as an ice chip on my tongue. 'I want to help, but I don't think you're being honest with me. What is it that you're not saying?' All my prodding, and she was still holding back. I could sense it.

Sylvie thought for a moment. At last, she said, 'I think there's a chance Cary wanted to disappear.'

I spoke her name quietly, creeping up as if trying not to startle a mouse. 'Are you saying you think Cary was suicidal?'

She drew a shaky breath, closed her eyes, and nodded.

The woman's words had set my limbs to tingling. I was known for closing missing persons cases, but suicide was something I had experience with, too. The last self-inflicted death Alexandria Bay had seen played out right behind Tim's cabin on Goose Bay, and it was woven into the fabric of the community like a blood-soaked skein of yarn. Sylvie was from Kingston, close enough that when the devastating events of that spring took place, she would have heard about them. That particular death had been told and retold by the press. A story with no end. If Sylvie knew about the suicide I'd witnessed, she might see me as an ally. A hand to hold while this nightmare rolled over her life like noxious fog.

Even so, my sympathy wasn't so easily won. For hours now, she'd watched our team fan out, the crew putting themselves in imminent danger while she hid the fact that Cary might have offed himself. Hoarded significant information like a secret candy stash.

If what she was saying was true, there was a chance we wouldn't find Cary for months, if we were lucky enough to recover his body at all. There were a dozen different ways a person could take their life on an island in winter, a dozen places they could dispose of themselves. We'd been working under the assumption that Cary was the victim of an accident. Either he'd stumbled upon a weak spot on the ice, or ventured out into the woods for a photo and been unable to get home. Hypothermia could set in within minutes of plunging into freezing water, death possible within an hour if someone was stuck in minus-fifteen-degree cold. This revelation, this *confession*, meant Cary could indeed have walked toward the channel, where currents thinned the ice further. He might be on the other side of the island, which abutted Canada, or miles deeper into the dense woods than our team had previously thought.

When she handed Sylvie a cup of tea, Emmeline Plum's veins bulged blue where they spanned gnarled knuckles.

'You're sure about this?' I asked Sylvie Lavoy.

'Positive.'

It was the last thing I wanted to hear.

It meant, without a sliver of doubt, that Cary was never coming home again.

TEN

New York City

Four Years Ago

D ave and I had agreed to meet at One Police Plaza, but I got there first. I didn't mind the wait. There was an independent bookstore not far from my apartment, and I'd made a stop on my way to Park Row. The weather was hot, the midday air rippling with humidity, and the dappled shade cast by the tree next to the park bench provided little relief. Sitting as still as possible while droplets of sweat rolled across my scalp, I started to read.

Murder Mind: Mapping the Brains of Killers was new, having released at the start of summer, and according to his website Starkweather had done a small tour with stops in Atlanta, Boston, and D.C. He was more of a celebrity than Dave had let on, a true authority in his field. He was a good writer too, and it wasn't long before the book pulled me in.

A broken limb, a knot of bruises on a wrist or thigh . . . on a corpse, such marks were as distinctive as eye color or nose shape when it came to identifying a killer. The condition of a body told investigators so much about the monster who'd inflicted harm. The context of a crime.

I swiped at my forehead and dried my hand on the leg of my polyester pants. Across the courtyard, a man was singing – or trying to, anyway. I lifted my eyes from the page. The man stumbled, hands sunk deep in his pockets as he walked. He wore a fisherman's hat and kept his head low, watching the pavement as if it might rear up and toss him like a rogue wave.

To Starkweather, violent crimes weren't whodunits; what he cared about was why. How a person's mental and emotional state might impact their actions. The connection between what they did and who they are.

'Happy Thanksgiving!'

This time when I looked up, the man was right in front of me, swaying in his soiled shoes. He looked to be homeless. Smelled that way, too. Though the hat masked most of his face I could see crumbs of food in his scraggly beard. He was drunk maybe, or suffering mental health issues, but he seemed harmless enough.

'You're early,' I told him. 'It's only August.'

'I wrote a poem about Thanksgiving once.'

'Oh yeah?'

The man's head bobbed. 'For my mother. I wrote it in jail.' He started to sing once more, his voice deep and raspy. The sound of a donkey mid-bray.

'OK, buddy, move along. Happy Thanksgiving to you too.' To my surprise he gave a salute and lurched away as I returned my attention to the book splayed on my lap.

In law enforcement, patterns are important. Recognizing them in crime data sets can expose habits, and when seemingly disparate criminal incidents demonstrate the same method of operation, that's vital. Finding patterns in historical data is helpful too, since it allows investigators to predict and forecast future crimes. Starkweather liked to use patterns – the nature of the attacks, where victims were found, indications of torture – to diagnose a series. Three kills made a serial murderer. But it only took two similar events to make a pattern.

'Hey there, lady.'

'Listen, man—'

I looked up, expecting to see the homeless guy again, and found Dave grinning down at me.

'Damn,' he said. 'Didn't realize we were doing storytime today. I left my copy of *The Very Hungry Caterpillar* at home.'

'It's good,' I said, flashing him the cover. 'Really good.'

'Haven't read it. *Golf Digest*'s more my speed. If I want to keep my marriage intact, I've got to give this job up soon anyway. Made a deal with the wife,' he said, 'so I think I'll invest my reading time in leisure sports, thanks.'

'Suit yourself. It got me thinking, though. I'd like to take a look at some other Jane Doe homicides. See if there are similarities.'

Dave studied me. 'Tell you what,' he said, nodding at the building that housed the Deputy Commissioner for Public Information. 'I was just here for another case a week ago. These guys know me. Let me handle the request and meet you back at the station. You can get a head start on those homicide files.'

'Yeah? OK, great. You sure you don't mind doing this yourself?'

'Nah.' Dave winked at me. 'I'll see you back there.' Hiking up his waistband, he said, 'Time to convince the DCPI to get Jane Doe's face in the news.'

As Dave sauntered off, I caught sight of the homeless man again. He was slumped on a bench on the opposite side of the courtyard, and though his eyes were half-closed, I had the distinct feeling that he'd been watching me.

ELEVEN

Emmeline Plum couldn't stop staring at my scar. Whereas Sylvie's cluttered cabin had been dim as a tomb, stark winter light streamed into Emmeline's home to put my disfigured cheek on full display.

'It's a hard life up here,' she said with a shake of her head. She'd mistaken me for a local, assumed I'd suffered some freak accident on a farm or a boat. She probably thought I had a lot of scars like the one that curled down my jaw.

She didn't know the half of it.

After I'd finished questioning Sylvie, Emmeline had suggested we let her get some rest and invited me over to her place. Tim and Val were still investigating the source of the blood we'd found outside Rich and Jane's cabin, and I hadn't been able to reach them. I wanted to see Cary's ice fishing spot during my time on the island, while I had the chance, but I didn't know where to look without my team. On top of that, I had more pressing concerns. Like the fetus reclining against my bladder.

After using the bathroom, I'd allowed Emmeline to settle me on her blue sofa. It was just a five-minute walk from Sylvie's place to Emmeline's property on the bay, but she seemed convinced the trek had left me winded. Went straight to the kitchen for juice and a sleeve of saltines to tide me over while she boiled water for more tea. Tea was something of a staple on Running Pine, it seemed, and that was fine by me.

It wasn't just the lighting that set Emmeline and Sylvie's cabins apart. Sylvie's rooms were crammed to bursting with props, but this living space was lined with metal shelving that held all manner of shelf-stable food. Commercial-sized tubs of oatmeal and ground coffee sat alongside boxes of crackers, rice, brownie mix, and enough cans of tuna to build a small fort. Airtight containers of spices and every canned vegetable under the sun. There was a clear bin sitting on the floor that must have held a hundred pounds of flour. It all gave the cabin the air of a doomsday bunker, as if Emmeline was preparing for the end of days, but it also made me worry that Sylvie and Cary were underprepared. Emmeline must have dropped a thousand bucks at Price Chopper to stock up for winter. At Sylvie's, I'd seen no food stores at all.

'It's kind of you to stay with her so much,' I said, thinking of Emmeline's hand on Sylvie's arm.

The woman nodded. 'She shouldn't be alone at a time like this.'

I said, 'I should warn you. Investigator Ott and I saw a coywolf earlier, right behind Rich and Jane's cabin.' I watched Emmeline's expression closely. The woman's lips thinned.

'They come with the territory. There are quite a few roaming the island. We get big herds of deer sometimes, too. That's a sight to see. All those deer crossing the ice.'

'Any dangerous encounters we should know about?'

'Oh, sure.' She'd returned from the open kitchen to stoke the fire. The electric heat was doing its job, but a thread of icy air from the window kept licking at the back of my neck. 'Not a year goes by when someone isn't chasing off a beaver on a mission to kill all the trees. There was a mountain lion sighting once, back in the forties, but these days the animals are mostly harmless.'

Mostly. It wasn't the answer I'd been hoping for.

How much had the newest arrivals known about Running Pine before deciding to spend a year here? Based on my conversation with Sylvie, she and Cary were ill-equipped in more ways than one. The consensus among the islanders was that the couple was in over their heads. Ewan's comment to Tim about his five-year-old daughter being better prepared than the newcomers suggested the Fowlers, Rich and Jane, and even Emmeline viewed Cary and Sylvie's pet project as reckless.

It was another reason why Sylvie's suicide theory wasn't without its merits. Running Wild had gotten big, the burden to maintain it like a pair of concrete shoes. All the while, behind the scenes, the focus was on survival. Meeting their basic needs and making sure they didn't get injured, or worse. Cary looked happy enough in pictures, but social media could be deceiving. Who better to gauge the man's emotional state than his live-in girlfriend?

There was a flaw in Sylvie's logic, though. *Running Wild had gotten big.* Ewan claimed the couple was doing well – so why wouldn't Cary stay to cash in? What kind of person took their life right after hitting paydirt? After working so hard to get here? I had to consider the possibility that Sylvie had imagined suicidal thoughts where there were none.

'Did you notice anything strange about Cary?' I asked now, leaning back against the couch and cupping my stomach. I hadn't had many opportunities to use my pregnancy to my advantage at work. If it kept Emmeline at ease while I questioned her about her missing neighbor, playing up my delicate state seemed harmless enough.

'Strange?' She eased a strand of clipped and colorless hair behind her ear. 'A lot of things he did were strange to me. He and Sylvie would spend hours setting up for a picture, even outside in the cold. All that time and effort for one single photo. But I didn't know him well enough to judge.'

'Moving to Running Pine must have been a difficult transition,' I remarked while nibbling on a pale cracker.

'It's not like moving to a new town, where your main concern is finding the hardware store and hunting down the best tuna fish sandwich.' Crouching next to the fire, she tucked another log into the hearth. 'It's life or death out here, and that's no exaggeration. I think we all feel a little responsible for this. I know I do.'

My eyebrow twitched. 'What do you mean by that?'

'We should have done more to prepare them. For this life. But it isn't as though we didn't try. Ewan and Rich, they gave Cary a crash course in the important stuff – make sure to let someone know where you're going, always carry a boat bag with a whistle, flashlight, flare. To be honest,' she said with a downturned mouth, 'I'm not sure he paid attention. He was more interested in getting the sunrise in his selfie.'

'Part of the job description, I guess. As unorthodox as that job may be.'

'I guess. But out here, safety needs to come first. You can't let yourself get distracted. The consequences are too dire, help too far away. I don't think Cary understood that at all.'

Green as they come. That was something else Ewan Fowler had told Tim when questioned about Cary's disappearance. 'Is Sylvie better equipped for this rugged life?'

'She'd been out here before, at least,' Emmeline said. 'She used to come to Running Pine as a child. Roscoe – that's her father – brought the family here most summers. That cabin's been around since the fifties, built at the same time as mine, I believe.'

'Roscoe,' I repeated. 'Do you know what Sylvie meant when she said her family had a bad reputation?'

'I hate to think that poor girl has been maligned because of her relatives' misdeeds, but people like to gossip. I don't know how much is true,' she went on, 'but Roscoe Lavoy got into some trouble back in the day. Nothing to do with her at all.'

I made a mental note to look into that. 'Well, I'm glad she's got you to show her kindness.'

'It's the least I can do,' Emmeline said, 'and what the others did for me. Until Cary and Sylvie arrived, I was the baby of the bunch – just two years living on the island. It was Oscar's idea to come. My husband. I lost him last April.'

'I'm sorry,' I said.

'Thank you. It's a horrible thing, losing your partner in life.' Her eyes trailed to the front door, and the road we'd taken from Sylvie's. 'Oscar died very suddenly. Bad heart.' With a fisted hand, she thumped her own chest. 'We met in Sacramento, but he grew up here and always wanted to move back. He'd been talking about overwintering for years. I thought he was nuts, of course, having been raised where I was. I never liked the cold. Oscar could be convincing, though.' With a smile, she added, 'He wore me down.

'The first year was an experiment,' Emmeline went on, needling me to eat another cracker as she made her way back to the stove for the tea. 'I didn't think we'd make it past Christmas. But we did. And here I am.'

'Even after your husband's passing.'

'It reminds me of him, being on the island. It was the last place we were together.'

'You live here full-time, then?' I said. 'All year?'

'Oh, no. I have fifteen grandchildren, and they all want a piece of Nana Emmy.' She laughed, and the sound was dazzling. I was starting to like Emmeline Plum. 'With the exception of my youngest son, who lives in South Carolina, my brood is on the West Coast, so I go back in late spring and stay through Halloween.'

'I guess the island life isn't for them?' If I'd had access to a place like Running Pine as a child, I would have loved to visit in summer. It struck me as odd that Emmeline's family, the grandchildren in particular, didn't petition to spend time in Upstate New York.

As she returned to the living room with a teapot and two mugs on a tray, her expression darkened. 'The trip is a hassle. Airfare's not cheap, especially with a gaggle of kids.'

'Well, you're one of the hardy ones, then,' I said. 'Most people do the opposite. By October, they're long gone.'

'My children would love that, believe me. I'm the only one of the islanders who still leaves – but I always come back. This place is like a second home now. Rich and Jane, Ewan and Miranda, and little Imogen . . . they're family. I love it here in winter.'

'And Sylvie and Cary? Do they love it too?'

The woman's brows dipped as she busied herself with the tea. 'I thought so. Now I'm not so sure. To be honest, last night was the most time I'd spent with Sylvie in quite a while. They keep to themselves,' she told me. 'We did try to welcome them into the fold. I offer to walk Bash with Sylvie sometimes, or ask her over for coffee. And we always invite them to Supper Club.'

'Supper Club?'

'It's a tradition. Something to look forward to. We take turns hosting,' she said. 'Make a big event of it. Sometimes even dance a little. We're limited with what we can cook out here, of course, but we do our best and dress to the nines. I look forward to it all month long.'

'A monthly dinner. That sounds like fun. Do Sylvie and Cary join you?'

Emmeline's lips wriggled into a tentative smile. 'They did at the beginning, for the first few months after they got here. Now they always seem to have an excuse. One of them isn't feeling well, or they're working on a new blog post.'

I thought about correcting her, but explaining social media to a septuagenarian wasn't a priority.

'Don't get me wrong, they're lovely. And generous, too. Sylvie gave me this.' She ran a hand over the scarf that was looped around her neck, seafoam green and fringed and, quite possibly, cashmere. 'We don't want them to feel pressured, but it's always a little odd when the day arrives around and they stay holed up in their cabin. What with everyone else joining in.'

Just seven adults living on the whole island, and when a party came around, two opted to stay home. 'I guess you have to make your own entertainment when there are no restaurants or movie theaters for miles. Not too many activities to choose from. Or people to spend time with.'

'It's not just that. We all came here by choice because we like the quiet. The slower pace. Being out here for months at a time, though . . . it can make you a little crazy.'

I'd been about to take a sip of tea, but as the rim of the cup met my teeth, I paused. 'How do you mean?'

'Have you ever been in an anechoic chamber?'

I gave the woman a puzzled look, and set down my cup.

'Anechoic means no echo,' Emmeline Plum explained. 'Think of it as the quietest room on earth, a place so silent that noise is measured in negative decibels. Oscar was an electrical engineer, and he used one in his work. Six layers of steel and concrete and these foam spikes that look medieval. It was quite impressive in there. Terrifying, too. The total absence of sound is deafening.' The woman closed her eyes and I studied her eyelids, lavender and gossamer-thin. 'It was so quiet I could hear the woosh of blood flowing through my own veins. Bones cracking in my neck when I turned my head sounded like tree branches split by lightning. The feeling is claustrophobic, the silence so total it left me gasping. No echo means the brain can't interpret space, you see. I imagine it's like being locked inside a padded coffin.'

Silence and isolation. It seemed that Ewan Fowler had shared an interest with Oscar Plum.

I waited, giving the woman time to go on while making a mental note never to set foot inside one of those chambers. 'Being out here isn't so different,' she said at last, 'standing in the woods at night after a snowfall. Winter's endless, sweeping silence. I happen to enjoy it, but it can be distressing if you don't make a point of stimulating your mind.'

Emmeline's gaze skated to the door once more as she said, 'Look at their day-to-day lives.' There was no chance of Sylvie hearing her, but I noticed that Emmeline had lowered her voice. 'They spend most of their time on their screens, talking to strangers and emailing with companies that want their products on Running Wild. Sometimes I wonder if, to them, this whole island isn't just another prop. If that's the case, the silence might be a lot to handle.'

'It sounds like you're saying you agree with Sylvie,' I said. 'About Cary's state of mind.'

'Does it?'

This time, when she looked away from me, Emmeline's stare came to rest on the window.

To the white and silent world outside.

TWELVE

The whine of a snowmobile approaching brought me to my feet. Emmeline beat me to the door.

'It's just Jane,' she said, letting the curtain fall back into place. 'She may have news about Cary.'

I tried not to let her see me exhale. Like Emmeline, Sylvie, and little Imogen, Jane was safe. Whatever the source of the blood, it hadn't come from her. We waited while she turned off the engine and shuffled up the cabin steps. Watched while, inside, she freed her head from her helmet and dug out a wad of tissues.

'Nothing new, I'm afraid,' Jane said. 'Rich thought he heard someone in the woods, but by the time he made it over there it was all quiet.'

'Any sign of my team?' I asked eagerly. 'Or the other searchers?'

Jane buried her nose in the tissues and blew. 'They're pretty well spread out. I heard a couple of them say they were going to the vineyard. It's closed for the season, of course, but if Cary made it up there, he might know to look for food. Or wine, anyway.'

If Sylvie was right about Cary, and he was a suicide risk, I didn't think it likely that he'd break into a winery. The more thorough the search, though, the better.

'Don't worry,' Jane said, watching me closely, helmet in hand. Melting snow coursed in rivulets off her heavy black boots. 'Rich runs hunting parties in the fall. He knows where to look. If he hasn't found Cary yet, he will.'

That might be true, I thought. *But will Cary still be alive when he does?*

Would the rest of the search crew?

I didn't like what I was hearing. At the moment, our team was scattered across more than five thousand acres. No doubt Tim, Val, and Teddy were doing their best to confirm everyone was safe, but the blood we'd found was smack in the middle of the winter community. I didn't like that Tim and Val hadn't called with a head count. It meant someone else might be missing, or worse, they were the source of that blood.

I hadn't intended to bring it up yet, but I feared we might be staring down the barrel at more trouble. 'I need to tell you both something,' I said.

Emmeline and Jane turned expectant faces my way.

'My investigator and I found blood outside your cabin. In the back,' I told Jane. 'Close to the trees.'

The women's silence only lasted a few seconds, but those seconds felt like bricks stacked on my shoulders.

Bricks that tumbled to the ground when they both began to laugh.

'I told him,' Jane said, turning to Emmeline. 'Didn't I tell him? It looks like a crime scene out there every time.'

'I hope you weren't worried.' Emmeline showed me her teeth. 'I can see why something like that would alarm you.'

'The blood's from the turkey,' Jane told me.

'What turkey?'

'The wild turkey. The one Rich killed last night.'

I said, 'Rich went *hunting*? In the middle of a search for a missing man?'

'Not *hunting*,' Jane replied coolly. 'The turkeys come right up to the cabins, looking for food. He didn't even have to leave the property.'

'He fired a weapon while unsuspecting people searched the island in the dark. They could have been close. Someone could have been injured!'

'I . . .' Jane was blinking furiously now. 'We needed that turkey. We didn't think.'

'No, you didn't.' What Jane's husband did was irresponsible. Apart from the dangers associated with firing a shotgun in the midst of a ground search, the blood Rich left behind had been misleading. Instead of continuing the hunt for Cary, who we now knew might have contemplated self-harm, Tim and Val were wasting still more time confirming the team and islanders were OK.

I did my best to contain my frustration as I explained all of this to the women before me, who, if nothing else, had the good sense to look shamefaced. Did our team really have to tell people to keep their firearms locked up while we doubled the current population of the island? I hadn't met Rich Samson yet, but his behavior made me want to punch a wall. More than that, it made me wonder whether we could trust his judgment. That was a problem, given he was currently assisting with the search.

'What's done is done,' said Emmeline, reaching for Jane's hand. At the older woman's touch, Jane's posture softened. 'Come in for tea, Jane?'

She gave a silent nod and started to take off her boots while I excused myself to call Tim from the bedroom.

'I'll send Val your way,' he said once I'd explained what I'd learned, which left him as exasperated as I was. 'She can take you to where Cary was last seen. You'll stay close to shore?'

'I won't go farther than the fishing site. And Val will be right by my side. Nothing new?'

'No. If Sylvie's right,' he said, 'and Cary doesn't want to be found, there isn't a lot of hope for us. Between the weak spots on the ice and the woods and all this snow, there are a lot of ways for him to disappear, and it's been more than twenty-four hours already. I really hope there's nothing fishy going on out here.'

That got my attention. 'You thinking foul play?' Our last island search for a missing man had taken just such a turn.

'No indication of that yet,' he said. 'But this whole thing strikes me as strange.'

That was putting it mildly. The place felt dystopian, ice-encrusted land and water stretching for miles in all directions and just a handful of humans living off frozen chops and gutted fish. Overwintering had an air of survivalist living. Personally, I favored a neighborhood to the idea of a remote home that was cut off from critical services like snow removal and first aid. Running Pine in winter was seclusion to the extreme. *Beyond the Wall*, just like Tim had said, and something about it was making him edgy.

'Could be the isolation,' I offered.

'Could be the people,' said Tim.

A cold dribble of apprehension made its way down my back.

My husband was loyal to his core, not just willing but eager to give friends and neighbors the benefit of the doubt. It was one of the things that had challenged us when we first met. Skeptical was my default setting, and I'd always made an effort not to let personal bias influence my investigative methods – but I'd also learned that Tim's approach wasn't half-bad. His outlook was hopeful, his attitude buoyed by the optimism that powered him like a car battery, and seeing the good in folks gave him a unique perspective on what might compel someone to commit a crime. He was an empath with a rare ability to connect with others on the deepest level.

Over the years, though, he'd come to understand a hard truth: a hunger for violence doesn't discriminate. If Tim had a bad feeling about someone, he was usually right.

'There's something off out here. I think it has to do with Sylvie and Cary. I'm not convinced they're welcome.'

I'd gotten the same sense, and told him so. 'They've been here for six months, right? Could it be the islanders are slow to open up? They're friends and family, long-time neighbors with history. Shared experiences that go back a bit. Communities can be funny about accepting strangers.'

'You of all people should know.'

I met Tim's comment with a snort. I did know what it was like to be the new kid on the street, and was willing to bet the islanders were even tighter than folks in A-Bay. Emmeline Plum, Rich Samson and Jane Budd, and the Fowlers lived in a place that required intense collaboration. They'd formed an alliance against the elements, and their success – their very lives – hinged on mutual trust. Maybe they were a close group, not 'off' so much as cliquey. And given Cary and Sylvie preferred not to socialize, they might have given up on welcoming them into the fray.

'What's your plan?' I asked. 'Give the search another day?'

Tim fell silent. This was not an easy decision to make. Cary had a girlfriend right here on the island, and a mother across the border in Ottawa who'd want to know we'd done everything we could to recover her son. As I thought about her, a fresh wave of guilt over Jane Doe rolled in. We'd given her case the requisite two weeks before moving on, but it wasn't enough. The early days of an investigation were critical; once we reached that liminal time when new crimes redirected our focus, our faith began to dwindle. The situation that had bedeviled me and Dave wasn't so different from what was happening to Tim and Val. With every passing hour, our team got less bullish, the likelihood of success skidding away.

'Let's see what today brings,' Tim said. 'Take it one hour at a time.'

After reassuring him once more that I'd be fine on the ice, I ended the call and stepped back into the living room. Immediately, Emmeline and Jane leapt away from each other like they'd been stung. They'd been whispering, heads and bodies close. Conferring about something I wasn't meant to hear. It didn't escape my attention that, when they saw me, both women slapped on guileless smiles.

'I should get going.' It was Emmeline who said it, all at once eager to leave her own house despite having just offered Jane tea. 'I promised Miranda I'd keep Imogen busy while she cleans up – and the soup! It must be time to replenish that pot by now.'

Jane said, 'I'll take you, Em. The search team has your Ski-Doo, right?'

'That's right. You're welcome to stay,' she told me. 'Warm up some more while you wait.'

'Shout if you need anything,' Jane threw in before zipping her bulky snowmobile suit. Moving far faster than she had before.

And with that, the two women were gone, and I was alone in the cabin.

THIRTEEN

'A turkey,' Val said as we plodded from the snowmobile down to the bay. 'For the love of Christ. Please remind me never to accept a dinner invitation from Rich Samson.'

After Val picked me up at Emmeline's cabin, we'd gone to see the bird for ourselves and found it in the outhouse, of all places. When Jane had explained that part to me, I'd been disgusted too, but apparently Rich had converted the slim building once the cabin got indoor plumbing. The turkey would be suspended in there for a day or two until Rich finished processing it.

But first, it had hung from a tree branch in the yard while the man slit its throat.

Now, down by the river, I was still fuming over the fact that Rich had shot a turkey while our team was on the island. It was a big place – amazingly, no one had heard the shot – but accidents could happen, and he hadn't even given Val and Tim a heads-up. 'He must have known we'd find the blood,' I said, screwing up my mouth as I tried to make sense of his actions. 'Strange behavior, under the circumstances.'

'Maybe living out here killed his manners. Excuse the pun. It's right there,' said Val, pointing to a spot on the ice while stepping over a colorless clump of dried brush. 'But we've been all over this bay, both yesterday and this morning. If there was anything else to see, I gotta think we'd have found it by now.'

I agreed with her, but wanted to check out Cary's last known location for myself. 'Tell me more about the search this morning,' I said.

'We thought we were getting somewhere with this one barn. There's an abandoned farm out by the cheese factory, which is abandoned too. I thought for sure I saw movement in the window,' said Val. 'A shadow or . . . something.'

'A shadow? In a barn that should have been empty? What was it?'

'I was with Jane at the time. She said she thought maybe a bird. They nest on the windowsills, apparently. I didn't see any birds when I looked inside. But then, I didn't see Cary either. You sure this is safe for you?' she asked as we stepped onto the ice.

There was a jacket of snow on the bay, not the streaky, wind-blown kind I'd seen on the ride over but a dense layer that concealed most of the ice. The snow's surface was ever-changing, crusting and condensing to take on a new texture depending on factors like temperature, sun, wind, and rain. I shuffled my boots and was happy to find we had traction. 'We won't go past the fishing site – and it got colder overnight. This ice isn't thinner than it was yesterday. But let's stick close to the shoreline all the same. That way if it cracks, all we'll get is cold feet.'

Val nodded, flinching when the ice creaked under her insulated boot. Dragging a hand across her nose, she said, 'What do you make of Sylvie?'

'She's oddly calm, under the circumstances.' The prior day, Jane had painted the woman as frantic, so panicked about Cary failing to come home that Emmeline had felt it necessary to medicate with brandy. Today's composure could be chalked up to emotional exhaustion, maybe even a hangover. It bothered me all the same. 'She seems confident in this suicide theory.'

'Confidence and delusion can look a lot alike.'

'You don't trust her?' I asked.

Val rubbed her mittened hands together while we walked, a feeble attempt at keeping warm. With her snowmobile helmet on and two long pigtails flopping over her shoulders, she reminded me of Bobby. At thirteen, Val's daughter had the same dark hair and build as her Pacific Islander American mom. The girl may have lacked Val's titanium shell, but I could sense that forming already.

'If you're asking whether I think she killed her boyfriend, I'm not convinced of that,' said Val. 'Not yet, anyway. But no, I don't trust her. Do you?'

Did I trust Sylvie? This woman who'd lured me to the island with important information she'd withheld from my team? 'We aren't getting the whole story, that's for sure. What do you know about her family?'

'Not much. Should we have Sol work on that?'

'Let's,' I said, taking out my phone to send Jeremy Solomon a text. When I was done, I snapped a photo of the bay. 'You're a few years younger than me. Have you ever heard of a couple in their twenties ditching dependable government jobs to become online influencers?'

'Don't keep that phone away from your body heat for too long.

The cold drains the battery crazy fast. Yeah,' Val said as I stuck the device safely back in my pocket. 'That kind of thing definitely happens. Bobby watches this couple on YouTube who sold everything they owned to buy a sailboat. Now they're circumnavigating the world with their cat, dodging lightning storms and grilling fresh-caught fish. They've got two million subscribers.'

'We're doing life wrong, Tim and me. How'd we end up in the frozen north rather than sailing the Portuguese coast?'

'Come on,' Val replied through a grin. 'You know you wouldn't have it any other way. It doesn't seem like it was planned, though, this Running Wild thing. Sylvie only inherited the cabin from her dad in early summer, and she and Cary didn't move here until a week before Labor Day.'

'Remind me what happened to the father? Roscoe Lavoy?'

'Lung cancer. It was a long illness. He was Canadian, so she's a dual citizen. Sylvie never lived anywhere but Cape Vincent and Kingston. Guess she was looking to make a change.'

'Yeah,' I said, though choosing a community of six strangers over friends and Cary's family seemed like a drastic choice. Shielding the harsh winter light with my gloved hand, I squinted at the frozen river. 'There have been links between suicidal tendencies and extreme sports. Cary took some big risks to get his dramatic photos – and those are just the ones we know about.' Waterskiing with a carved pumpkin on your head was bad enough, but Sylvie's mention of a proposed polar plunge in thirty-five-degree Fahrenheit water was deeply unsettling. 'Sylvie made it sound like he was desperate for an escape, though you'd never know it by looking at Running Wild.'

'Social media's a highlight reel,' said Val. 'People use it to showcase the good in their lives, which also makes it easy to detract from the bad. If Cary and Sylvie have sponsors, big brands expecting upbeat content that convinces people to buy their products, Cary would only post happy times. Glowy cheeks and twined hands and brandy by the fire. See those two fishing poles frozen in place? Those are his.'

I followed the trajectory of her arm, and took a few more steps onto the bay. I could just make out the ghostly impression of footprints next to my own. This must have been the trail the fisherman took the previous morning. Just as Tim said, the holes Ewan augered to test the ice had closed up. If there had been a bigger hole, like from a break, that was gone now too.

Reaching down, I scooped up a few bits of ice and popped them in my mouth. My stomach had started to growl.

'Let's head back and warm up,' said Val. 'Emmeline's been really generous with her place. I'm sure she has some soup for us, too.'

Staring out at the river, I said, 'Yeah. OK.' Seeing the fishing site for myself was eerie, but it confirmed my suspicions. Wherever he'd gone, Cary probably wasn't coming back.

The cold had hardened the newer footprints we'd followed out, so we made a fresh path on the way back to shore. Though I couldn't see the state helicopter, the thwack of its blades reverberated across land and ice. 'The Huey can be a game changer, but if Sylvie's thinking suicide, then . . . oof.'

I stumbled, arms windmilling as I struggled to regain my balance. My foot had connected with something hard, toes tingling inside my boot. Something else happened then: I felt the ice shift. Val reached for me, pulling me close just as a crack fractured the surface. I looked down. The thing I'd tripped on was a baseball-sized mound.

'What the . . .' Gripping Val's arm for balance, I nudged the mass with my boot. 'I think it's a glove.'

'Shit,' said Val. 'Could be Cary's.'

'It's stuck.'

Widening my stance, the weight of my belly towing me down, I strained to reach the object and used my foot to clear away still more snow. The glove was a man's, ice-caked and frozen solid. Standing upright like a Halloween centerpiece, fingers curled into a menacing claw. Again I dragged the side of my boot across the ice, scooping still more snow away. One more hard swipe, and I saw it.

A man's face, ghostly pale with mouth agape. Hovering below the bluish ice.

I reared backward, mint-cold air searing the back of my throat. 'Dig,' I gasped, widening my stance. 'Dig!'

Val dropped to her knees and raked at the snow in a frenzy, pulling on the hand that punched out of the ice. Bile formed in the back of my throat as I waited for the ice to crack again and black water to creep up on us like spilled oil, but it held. I whipped out my phone. We needed Tim.

We needed a chainsaw.

In Vermont, I'd lived near Lake Champlain, and one year the local news had reported that a fox fell into the shallows, freezing solid. The man who found it had cut the fox out and displayed it on the shore as a warning. The animal was perfectly preserved, memorialized in a brick of white ice. Local authorities wasted no time removing the morbid exhibit, but I'd seen the photographs. Remembered that poor creature's legs, outstretched as if it was still out for a stroll.

It took Tim and Teddy ten minutes to get from wherever they'd been to the bay, and five more to free the corpse from the river with Rich's chainsaw. Wherever Cary had gone into the water, the current had carried him back to shore. It was impossible to say whether he'd been alive when his gloved hand caught in that soft spot, but in all likelihood he'd been under our search team's feet the whole time.

As Val and I watched from the shore, I thought about Sylvie. I'd been tough on her during our talk, a fact that pained me now. There was no telling what this news would do to her, or how she'd cope while we began the arduous task of transporting Cary back to the mainland. Moving the dead required a license; if the funeral home's boat was occupied, it might take hours to arrange an alternative. In the meantime, we'd have to inform the islanders, and offer whatever support we could.

'Shana.'

I blinked twice when Tim called my name, and made my way to where he stood. Looked down at the jagged black hole, the water gently lapping at the ice. Cary's face was chalky, eyes dull, mouth slack. I heard myself make a sound of surprise.

The front of Cary Caufield's lurid red jacket was split wide and shredded, bits of white feather down peeking through. The fabric so ragged it looked as if he'd met a creature with the sharpest of claws.

'He was shot,' Tim said. 'The damage to his coat. It's from a rifle.'

'He was shot,' I slowly repeated. 'While on a fishing trip.'

This wasn't suicide.

Sylvie had been wrong about Cary.

She'd been wrong about everything.

FOURTEEN

New York City

Four Years Ago

'Everyone wants to hear about the offender,' the man at the microphone said. 'Why they did what they did. The thing is, those answers don't only come from the offender's life. Sure, a killer's relationships, job, and childhood may factor into a crime, but some of the most critical insights lie with the people they choose to target. And yet, time and time again, one investigative tactic is ignored.'

'Profiling the victim,' I muttered under my breath, thinking of what that might look like. Studying the thirteen-year-old boy shot on his way to school, the eighty-two-year-old widow pushed down three flights of stairs. The unidentified body dumped into a river.

'Profiling the victim,' Adam Starkweather said, echoing my words, and for a fleeting second, his eyes met mine.

Wednesdays were the days I looked forward to most. Karate offered an escape from the emotional burden of my job, a chance to channel my anger over all that ugliness and pain into something useful. That night in August promised to be even better. My sensei had kept me a few minutes late to perfect a new form – 3 Kata, more about strength and conditioning than self-defense, but important all the same – so I was still in my gi pants when I arrived at the Barnes & Noble to find every folding chair taken, the event already underway. I dropped my backpack at my feet, leaned against a shelf of cozy mysteries, and settled in to watch.

The timing of the talk, right days after Dave told me about Starkweather, felt like kismet. It was the last stop on the tour, and I had just finished Starkweather's book, tearing through it faster than I'd read anything before. Against his dark skin, his sideburns looked grayer than in the author photo on the back of *Murder Mind*. His eyes narrowed in a perpetual squint that gave him a gravitas at odds with the droplets of summer rain sparkling in his tightly coiled hair.

'Knowing more about a victim – from marital status to hobbies and career – expands the network of that individual's relationships, which in turn can lead to information about why they were a target. Yes, psychological profiles are a must. But the victim can hold the key to a whole crime.'

There were questions, after which someone steered Starkweather to a table piled high with shiny hardcovers. It was only then that I realized I'd left my own copy at home. I thought about calling it a night, but I'd gone to the trouble of coming. I couldn't let the opportunity to meet him slip me by.

Ten more minutes, and it was my turn. When Starkweather saw me empty-handed, he cocked his head.

'I do have a copy,' I told him. 'I forgot to bring it.'

'Ah. So . . . just wanted to say hi?'

'I guess. Hi.' I felt myself flush.

'True crime fan?' he asked.

'Detective, actually. Shana Merchant, Ninth Precinct.' I extended my hand.

With a quirk of his eyebrows, he took it. 'Good to meet you, Shana. I don't get a lot of colleagues at these things. Jiu-Jitsu?'

It took me a moment to clue in, but when he gestured at my gi pants, I smiled.

'Karate, actually. Do you study martial arts?'

'My son does. He's into the tournament scene.' Though he was still smiling, his gaze had flicked to the people in line behind me.

'Thanks for the talk,' I said quickly. 'It was fascinating. Really.'

'It was nice meeting you, Shana.'

'You too.'

'Wait.'

When I turned back around, there was a business card in his hand.

'So I can sign your book sometime,' Starkweather said.

Wordlessly, I accepted the card from the guy Dave had called a legend.

He was just the man I'd been looking for.

FIFTEEN

Waxy skin the color of chilled skim milk. Cloudy eyes sunken in their orbits. Two faces, Jane Doe's and Cary Caufield's, played on repeat in my mind.

Two people lost to the water.

After extracting Cary's body from the ice, Tim, Val, and I decamped to Emmeline's to peel off sweat-soaked clothing and devise a plan. After that, Tim and I made our way to Sylvie's to break the gut-wrenching news. I hadn't expected to find Emmeline there yet again, but it was she who responded to my knock. 'You're back,' she said softly, her gaze lingering on the hats clutched in our hands.

Sylvie was still on the couch, her Golden Retriever panting in the suffocating heat from the fire. She was sipping from a black and green mug that said, 'Stone Cold Witch,' a vestige of Halloween time. Another one of her props. Reality was about to come into stark relief for Sylvie, Running Wild fading into the background as her life took a startling turn.

'I fell asleep,' she told us, turning vacant eyes our way. 'I was hoping this was all a bad dream.'

'Oh honey,' Emmeline said, bringing a hand to her heart.

We did our best to explain the procedure while Sylvie gave in to body-racking sobs. The medical examiner was on his way to photograph the crime scene before Cary was transported to the mainland. The missing persons search had upgraded to a homicide, our criminal investigation already begun.

In the small island community, there were just seven residents left.

By all indications, one of them had shot the eighth and hidden him under the ice.

If I'd had any doubt left that Emmeline sought to solve problems with food, it was driven out when she set a tray on the coffee table. Slices of bread and pound cake next to jars of honey and jam. She was trying so hard to provide a moment of comfort that I hated what I was about to say.

'I'm sorry, Emmeline. Could we have some time alone with Sylvie?'

The woman's broad forehead, nearly the same shade of ivory as her hair, furrowed.

'We know this is awkward,' said Tim, 'since you've been so kind to loan our team your home.'

'Val may still be over there,' I went on. 'Maybe you could wait at a neighbor's?'

She nodded once, and then more vigorously. 'Of course. I'll go to Jane's. You call if you need me, sweetheart,' she told Sylvie. 'I'm just a few minutes away.'

Sylvie, Tim, and I waited in twitchy silence as Emmeline abandoned the coffee service and slipped on her coat. 'Can you think of any reason why someone might want to hurt Cary?' I asked after she'd gone.

It was a long time before she answered. 'We get haters sometimes,' Sylvie said through her tears. 'Everyone does. It's jealousy. Some people are just mean.' Her attention was on the picture window. That cluster of rod-straight pines outside. 'The messages I get . . . there's this one troll who DMs twice a week. Keeps calling me a spoiled bitch and telling me I should drop dead.'

'DM,' I repeated, my antennae up as I fished my notebook from my pocket. 'He messages you on Instagram?'

'Through Running Wild. He's horrible.'

I'd dealt with cases involving such messages, the kind that could slide from professions of admiration into insults and intimidations like slow, sticky sap from a tree. 'Can you show me?'

She shook her head. 'I delete them as soon as they come in. I don't like having them on my phone.'

'The troll who's been bothering you,' said Tim. 'What's his name?'

'His profile's a fake, all gym selfies and anti-gun-control posts. I keep blocking him, but it doesn't help. He just starts over again with a new handle.'

We couldn't know where this so-called troll was from or who he was, at least for now. It was obvious that Sylvie found his DMs upsetting, which suggested the threats were convincing. The couple made no qualms about sharing the details of their life online, including the fact that Running Pine was in the Thousand Islands.

Before I could voice my concern, Sylvie said, 'I guess one of them could have come here. Everyone knows where we are – we post about it all the time, and tag our location. Anyone with a map could find us. Do you think someone followed us here and *shot* Cary?'

In any other scenario, the notion might have held water. Cary and Sylvie were famous enough to attract a troubled, obsessive fan. But Running Pine Island was a thirty-minute airboat ride from the mainland, the St Lawrence a deadly fusion of subzero water and slabs of rough ice. Even the parts that didn't freeze solid could be lethal if a traveler encountered Sol's frazil ice clogging the river like post-tsunami debris. Crossing, making landfall, getting back to the mainland, and doing it all undetected was no minor feat. There were snowmobiles aplenty in town, but they were conspicuous and loud.

Neither Tim nor I had answered Sylvie's question. 'If you get any more of those messages,' Tim said instead, 'don't delete them.' We needed to determine the validity of those threats.

Sylvie sunk her hand deeper into her dog's fur. 'You said why. *Why* someone might want to hurt him. Not who. Does that mean you know who did this?'

'Not yet,' Tim said.

'But there's no one else out there,' said Sylvie. 'Just them.'

Them. Her neighbors. Some, like Emmeline and Jane, closer to friends.

Tim said, 'We don't want to make assumptions, but you do live on a remote island that's difficult to access. Which is why we need to know whether Cary and your neighbors got along.'

All of a sudden Sylvie looked panicked. Her eyes searched the room as if for an escape route. 'We didn't spend much time with them. Just a few dinners early on. Ewan and Rich showed him around a little. Not recently.'

'How often did they go fishing together?'

'This was the first time. Honestly, we hardly see them.'

'And Emmeline?' I said. 'Miranda and Jane?'

'They didn't do this. You've got it all wrong.'

I hadn't expected her to throw an islander under the bus. Sylvie hadn't so much as hinted at a rift in prior conversations. Even so, the vehemence with which she defended them was surprising.

'Hardly see them,' Tim repeated. 'Why is that, Sylvie? Not a lot of choices for friends in these parts.'

'They're . . . older,' she said. 'We're busy with Running Wild. We're just not very social people.'

That didn't exactly square with social media stardom, but I nodded all the same. Tim and I often opted to stay home rather than go out with friends – but not always. At least once a week, I'd get coffee with Maureen McIntyre; she'd drive in from the sheriff's office in Watertown, or I'd make the thirty-minute trip south. More recently, Tim and I had been meeting Val at our go-to bar, or hosting pizza nights for her and Bobby. The day after tomorrow, we'd be at Tim's moms' eating that amazing onion dip. I could never imagine tiring of Tim, but spending every minute together for months on end with very little outside contact sounded like a recipe for trouble.

'Just a few more questions.' Tim had softened his voice, and I knew what was coming. 'Do you or Cary own a rifle?'

'Asking is standard procedure, that's all,' I said when Sylvie's eyes got bigger.

'No,' she told us, tensing her jaw. 'No, we don't own a rifle, and I wouldn't know how to use one if we did.'

'OK,' said Tim. 'Thanks. You're doing great.' As he reached out a hand to pet Bash, he gave Sylvie an encouraging smile. 'What about you and Cary, Sylvie. Any problems in your relationship?'

'Our relationship was great,' she said coolly.

I made a note of that as well. 'We'd like you to come back with us. Stay on the mainland for a while. I know this is all incredibly hard, and I know it feels like you're alone, but we have people who can help you.'

Sylvie shook her head again. 'I can't leave here.'

'Just for a day or two.' *Until we know what we're dealing with. Why your boyfriend went fishing, and ended up shot.* 'We'll be notifying Cary's family,' I said. 'I'm sure they'll want to see you.'

'What? No. I have to stay here.'

I drew in a breath. 'We know you don't have family of your own close by, but we could call someone for you. It might help to talk about this.'

'It won't.'

Tim said, 'If you're worried about your dog, I'm sure we can find a hotel that—'

'It's Running Wild,' she said. 'I have to be here. I have to stay.'

She must have seen the shock in our expressions, our stunned reaction to the notion that she wanted to stay in a place where every view smacked of her immense loss because a bunch of strangers expected fresh content. Sylvie said, 'This isn't, like, a hobby. Running the account is my *job*. We're under contract with dozens of brands to feature their products, brands with entire teams of executives and lawyers watching to make sure we deliver. Some of them already paid us for posts we haven't created yet – and what they paid for is *this*. Look around,' she said with a note of derision in her voice. 'You can't recreate this island. It can't be faked.'

I wasn't so sure about that. Much of what I'd seen online already was an act. As a graphic designer, Cary might have borne the brunt of that work, but surely Sylvie had a sense of how to doctor photos too.

Tim said, 'I'm sorry, but we have to insist. We need to take a formal statement, Sylvie. There are papers to sign related to the death.'

'Grief can sneak up on you,' I put in. How many times had I thought I was fine, good even, only to go jelly-kneed when a torturous memory slipped a switchblade through my ribs? 'It can be overpowering. You staying out here tonight, alone, isn't safe.'

I watched her take the measure of our request. In the set of her eyes, I could see her recalling what she'd already told me. The isolation of Running Pine had messed with Cary's head. *It got to him. It got him.*

I also catalogued the moment when Sylvie realized that, despite the light touch with which we'd handled her, she didn't have a choice.

The young woman swept the tears from her cheeks with the side of her thumb, the motion so tender she might have been soothing a child. 'I can bring Bash?'

'Of course. We'll bring you both to Clayton.'

It didn't take long for her to pack. A duffle of clothes and some toiletries. A Ziploc bag of kibble for the dog. The rest of the items she'd used to stage an enviable life stayed behind. Tim called Emmeline to let her know we were taking Sylvie off the island, and that we'd be back the next day. It would be a tight squeeze on the airboat this time, even if Teddy took two trips, but we had to work within the confines of the situation.

At last, we bundled ourselves up and headed back into the cold.

Winter days upstate were frigid, but on that particular afternoon the very air felt rimy, infinitesimal shards of ice stinging our cheeks as we rode Rich's three-person snowmobile to the river. All the while my mind was churning, projecting the tasks to come. I kept an ad libitum to-do list, and Tim was endlessly amused by my need to plan next steps. *So OK, when we get home you'll grab the groceries from the back and put the meat and dairy in the fridge while I start on the sandwiches and make the fire.* I craved order, valued efficiency, so by the time we reached the airboat I'd already devised a procedure for when we were back on the opposite shore. We'd get Sylvie settled at the hotel, and I'd drive with Tim to the barracks where, at my desk, I'd check the islanders' criminal histories. Then home to scrounge up some dinner and finish the laundry already underway. I hadn't made it to the store – chicken chili was out of the question – but there was leftover tomato soup that, paired with scallion-studded grilled cheese, would hit the spot.

'What the hell?'

Sylvie's tone brought me out of my reverie. We were back on our feet, walking down to the river, and she was staring slack-jawed at Ewan and Rich, both of whom stood with Teddy next to the boat. It was my first time seeing Jane's husband, who had cropped gray hair and the hardened look of an ocean fisherman. Both men wore expressions of regret, but neither looked up from the ice on our approach.

Val had beaten us to the bay. I could guess what she'd told the men when she managed to track them down. *You were the last ones to see Cary alive. We need to bring you in for questioning.* I imagined they'd kissed their wives goodbye, Ewan brushing his daughter's cheek with his hand before being marched to the airboat. Cary had been shot at close range, seemingly by a rifle, but Rich had used a shotgun to kill a turkey. His weapon was in Val's possession now, on its way – like the men – to the barracks. We all knew the difference between a rifle wound and that from a shotgun slug, and the odds that Rich's gun had killed Cary were nearly non-existent. That didn't change the fact that these two were currently prime suspects.

'Let's get you and Bash on board,' I told Sylvie, unsure how she'd feel about sharing a boat with the men. She'd told us we had it wrong, that the islanders were innocent. And yet, here we were taking them to the station.

'No.' Next to me, Sylvie shook her head. 'I changed my mind. I'm not going.' The woman looked haunted, her fear pure and cold.

'It's a short trip,' I said, though I knew that wouldn't appease her concerns. Her face was going whiter by the second. I caught Teddy's eye where he waited. The man shrugged. We were riding together whether Sylvie liked it or not.

As I led Sylvie farther down the dock, Rich said, 'I'm so sorry for your loss.'

'He was a good man,' added Ewan Fowler, bringing a hand to his heart.

I reached for Sylvie's elbow to help her past Teddy and into the boat. She bucked like she'd been jabbed with a cattle prod, though my hands were still on her arm.

My boots had good grip, unlike Sylvie's, which looked more suited to a catwalk runway than the island's rugged terrain. It didn't matter. The dock was coated with a pulpy layer of snow, under which sat solid ice. And when Sylvie convulsed beside me, straining away from the airboat, my feet went out from under me sure as if I'd been struck with a bat.

I wasn't used to my ungainly shape, or the odd new distribution of weight. I fell sideways, the length of my body striking unrelenting ice.

Pain shot through my arm and the bone of my hip, and for a second I was breathless. By the time he reached me, my husband's face was gray.

'Oh my God,' said Sylvie. 'Is she OK?'

'Oh my God,' said Tim, hands fluttering helplessly around me as an array of tiny, dizzying lights swirled in my field of vision.

'Quick,' said Val, 'get her in the boat. We'll dock at the hospital.'

The hospital.

The baby.

SIXTEEN

New York City

Four Years Ago

The bistro was filled to bursting with diners dressed in linen and expensive shoes. He waited in a booth by the window, his face flickering in the mullioned glass.

As I crossed the candlelit room toward Adam Starkweather, he looked up at me and smiled.

I hadn't been able to get the man out of my head. His book validated what I'd suspected: the cut on Jane Doe's face wasn't born of some random sadistic impulse. It meant something. And so, the day after meeting him, I'd taken a chance and called the number on his card. Dave had insisted that Starkweather's expertise was out of our reach, but somehow, the criminal profiler had agreed to meet me.

I would finally get my chance to ask him about Jane.

'For your son.' I held out a patch, the black crest outlined in red and surrounded by a twisting green and gold dragon. Starkweather had only mentioned his kid in passing, but I was proud of myself for having thought to bring a gift. My own first patch, I'd received from my sensei after an especially grueling belt test. It had meant a lot to me.

'Wow. This is great,' Starkweather said, accepting the iron-on emblem. 'Vincent would have gone nuts for this as a kid.'

'Oh. How old is Vincent now?'

'He'll be thirty-five next month.'

My mouth filled with acid. 'Oh,' I repeated, mortified. The man before me didn't look anywhere near old enough to have a son that age. 'I—'

'I'm messing with you,' he said, smirking. 'Vince is ten, and he'll love this.'

'Was that some kind of test?' If so, I'd clearly failed.

'More like a reminder. Never doubt your instincts. They're the only thing you can trust. So, want to tell me about your case?'

I hadn't mentioned a case, not Jane Doe's or any other.

'I don't get a lot of cops at my readings,' he explained in response to my baffled look. 'Not unless they're after something.'

'Guilty,' I said through gnashed teeth. 'There is something I wanted to ask you about. It's a Jane Doe homicide, and she has this facial wound – a cut given to her postmortem.' I told him everything we knew, which wasn't much. 'Any thoughts on what kind of person would do that? Disfigure a woman after she was dead?'

'Plenty,' he said. 'You're working with some interesting traits. Historically, both asphyxiation and drownings have been linked to expressions of dominance. They're a means of controlling the target – what they see and feel – in the most visceral way. The idea of taking another human to the brink, withholding something so vital as oxygen to mete out pain, can be appealing to the monsters among us. You have to remember, though, it isn't always spontaneous.'

'Patterns,' I said. 'Leading up to the crime. Like distorted thinking or feelings of inadequacy. Real or imagined events that might motivate someone to act.'

'Chapter Nine. You've been paying attention. Tell me more about the cut.'

I did. He was too much of a gentleman to ask about my own scar, or ponder aloud the peculiar fact that it seemed to match the victim's. I knew he was wondering, though. On those rare occasions when someone asked, I would say it was a childhood accident. *Nothing too exciting.* It wasn't the truth, and I suspected that Starkweather would see right through it.

'Wounds like that can be about dominance too,' he said, softly now. 'But often, they're also more intimate. A desire to connect with the victim in a tangible way. Leave their mark, so to speak.'

'Leave their mark.' It was possible whoever had disfigured Jane Doe wanted to forge some twisted connection. Create a bond.

'You're right to pursue this. The cut could be important,' he said. 'But it isn't the place to start.'

'Yeah,' I said absently, my mind someplace else.

I hadn't thought about Abraham Skilton in a long time, but the pain rushed in unbidden. In spite of all he'd done, to me and others, I rarely found the courage to face the truth: Abe had left home with nowhere to go and very little money, and there was a chance he had not survived that. A strong possibility that, like countless others – like the woman I was investigating now – he had become a nameless victim, fate undefined to those who had known him before things went wrong.

Abe was a persistent hangnail, the memory of him prone to snagging. I didn't always feel it, but in talking to Starkweather, it was dangerously close. One careless move, and I'd be bleeding again.

One day, I thought, *maybe I'll tell Starkweather about my cousin.* What our relationship had been like all those years before I saw his darkness, a toxic smudge I'd tried and failed to scrub away.

One day, maybe I'd explain my scar.

SEVENTEEN

The River Hospital was steps from the St Lawrence, directly across the channel from Heart Island. I'd been stunned by the views from exam rooms before; though the windows were small, they framed Boldt Castle like a painting on an English drawing room wall. My prior visits had been professional, accompanying victims for medical assessment. Escorting the dead.

Tonight, while healthcare workers bustled around the ED, it was me on the exam table, a thin sheet of paper crinkling beneath my weight.

There would be bruises; already I could feel a constellation of hematomas forming along my forearm and hip. I didn't care about that. The ER doctor had arranged for a consult from the on-call obstetrician, who'd performed an ultrasound to measure fetal heart tones. After several rounds of reassurances, question upon question from both me and Tim, we left feeling safe in the knowledge that the baby was OK.

'Your mom's going to kill me,' Tim said, still looking bloodless as we made our way back to the car. Both his hands were on my body as we navigated the checkerboard asphalt of the icy parking lot.

'It was an accident,' I said. 'It could have happened anywhere. On our driveway. While hauling groceries into the trunk.'

He nodded, but I wasn't sure he believed me. Wasn't sure I believed myself, either.

I was a woman who'd never balked at danger. I charged headlong into every situation, even when I knew it might end badly for me. I wasn't always fearless, but I could be reckless, and carried the scars to prove it.

Always, the decisions I'd made had been for someone else. When the serial murderer I was investigating turned the tables and took me captive, it was a vision of my parents and brother back in Vermont that motivated my escape. Years later, when I waited in a dark Clayton cemetery for that same murderer to appear, I'd done so for the victims he'd killed and those he might prey on next.

I needed to accept that my decisions had to be about me now. To defend my body. Protect this kid. My mother had been right to be concerned. My priorities needed recalibrating. And though I didn't want to make a change, that meant aspects of my job might require rethinking, too.

Tim insisted on dropping me off at home before meeting Val and Sol at the barracks, where they were already interviewing Rich and Ewan and would handle the background checks, too. By the time he got back I was cocooned in bed, feeling thoroughly warm for the first time all day.

'Brought you something,' he said as he entered the room, a small bowl of ice cubes in hand.

'You're a star.' Though he was still in his work clothes, I flipped over the edge of the blanket and beckoned for him to scooch in.

Tim kissed my forehead and asked about my pain. Only once I'd managed to convince him it was under control did he tell me the status of the investigation.

'They're both clean. No priors – although Rich Samson filed for bankruptcy six years ago.'

'Is that right?' I said, molars grinding on the ice.

'Yeah. He used to be a contractor. Looks like a bout of bad luck – his partner was shady, and the two of them owed money to home-owners all over the county.'

'That's terrible.' Tim and I had narrowly escaped contractor fraud ourselves when kicking off renovations on our antique house. Even if Tim was right and Rich hadn't been the ringleader of that con, the news altered my impression of the man. Between that and the turkey, I was sure we couldn't trust him.

'I truly expected one of them to admit it was an accident. An involuntary manslaughter charge is no picnic, but if the alternative's homicide . . .' Tim puffed out his cheeks and sighed. 'Both are claiming they had nothing to do with the murder. Forensics will look at Rich's gun, but I'd be shocked if it's a match. Both men have alibis, albeit weak ones. Their wives say they came straight home after leaving Buckhead Bay, and stayed there. Both swear Cary was alive when they left him at the fishing site.'

My tongue was pleasantly numb, the ice like a dose of valium. 'Do you believe them?'

He ran a hand over his head. 'What's the motive? That's what I keep coming back to. Maybe they *could* have done it. But to what end?'

Tim's words called to mind Adam Starkweather's book. Always, it came down to why. Murder was a heinous crime, one of the most extreme of human acts, the suffering it caused for those left behind immeasurable. Motives could be rooted in anything from social reciprocity to greed or personal revenge, every crime riddled with veiled secrets. The why was the key.

'I've been spending some time on Running Wild,' I said. 'A lot of followers have said they plan to visit the island this summer.'

'What you're suggesting,' said Tim, 'is that the islanders might not like their home overrun with tourists.'

I corkscrewed my lips. 'Just a thought. Here's another: when I got out there today, Ewan mentioned he's anti-social-media. He said it exploits kids and incites impulsive behavior. Must be hard for a guy who feels that way to swallow the fact that his island is all over Instagram.'

'Kill off Cary, and you kill Running Wild.'

'Like I said, just a thought. I buy that they're not all that close. Everyone has confirmed Sylvie and Cary did their own thing. Her behavior on the dock sure drove that point home.' Sylvie's reaction to seeing Ewan and Rich had been visceral, a response from the gut. We had no evidence that the men were involved in Cary's death, but there was no question about how Sylvie felt, either. The woman was afraid.

'That was weird, right?' said Tim. 'She was quick to defend them before, but as soon as she saw we all had to share a ride, she freaked.' He laced his chilly fingers with mine. 'Oh hey, good call asking Sol to look into her family. He put together a nice little history lesson for us.'

I listened as Tim talked about Roscoe Lavoy, whose family had been founding settlers of the island along with the Budds, Plums, and a handful of others.

'Ewan mentioned that Emmeline is Miranda's aunt by marriage,' I said.

'Right. So anyway, Roscoe was mixed up with a murder case – never convicted,' he added before I had a chance to express my shock. 'I'm sure that's what Sylvie meant about his reputation. The family's history is bound up with booze. Roscoe owned a wholesale liquor distribution company that covered Jefferson, St Lawrence, and Oswego counties. The victim, Alan Nevil, was a client of his. At the time, Nevil owned Frontenac County Distillery over in Kingston.'

'I know Frontenac Distillery.' When it came to drinking, Tim stuck to beer and wine, but my brother was a distilled spirits man. On his last visit, Doug had picked up a bottle of Frontenac whisky from a shop in town.

Tim said, 'Nevil died in a home invasion in 1999. It was common knowledge that he and Roscoe didn't get along, and Roscoe had met with the guy on the day of his murder. There was no DNA or evidence, so the Ontario police never closed the case, but the papers sure made it sound like Roscoe was good for it.'

I said, 'Ninety-nine. Sylvie would have been, what, eight years old? That's old enough to remember accusations of murder swirling around her only parent.'

'For sure. Things would have changed for the family after that. Roscoe closed the business post-scandal. Having your name attached to a murder investigation's bound to cost you a few customers.'

'No doubt.' Was it possible the islanders held a grudge against Roscoe Lavoy and, by association, Sylvie? They were people who took pride in their island. If Roscoe had tarnished the Lavoys' reputation, I could understand why the few families who were left might give Sylvie the cold shoulder. At the same time, she and Cary had only planned to stay for a year. All the islanders had to do was wait out their departure, and they'd have their utopia back.

Only now it was marred by something far worse than a disgraced name.

'Anything on the great-grandfather?' Sylvie had mentioned the men in her family – plural.

'Sol didn't get around to looking before Rich and Ewan showed up. It's on the to-do list, but that seems like ancient history. By the way, I put in for a search warrant. I can't see why Sylvie would kill her boyfriend with Running Wild such a hit, but lots of folks in these parts do keep rifles.'

I nodded. We had to be sure she wasn't concealing a weapon. 'How is Sylvie doing?' I asked.

'OK, I think.' Disentangling himself from me and slipping out of bed, Tim unbuttoned his shirt. I watched as he peeled off his undershirt, too. Admired the solid muscle underneath. 'Val talked to her after the interviews. She's already pushing to go back. I can't believe she wanted to stay there,' he said, 'especially after today.'

'I don't see why she couldn't post from Clayton, at least for a day or two.' There were just as many posts starring Sylvie in stylish scarves and hunter-green wellies as Cary posing with those dimpled cheeks, so I had to think she could buy some time, at least until word got out about the murder. 'I'm no social media expert—'

Tim feigned shock. 'You mean spending three minutes a year on Facebook doesn't make you a leading authority?'

'Ha. If they've been running this thing like a business,' I went on, 'with real advertisers and sponsors, they must have some content stowed away. Cary's photoshopping skills were impressive.' If I didn't know better, I would have bet a week's worth of ice cream that Bash's luxury SUV had been parked on Running Pine. 'That's another thing,' I said. 'When I first talked to her, Sylvie asked that we delay making Cary's death public. Did she mention that to you too?'

'Yeah.' Tim stepped out of his pants and hung them neatly in the closet. 'I wonder what happens when the sponsors find out he's dead.'

It all came back to Running Wild. No island, no photos. No photos, no account. Running Wild was about a lifestyle, and a life had been lost to brutal violence.

'I could withhold his name when I do the press conference in the morning. Keep reporters off her tail for a bit,' said Tim. 'But that's just delaying the inevitable, and now that his mother's been notified . . .'

I nodded. There was little point in suppressing Cary's identity. The media would make the connection soon enough.

A thought occurred to me as Tim pulled on his flannel pajama pants, the only other theory that might actually have legs. 'That internet troll Sylvie brought up. Could we be looking at an obsessed fan?'

'We talked about that, Val and I. Those deleted messages.' He issued a sigh. 'I've got Sol doing forensics on the account – looking at comments and such – but I'm not holding my breath. Val asked Ewan and Rich about it, but they claim neither Sylvie nor Cary ever mentioned having a stalker, and they haven't seen a stranger on the island. That's what sets our vic apart, though, isn't it. The fact that he's Instagram famous.'

Celebrity attracts hate; I'd seen it first-hand when my connection to a killer led to far more than fifteen minutes of fame. People had judged me then, propagating false rumors about my life. For their part, Sylvie and Cary had isolated themselves from society, carving out a new existence in nature and on their own terms . . . but if that life was underwritten by social media, were they really alone? I thought of Billy Bloom in the diner, crumbs in his beard and that rotting-fish smell. *She involved in this at all?* he'd asked. The social media star. The girlfriend.

'There will be rumors,' I warned. 'I'm already getting questions. Remember Billy Bloom? From Tern Island?'

'That old geezer? Sure. I see him around town now and then. Drinks too much, but he's harmless.'

Succumbing to a yawn, I said, 'He was in the diner with me last night. He asked what was happening on Running Pine.'

'Well, he'll find out tomorrow. I'll search the perimeter. Look for rogue snowmobiles and ATVs.'

'We should check for chimney smoke too. Pass me that?' I'd heard my iPhone chime as I crunched down on another piece of ice, the warble indicative of a new text.

'*We?*' Tim repeated as he plucked the device from the nightstand and handed it over. 'Hon, look at yourself. You're almost seven months pregnant. That ice is treacherous, in case that wasn't blatantly clear. If you'd landed differently, or broken through to the water . . .'

I felt a flutter behind my navel. A delicate shift. My eyes were still on the screen in my hand.

'I know,' I said. 'You and Val have got this.' I hardly needed to say it. Valerie Ott wasn't as experienced as me and Tim, but since her trial run in A-Bay last fall I'd found she excelled at conducting interviews, interpreting doubletalk, and cornering liars so deceptions had no place to hide. With her good looks and expensive slacks, people didn't see her coming. Val could fell a killer with the best of them.

'Wait a second, what is this?' Tim's expression had grown wary. 'It's not like you to give in so fast.'

'I won't help with the search,' I assured him, opting not to expound.

I'd only walked away from a homicide once in my life, and only because I had no choice. Had I not become a serial killer's new target, I might have put Jane Doe's case to rest. The criminal profile

I'd been creating was starting to take shape. With Adam's help, and a little more time, I might have found Jane's killer.

'So you're staying home tomorrow,' Tim confirmed.

'I didn't say *that*.'

'Shane,' he said, reverting to the nickname he'd given me before our first case.

'Don't worry.' I reached for the bowl of ice once more. With a cloudy cube pinned between my front teeth, I mumbled, 'I have an idea. And it'll keep me about as far from this river as I could possibly get.'

EIGHTEEN

'Tell me again why we're doing this and how on earth you got me to agree?' Mac said as we sped down the highway.
'We both know how,' I replied. 'I swear this little guy – or girl – I'm carrying is the best bargaining chip I've ever had.'

In truth, I'd been surprised the sheriff had endorsed my plan, especially since it involved getting up at five in the morning, but somewhere between Sandy Creek and Syracuse, she confessed she'd talked to Tim. They'd hemmed and hawed and come to the conclusion that a trip would keep me busy and diminish the chances that I'd argue my way back on to Running Pine. With Sylvie still in Clayton and a new search underway, the timing was the best I was likely to get – so, the first female sheriff of Jefferson County, who also happened to be my best friend, had taken the day off work and taken the wheel.

I looked into that Jane Doe case you called about, Dave had texted the previous night. *It's ice-cold. Nobody left around here who gives a shit about her but me.* I'd been hoping for the best news a former New York homicide detective could get: an ID on the victim, the offender apprehended. Instead, I'd learned the woman I'd abandoned never got justice and that her family, whoever they were, never learned what had happened to her. At the same time, Dave had implied that he cared. That was something.

After talking with Tim, I'd texted Dave back. Thanked him for the intel, and asked if he could spare an hour.

Now, Mac and I were on our way to the East Village.

I had a meeting to make.

The restaurant sported bright yellow walls and Bob Marley on the stereo, but my focus was on the man before me. Same grizzled stubble, same tapered eyes; even his blue checked shirt with the stretched-out collar looked as familiar as though I'd just set eyes on it. I hadn't sat across from Dave Johansson in four years. It felt like a week.

Back when we were partners, we'd started our days with breakfast sandwiches at my desk. We'd take turns supplying the food, wolfing down our meals while discussing the investigation. I had wanted to do the same thing today, for old time's sake, but Dave said we could do better than shitty break room coffee and gummy bodega bagels. Which was how he and I ended up at the Jamaican café on Avenue A.

When Dave cracked open his Ting soda, I could feel its citrusy bubbles in my nose. I'd insisted that he fill me in on his life first, but he was reluctant to talk about work and deftly piloted the conversation back to me.

'When I heard you married Gates and moved up there, I thought you'd bought the farm – in more ways than one,' he told me. 'But it clearly worked out for you.' A flutter of the hand in the vicinity of my belly emphasized his point.

'Ah. No,' I replied tightly. Dave was smiling, so sure he understood. Yes, I'd moved north. Yes, I'd done so with Dr Carson Gates. From where Dave was sitting, despite what had happened with Bram, I'd lucked into an idyllic life with my handsome former therapist.

Dave was dead wrong.

'The baby, it's not Carson's. Carson . . . died, actually.' I rolled up my sleeves as I spoke, just to give my hands something to do. 'My husband is Tim – Tim Wellington. He's an investigator up there. Like me.'

The explanation was indelicate, my cheeks aflame. For his part, Dave appeared to be stunned into inertia. I followed his stare to my bare forearm and the string of wine-red blooms that tripped up my bone. He'd spotted the bruises. Dave drew in a breath that inflated his chest.

'Your husband. He's not . . .'

'What? Oh God, no. I fell on the ice. Tim would never hurt me.'

'I'm sorry, I didn't—'

'It's OK. Really.' I laid a hand on his arm. The man looked like he was in agony.

'I'm glad,' Dave said. 'That you're doing well. That you're . . . happy. I'll never forgive myself for what happened to you. You know that, right? Never.'

The cellophane-wrapped flowers. His unsteady hands. Dave aged ten years before my eyes the day he came to the hospital, and thinking of that now flooded me with shame. Our estrangement went both ways. Gutted by my ordeal, he hadn't kept in touch. But I hadn't either.

How had it never occurred to me that my rapid departure had hurt him too? We'd spent countless hours together in the days leading up to my kidnapping. We hadn't been close for long, but we were partners. Colleagues sworn to defend and protect.

'What happened to me wasn't your fault,' I said. 'I should have been more careful. More alert. I didn't realize I'd become a target.' If I had, then I would have stood a chance against Bram, instead of almost becoming his next victim.

It was Dave who'd raised the alarm. I didn't have a roommate, and though I talked to my folks on the regular, our chats weren't consistent enough for them to notice my absence right away. I'd moved on from the Jane Doe case by then. Dave too. He should have forgotten about me, but he didn't. Instead, he'd buzzed my apartment one day. Tried to call when he got no response. It was only due to Dave's stubborn streak that he came looking for me at the precinct, which led my NCO supervisor to realize I hadn't come into work. Dave's efforts had almost died right there, when De La Cruz dismissed his concerns. News of the argument we'd had on the steps of the station house had made the rounds, and my supervisor thought my disappearing act had something to do with the fight. That I was embarrassed, maybe, for losing my shit in public. By the time Dave managed to convince him otherwise, I'd been locked in the basement boiler room of a crumbling apartment block for thirty-six hours and was sure I was going to die, cheek pressed against dust-sticky concrete in the presence of a psychopath.

Dave helped with the search, I'd been told. When at last I was reported missing, and my parents and brother showed up demanding answers, it was Dave who took them to dinner and tried to persuade them things would be OK. He'd been talking through his hat, of course. I hadn't informed Dave, or anyone else, that I'd decided to stop at a pub for a drink on my way home from work. Why would I? It should have been a quick detour, a pint or two to take the edge off another fruitless day of tracking the killer from Swanton, Vermont. Blake Bram had other ideas. It took several days for the bartender with the Irish brogue to realize the missing Ninth Precinct detective from the news was the same woman who, after a drink and a half, was inexplicably wasted. So wasted that she'd let a strange man guide her to a waiting car. The search continued until a tenant in the building where Bram worked got a creepy feeling, and brought in a rookie cop from the street.

It was hard to rejoice in the fact that I'd survived when so many others had not. I should have recognized Bram as my cousin sooner. Made sense of his crimes. Instead, I'd emerged from that basement a broken woman, the damage he'd caused as real as my scar. I was a detective trained in martial arts who'd failed to defend myself against the very suspect I'd been hunting. Someone I was connected to by blood.

'You don't need me to tell you that's horseshit,' Dave said. 'You should have *been more careful*? You were a woman living alone in the city who had the bum luck of becoming a psycho's obsession.'

When he closed his eyes, my gaze went to that sagging collar, rising and falling with each distressed breath. 'You're right. What happened wasn't my fault. But it wasn't your fault either.'

In the restaurant kitchen, plates clattered. I looked up to find our server watching from the pass-through, our lunches congealing under the heat lamp behind her.

'Now,' Dave pasted on a smile. 'Since you have a track record of disappearing when we argue, and I don't want to make an enemy of your husband, how about we focus on the reason you're here. I know her cut always bugged you,' he said, 'but what makes you want to revisit Jane Doe after all this time?'

The change of subject had an instant effect, like hitting a reset button. 'There was a homicide up north,' I told him, grateful we'd moved on. 'A man – kind of famous on Instagram – killed while overwintering on an island. We found his body in the river. The case got me thinking about ours, and since I have some time on my hands . . .'

'You couldn't just take up baking?'

'I think you and Tim would get along,' I said with a laugh.

'Well, like I told you, the file's just been sitting there. Unless someone IDs the vic or we get a new lead, it'll keep rotting away.'

I gave a solemn nod. 'You were right about the cut,' I said. 'It bothered me then, and it bothers me now. Not sure if you heard – De La Cruz was involved with the investigation last year – but the FBI has linked Bram to more than a dozen other victims, many of whom he killed right here in the city. I'm talking nearly fifteen years' worth of murders. Jane Doe had a mark a lot like mine, and we found her just a couple weeks before Bram took his murder spree to my front door. We've always thought his third victim, Jess Lowenthal, was the first body he left in the East Village. But what if it wasn't?'

'Shit,' Dave said simply. 'You really think this could have been him?'

At last, the waitress delivered our lunches. I looked down at my selection, a rich Jamaican oxtail stew, and winced. 'I don't think I need to tell you my feelings about this are complicated. If my cousin had a hand in that woman's death, I want to know.'

Dave sat there, not reaching for his fork. Steam wafting off his vegetable roti like a cigarette left to smolder.

'How long are you in town for?' he asked.

'Just the day.' That had been strategic. Eleven hours of driving was exhausting, but I hadn't been back to Manhattan since moving north, and was unsure of how I would manage. I planned to get what I came for and get home. 'What are you thinking?'

'That *I'm* not going anywhere. Consider me your eyes and ears,' said Dave. 'I'll handle everything. And enjoy it, because this is the one and only time I'm gonna be your puppet on a string.'

'Are you saying what I think you're saying?' I asked, a smile tugging at my lips.

'One way or another,' he said, 'we're going to do what we failed to do last time. We're gonna get this solved.'

NINETEEN

'He's going to exhume everything we had,' I told Mac as we ambled down the sidewalk. 'Interviews, reports on evidentiary materials, the works. There was one lead that seemed promising, a date the vic took to see a concert. I'm going to make some calls myself and see what I can dig up.'

Mac's hands had been buried in the pockets of her coat, but as we approached our destination, she took them out and flexed her fingers.

'What?' I asked, studying her face. There was a cranny in the flesh between her fair eyebrows that only appeared when she was tense. 'You don't think I should be doing this?'

'I think working with an old partner on a cold case is just what you need right now. What worries me,' Mac said, 'is *this*.'

Her eyes pivoted to the building beside us. The green and gold sign read *O'Dwyer's*.

'We could leave right now,' she said. 'Beat traffic on the FDR and be home in time for a late dinner.'

'I have to do it, Mac. I have to find out if I can.'

The pub was near Tompkins Square Park, which was the reason I'd come the night of my abduction – that, and my frustration over the lack of movement on the case. This man we knew only as Blake Bram had murdered three women, and on the dating app he'd used to lure his suspects, he had claimed to be from Swanton. Same as me. All through the park, that fact pursued me like a phantom, until I found myself in a tavern packed with Friday night patrons escaping the rain. *One beer*, I'd thought, *to clear my head*. That night, I'd begged the universe for a lead.

The universe had delivered.

Mac followed me inside now, all the way up to the bar. I half-expected to see the freckled barkeep who'd served me on my last visit, but of course that young woman was gone. In her stead, a sinewy man with a neck tattoo and bone-white hair took our order. A beer for Mac and soda water for me. Extra ice.

Not much else about the place had changed. The bar top still had the color and finish of boiled caramel. Dozens of backlit bottles of liquor gleamed against the wall. There were twinkle lights up, striping tin ceiling tiles. It smelled the same, too. Yeasty, with the sour bite of dried sweat.

Mac said, 'OK, if you're sure, let's do this. Tell me about that night.'

All she knew was what I'd revealed to her when I took the State Police job upstate. The part I'd held back was the hardest to share.

'He followed me here. Probably all the way from the precinct. He spilled my beer – an opening. And when he bought me a new one, he drugged it. But before I realized that,' I said, 'before he stole me from this very spot, I liked him.'

Most people I met were startled by my scar. The guy with the silvery eyes – *snow in the moonlight, ice on a creek* – ignored it completely. How easy it was to talk to him. Like we'd known each other all our lives.

'I wasn't a rookie.' I dipped my fingers in the water as I spoke, fished out a cube. I needed grounding, something soothing and familiar to help me regulate my emotions. The ice on my tongue reminded me that, despite the thrashing in my chest, I was married and pregnant and, above all else, alive. 'I didn't know him, but there was this spark of recognition.'

'All those years apart,' Mac said. 'But you'd been close once.'

'The closest.' Back when he was Abe, he'd been my best friend.

'I think he suspected I'd feel something, and wanted to know if he'd feel it too. There's no other explanation for why he took the risk. He could have roofied me without showing his face. It was packed in here. But he lingered. Talked to me and the bartender, right in front of the security camera. He wasn't afraid of getting caught.'

I looked down at the ring on my finger, a simple gold band to match Tim's. I thought of him, more than three hundred miles away on the island, and my ex-fiancé Carson, who was in the ground behind St Cyril's Catholic Church. I thought of Dave Johansson, too. The argument we'd had that I'd been unable to shake. How had Bram known what I needed most at that precise moment in my life? That a sweet stranger in a pub could give it to me?

I shook my head to clear it. 'I thought coming back here would feel like closure. There are things I need to wrap up before this next phase of my life.'

Mac said, 'That's a tall order, and a short timeline. What happened here, that night, was deeply traumatic for you. It could take years before you fully move on.'

I don't have years. How could I make her understand? I was about to have a child. Tim and the baby were my fresh start. I couldn't be the mother this kid deserved until I'd done my best to purge the violence Bram had left behind. And McIntyre was right. I was running out of time.

The phone next to the till rang with a shrieky warble, and my arm flung out against my will. Fizzy water spread across the bar top, the sound like a hiss. As Mac issued apologies to the barman and started to mop up my mess, a man opened the door to the pub. He looked nothing like my cousin, but my stomach bottomed out, blood rushing my ears. In my head, the pub was packed again, a kaleidoscope swirl of color and sound and a soupy-hot fog that enveloped me. Filled up my throat like bubbling tar.

'You OK?' Mac asked, a wad of napkins in her hand. 'You look a little—'

I lurched from the stool. Careened into the stranger, and burst out the door.

It was daylight out, not night. I hadn't been drugged. I was safe. Bram was dead.

'It's OK. You're OK,' I told myself, shaking out my hands. My body wouldn't listen. Pitching forward, I barely made it to the nearest trash can before I was sick.

I had tried. I was trying.

But the darkness wasn't done with me yet.

TWENTY

I woke up feeling pummeled, the emotional strain of the previous day like a hailstorm on my heart. Sweaty, stale, and desperate for just one cup of fully caffeinated coffee, I hauled my body out of bed.

There was a note from Tim on the kitchen counter, next to a mint-flavored tea bag to distract me from the lingering smell of Breakfast Blend. *Search warrant obtained*, it read. *Press conference at nine, then back to the island. Take it easy, mamma. See you tonight.*

Take it easy. While I'd filled Tim in on my trip to New York when I got home, I hadn't mentioned my freak-out at the pub. I didn't want him to worry today, when distraction could be deadly, but my reaction to visiting O'Dwyer's concerned me. On the ride home, Mac had assured me it wasn't a relapse. People with PTSD had triggers, even years into therapy. The pub was the last place I'd seen before that basement prison cell – plus I was pregnant now, my hormones out of whack. *You weren't ready yet, that's all*, she said as she drove. *I should have talked you into ice cream instead.*

I hadn't given Mac a choice.

Dunking a tea bag into hot water, I took to the couch and slid out my phone. I was thinking about Cary Caufield, and my conversation with Tim. At the moment, Rich and Ewan were our most viable suspects, but my husband was right. We needed to establish motive.

'Morning,' I said when Sol answered my call.

'Hey, boss, how's tricks?' His voice sounded sunny and there was a radio on in the background, laughter from a morning show host. I'd caught Sol on the drive to work.

'You've been looking into Running Wild, yeah?' Tim had mentioned he'd put Solomon on social media forensics.

'*Looking into* is putting it mildly,' Sol replied. 'At this point I could tell you their dog's favorite treat, describe Cary's shaving regimen, and catalogue the couple's entire wardrobe – Bash's bandanas included.'

'You're nothing if not thorough. I guess we should be grateful that they overshare,' I said.

'I'm telling you, I may know more about these two than their own parents.'

Though he was joking, I suspected that was true. Where family was concerned, both Cary and Sylvie were lacking.

'Find anything squirrely in the comments? Particularly from Ewan Fowler?' Both men had been fishing with Cary, but it was Ewan who'd badmouthed social sites.

Sol chuckled. 'Tim asked me the same thing. I didn't find a single comment from an islander. There were some nasty remarks – typical troll fare – and I've got those on record, but none of the usernames match our persons of interest.'

He agreed to send them over anyway. If Ewan had been planning to murder Cary, I didn't think it likely he'd leave a digital trail using his real name. Still, the comments Sol had discovered were worth exploring.

So was Ewan's work in psychosociology. The man had told me he'd been researching the impact of silence and isolation, noting that humans are assaulted by noise. I got the sense he wasn't only referring to the decibel level in Times Square. As Sol told me about a comment that accused Sylvie of being a 'shoe whore,' I did a Google search. It took less than a minute to confirm that my theory had been right.

I explained what I'd found to Sol while he drove. The world of psychology journals was something I knew well; Carson had been obsessive about getting his papers published. It seemed that Ewan Fowler had notched a few accolades of his own.

The article was in an online-only magazine called *Psychology This Week*, and it addressed the impact of social networks on mental health. Ewan Fowler argued that, in spite of its name, social media didn't benefit society but rather created isolation and triggered loneliness.

On the line, a car door slammed. 'That's quite the coincidence,' said Sol. 'He publishes a paper like that, and someone starts a social media account about his island?'

'No coincidence,' I said, my eyes riveted to the phone screen. 'The article was posted last November. Three months *after* Sylvie and Cary moved to Running Pine.'

We spent a few minutes dissecting what that could mean. Sol saw the article as both a veiled threat and a dead giveaway: Ewan resented that Cary and Sylvie had monetized his island, and killed Cary to put an end to Running Wild. Just as I'd thought it unlikely that Ewan would troll the account before committing murder, though, I couldn't imagine a man with his pedigree advertising his intentions online.

I told Sol to keep up the good work, and we agreed to stay in close contact. As soon as I set down my phone, it buzzed against the table.

Val was shouting, the howl of the wind snatching half her words.

'—Our way. We'll—you—progress. But Sylvie—morning.'

'What?' I pressed the device hard against my ear.

What came next felt like a game of preschool telephone. After a minute of mixed messages and misunderstandings, I asked her to text me instead.

Whew sorry, she typed. *This wind is really picking up. Fingers freezing*

Go inside! Val was a hunt-and-peck typer to begin with, and her numb fingers were making our exchange painfully slow.

Needed privacy from the islanders. Sylvie's on her way back

Already? Tim had told me Cary's mother was headed down from Ottawa. Even if she and Sylvie had never met, I had to think the woman would want to speak with her deceased son's live-in girlfriend. To try to make sense of what had happened to Cary. Sylvie owed her that. Instead, she was making plans to leave the mainland. The quick turnaround smacked of an escape.

She get wind of the warrant? I asked Val. Maybe Sylvie's return to Running Pine was about wanting to be close when Tim and Val searched her home for the gun that killed Cary.

She says it's because of Running Wild

I blew out a frustrated sigh. Did Sylvie not see that her haste to get back qualified as suspicious behavior? The woman's partner had been executed while on a fishing trip, and all she could think about was Instagram?

I was starting to wonder if Tim and Val might actually find a weapon in Sylvie Lavoy's cabin – and that thought prompted another. Could Sylvie have found a way to keep Running Wild going without Cary? We knew the business venture had borne fruit, and that there were more sponsorships in the pipeline. Was it possible she planned to run the account without him? Use Cary's death to drum up sympathy, and keep future earnings for herself?

Don't take her, I typed, quick as I could. *Tell Teddy to hang back. I want to question her again about Running Wild.* Tim and Val were miles from her now, but I was a ten-minute drive away. Maybe I could squeeze out a confession – or at least delay her so she didn't interfere with the search.

Val's next message shocked me. *Teddy isn't bringing her*
What? I fired back. *Then who?*

I chewed the inside of my lip while watching the progress bubbles on-screen.

You know that bookstore in Clayton? Owner's husband has a homemade airboat

Cold flooded my body. A *homemade* airboat? Even if the vessel was sound, even if this guy was an experienced driver, the wind Val had described could make the trip deadly. It also meant we no longer controlled Sylvie's movements.

Val was typing again.
Tim wants you to call the ME
What for?
Ask him about the watch

For a full minute, she wrote nothing more.

Gotta run, she typed at last. *Tim said to call him after. He wants to know your thoughts*

The only ME in our region was Arthur Daisy. It was Art who'd helped transport Cary's body from the island. Val didn't know him well yet. But Tim and I did.

I pulled up his number as fast as I could.

'I'm not exactly sure why I'm calling,' I admitted when Art answered. 'Something about a watch?' I explained Val's cryptic message.

'I can help with that,' he said. 'I reached out to Tim this morning to report a visit I received from Sylvie Lavoy. She's the girlfriend of the decedent, yes?'

'Yes. She came to see you?' Art Daisy worked out of Watertown, which meant Sylvie would have needed to track down a taxi or Uber. No easy task this time of year. 'When was this?'

'Yesterday, late afternoon,' he said. 'I have to admit, it threw me for a loop. She was looking for a watch. A field watch, she called it. Said the decedent was wearing it when he died – or rather, that he'd been wearing it when he left the house that morning.'

'Did you give it to her?'

'I don't have it,' said Art. 'It wasn't with the body.'

Art Daisy wasn't one to misplace personal property belonging to the deceased. If Cary Caufield had been wearing a watch, it would have been inventoried. Kept safe until it could be released to the funeral home and family, or held until the close of our investigation.

A field watch. I'd seen a watch in a recent photo of Cary on Running Wild. Was this that same watch? Was it a gift from a brand sponsor? A loan? Could that be why Sylvie wanted it back?

This was what Tim had wanted from me, the reason he'd asked Val to call. He needed a read on the situation, and it was an odd one. If Sylvie had seen Cary wearing the watch the morning of the ice fishing excursion, it should have been found with his body.

'How did Sylvie seem?' I asked Art. 'When you said you didn't have it?' I put him on speaker, and opened Instagram. Found the image of Cary, the old barn, and the snowman, and zoomed in, pinching and pulling until the object filled my screen.

'How did she seem? Stressed,' said Art. 'Maybe a little impatient. She wasn't happy when I told her it wasn't in my possession. She even asked me to check again.' There was a sour tone to his voice. He hadn't liked the implication that he'd made a mistake.

'Thanks,' I said. 'This is helpful. I appreciate it, Art.'

'Anytime – and keep me posted on your bundle of joy. How many months to go now?'

'About two.' I glanced down, and for the briefest of moments I was surprised to see my rounded belly. Cary's watch was gone, and Sylvie wanted it back. Already, my mind was whirling.

Art signed off, and I zoomed into the image of Cary once more. The watch was partly concealed by the sleeve of his wool sweater, but it was on his left hand. I closed my eyes, and returned to Buckhead Bay. The gruesome image of that glove reaching up from the ice. It had been Cary's right hand. That meant his watch would have been underwater.

My eyes snapped open. If someone took Cary's field watch, they'd done it before he went into the river.

As I hovered over the photo, a tag popped up. *Longines Men's Nylon Strap Khaki Field Watch.* I clicked, and a shopping page appeared on my screen. The watch retailed for $2,675, inspired by the military timepieces of the 1960s. *Featuring a 38mm matt stainless steel case and premium quality strap that's built to last with double stainless steel buckles.* Wherever your adventure took you, the Longines Men's Field Watch apparently had you covered.

I took a screenshot of the watch strap.

Then I called Tim.

'Everything OK?' He'd picked up on the first ring.

'All good, but this thing with the watch is fishy. Sylvie tried to retrieve it, and when she couldn't, she made arrangements to go straight back to Running Pine. I'm wondering if that watch is the reason she agreed to come to the mainland with us.' I recapped my call with Art, including his description of Sylvie's behavior. 'I'm looking at an image of the watch now, and there's no way it could have fallen off, not even if it got snagged on a stick or a rock underwater. These things are designed to stay on in rough conditions. But it's missing, Tim. Why hasn't Sylvie told us? A stolen watch could speak to motive.'

'No idea – but if Sylvie doesn't want us knowing it's gone, we don't want to let on that we do. Not until we understand why she's been blowing smoke.'

'Have you done the search?'

'It's underway. Nothing yet. Rich and Ewan are back, by the way.' Without enough evidence to hold them, Tim explained, he'd had little choice but to escort them home.

'Where's Sylvie now?'

'Still on the mainland, we think. I've got Teddy keeping an eye on the river.'

I hadn't liked Sylvie for the crime, but her behavior was unsettling. The day Cary went missing, she'd asked for me, later citing her family's reputation as the reason why. She'd already withheld information by neglecting to share her suicide theory with Tim and Val, and now she was withholding potential evidence, too.

'I'm going to Clayton,' I told him. 'I'll ask about the watch, and delay her until you're done at the cabin.'

'You sure you're up to it?' Tim sounded deeply uncertain.

I prodded my bruises. Took stock of myself. I was tired, but I felt OK. The doctor had said not to worry. The baby was completely safe.

This would be my last case, probably for a long time. I was scheduled to go on maternity leave in just over a month, and planned to take a full three more off work. After that, we'd reassess. We had no firm plans for this transformative event beyond getting to know our new life and taking parenthood day by day, but I knew one thing for certain: nothing would ever be the same again.

'It's a short drive. Easy,' I said.

'All right. Let me know what you find out, yeah?'

I promised him I would.

'Come on,' I whispered, giving my bump a pat. 'Let's go for a ride.'

TWENTY-ONE

New York City

Four Years Ago

Three days since we dragged her corpse from the East River, and Jane Doe still hadn't made the news. By then the citizens of New York should have been acquainted with her face, instructed to call Crime Stoppers with any information that could help us make a positive ID. If their tip proved useful, they'd get some money for their trouble. It was a tactic that often yielded results. So I was furious when Dave confessed the request he'd made hadn't been approved.

'That makes no sense,' I said. 'Why wouldn't they sign off?' Not all requests merited dissemination, but with that forensic sketch, ours had been solid. I couldn't imagine the deputy turning it down.

'These things are never a given,' said Dave.

'Shit.' I paced the area around my desk. 'Well, I guess it's a good thing I have a backup plan.'

'Oh really?' Dave looked equal parts curious and dubious.

'A Facebook page,' I announced. 'If the press won't help us, we'll make a public plea of our own.'

The strategy had been on my mind for a while. Every detective had a collection of social media burner accounts that we could use to investigate victims, suspects, and their acquaintances. I'd heard that Facebook accounts for the missing could help identify bodies. Produce leads where there had been none. I planned to use the sketch and neighborhood in which Jane had been found to entice the public, throwing in an approximate age and death range to up our odds. If we were lucky, we might find someone who knew her. The approach might even lead us to her killer.

Already, Dave was eyeing me askance.

'That's a waste of our time,' he told me. 'You got no idea how many attention hogs are on Facebook, Shana. A lot of assholes think it's funny to mess with the cops.'

I'm aware, I thought, tamping down the desire to fire back a barb of my own. Dave meant well, but he had a grating habit of treating me like a rookie. Under the harsh overhead lights of the precinct bullpen, I could see a swath of pink scalp peeking through his thinning hair.

'Listen,' he said after a beat. 'If you really think there's value in this, I'll call my buddy with the cyber task force. He mostly deals with cyber crime, but he might know a way to build the page so it goes viral.'

'Sounds great,' I said. 'I'll compile the details.'

'Send me the wording you want to use, and I'll pass it along. Gotta take a piss.'

As I watched him go, I thought about bringing up Adam. I felt confident that the man's knowledge and insights could help us. At the same time, I didn't want Dave to feel belittled, a deuteragonist instead of the leading man. What mattered was that we got the solve, and I'd do everything in my power to make that happen.

It was dark by the time I left the station, having lingered to look over the crime scene and autopsy photos for the tenth time. August in the East Village was impossibly muggy, a mélange of skunky air and a gritty stickiness that clung to subway poles, door handles, skin. I couldn't stand the idea of mashing myself against sagging strangers in a subway car, so I walked the twelve blocks home, swiping sweat from the back of my neck all the while.

It had taken some getting used to, the sense I had of never truly being alone. I could walk back roads for miles in Swanton without seeing a soul, but in the city, I felt at once scrutinized and surprised by my own independence. There was always someone else close at hand, everyone living separate lives along a parallel plain. It was a heady existence, one I'd come to appreciate even when the weather was shit.

That night, though, I'd had the distinct sense that I was being followed. Casting cagey glances behind me like a tourist stuck in Central Park at night, I was aware that my fears were probably unfounded. I had no deranged ex to contend with, and if a mugger attempted an attack, my martial arts training would ensure I could handle whatever choke or wrist grab came my way. Even so, the walk left me uneasy, perspiration pooling in the space between my breasts.

I was letting the homicide get to me, allowing our search for

Jane's killer to ooze like a viscid poison into my life. Jane Doe was around my age. We appeared to share the same stomping grounds, and that cut . . . it linked her to me in a way that felt personal.

It wasn't something I could confess to Dave, or even my own mother, who called once a week to catch up but was never comfortable hearing about my work. I often got jumpy while working a case. But this time was different.

Back in my apartment, I opened a bottle of cold white wine and gulped down a glass to steel myself. *What matters is Jane*, I thought as I reached for my phone.

If it's a bad time, please ignore this, I typed, hoping I wasn't interrupting dinner with his family.

Not at all, Starkweather fired back. *What's on your mind?*

You said the cut isn't the place to start. What did you mean by that?

Pulsing dots, and then: *You read the book. Don't doubt yourself. Zero in on the victim – favorite haunts. Hobbies. Whatever secrets her body has to share.*

That, Starkweather wrote, *is how you'll get some movement on this case.*

TWENTY-TWO

In summer, the docks on Clayton's Riverside Drive were a gathering place for both tourists and locals. Shady maples and a row of public-use Adirondack chairs separated the street from the river, and if you visited on the Fourth of July, you'd see tiny American flags sunk into the edging of the well-tended gardens, their flowers now withered and buried by snow.

The fingers that made up the boat slips had been pulled from the water for winter, so a single dock remained near the tower of brown snow the town plow had dumped on the ice. The air felt as sharp as a knife on my throat when I stepped out of my car to survey the river.

The dock was where I expected to find Sylvie Lavoy, but there was no one around, though I did see the airboat Val had described abandoned on the ice-choked St Lawrence. Someone had bolted the engine from a paraglider to a beat-up duck boat, slapping a naked sheet of plywood onto the back of the fan to mimic a rudder. The vessel, if you could call it that, was straight out of *Mad Max*. I felt like I was going to be sick all over again.

Shrugging deeper into my scarf to stave off the wind, I assessed the street. With the exception of a few parked cars, there were no signs of life. My guess was that the airboat operator had gone somewhere to keep warm while waiting for Sylvie. It would take even longer than usual to make the crossing in that jury-rigged dinghy, so I knew there was no way I'd missed her. Like the boat's owner, I would have to wait.

Many businesses on the main drag closed for winter, Nelly's Bistro included. I wasn't sure about the bookstore, though. It was directly across the street from the docks, and I wanted to pick up Jane Budd's series about the Thousand Islands. With any luck, I'd find a sign posted in the window.

What I saw was movement, just behind the glass. A woman, black-haired with an earnest smile, noticed me on the stoop and waved.

'You're not open yet,' I remarked when the door swung inward.

There were boxes on the floor behind her, some inventory project in the works. 'I'll come back.'

'Oh no, please stay! Do you know how quiet it is around here this time of year? If you leave, you'll go straight home to Amazon, and I can't take that chance. I'm sorry, but you'll just have to do your shopping here instead.'

I liked her already, with her round glasses and butter-yellow sweater. 'You talked me into it,' I told her. 'But I only have a minute. I'm meeting someone at the dock.'

'Are you a friend of Sylvie's?' She scrunched up her eyes as she said it. 'That's Burt's airboat down there. My husband. He's grabbing some hand warmers at the store before he gives her a lift.'

'Sylvie's the one I'm meeting, yes,' I said, evading her question. 'I heard you helped her arrange the ride. Are *you* a friend of Sylvie's?' Val hadn't mentioned how Sylvie knew this woman, if indeed she did, and I was curious about the bookseller's perspective on the social media star.

'I've known her for years,' she said. 'Well now, let me rephrase that: I know the Lavoys. Sylvie called us yesterday. I'm Kath. Want me to keep watch while you browse?' She gestured to the window, which offered a clear view of the boat.

'Would you mind? I won't be long. I'm looking for some books by another resident of Running Pine. Jane Budd?'

'Jane! She's one of my top sellers. I have a hard time keeping her books stocked in summer, but I've got all four right now. Local author shelf behind you.'

I followed her gaze to the display, and there they were: Jane's complete works, from a title on Iroquois Confederacy pre-European colonization to books about river pirates, Prohibition, and the grand homes of the Gilded Age.

With one eye on the view outside, Kath said, 'They make great gifts. Maybe for your family back in Vermont?'

I hadn't told her who I was. As long as I lived in the area, I'd probably never need to introduce myself again. 'I'm sure you're right,' I said. 'These are for me, though. Fascinating stuff.' I flipped over one of the books in my hand to read the bio on the back. 'Third generation islander, huh? Jane must be a real expert on Thousand Islands life. It was kind of you and Burt to help Sylvie out.'

Kath still hadn't said a word about Cary.

'Well. I don't especially like the hubby joyriding in that contraption.

It's not the safest vessel, and I told Sylvie as much, but she was determined to get back. She offered to pay us. Not much.' Her eyes were darting all over the place.

'Did you say she called you yesterday?' The sign on the door had said the shop closed at four on weekdays. It had been nearly that late when we brought Sylvie to the mainland.

'She left a message,' Kath said. 'I didn't get it till this morning. I don't know how she found out about the airboat, but a lot of people in town know Burt has it. He can be a showboater.' A roll of the eyes.

I cast a glance at the window as I brought my stack of books to the counter. 'You said you know Sylvie's family?' I was fishing. I couldn't shake the memory of what Sylvie had told me. That she came from a family of disrepute.

Kath's tone turned salty. 'I know *of* them. Everyone does. I suppose it's no big secret,' she said with a sigh. 'Roscoe Lavoy – Sylvie's father – was a murder suspect. This was twenty years ago, but it sure caused a stir. And her great-grandfather was a rum-runner during Prohibition.'

I felt my eyebrows creep upward. 'Is that right?'

'A notorious one, at that,' said Kath, nodding sagely. 'Speaking of.'

I followed her gaze. Sylvie was making her way down the street, Bash loping along beside her.

Kath rung me up, handed back my credit card, and tucked the books into a bag.

'I have a lot of respect for Jane Budd. For all the islanders,' she said. 'It's not easy, how they live. Jane contributes a lot to the local community.'

'Sure sounds that way.' Crossing the wood plank floor, I thanked her for the books and yanked open the door.

Outside, I saw Kath watching from the window.

This woman wasn't a fan of Sylvie Lavoy. And by the sound of it, she wasn't alone.

My time in the toasty bookshop had weakened my defenses. No sooner was I back outside than my extremities started to ache. In a parka cinched around the waist, which she wore over a long tartan skirt and fur-trimmed boots, Sylvie moved toward the river. She cast furtive glances around as she went, and I thought again about the internet troll she'd mentioned the previous day. Walking at a clip and keeping Bash close by her side, it almost looked as though she thought that she'd been followed.

Burt, the airboat owner, had arrived too. I drew in a breath and coughed out Sylvie's name, cold punching the air from my lungs.

On the dock, she paused and turned. Her eyes widened.

'Be careful!' she shouted. 'It's slippery!'

I was grateful when she picked her way back toward me, saving me the trouble of navigating the slick dock ramp. Bash wagged his tail when he saw me. Misty breath coursed from his smiling mouth.

'Oh my God, are you OK? I've been so worried about your baby.'

'It's fine – really,' I said, because the woman looked distraught. It had been her, after all, who'd knocked me off balance when she saw Rich and Ewan at Teddy's airboat. 'What are you doing out here, Sylvie?'

With a flat look, she said, 'I'm going back. I found my own ride.'

'I see that. I guess I'm just surprised you're going so soon.'

Though she wore gloves – those were trimmed with fur, too – Sylvie reached for Bash's head and began to knead. 'I signed what they asked me to sign at the station. I just want to go home.'

'There are still some arrangements to make. Cary's mother should be at the hotel by now. I'm sure she'll want to talk to you. There will be a memorial service to plan, and she may want some of his belongings.' I didn't mention the watch, would rather Sylvie didn't know I was aware of her attempt to track it down.

'I really don't know Cary's mom,' Sylvie said. 'I'm sure she wants nothing to do with me.'

I studied her face, currently makeup-free. 'Why don't you come back to the barracks with me to warm up? We can talk some more about Cary, and how we can help you get through this. Then tomorrow, we can take you home ourselves.'

'Do I have to?'

'No,' I admitted, 'but—'

'Then I'm going back right now.' The toque she was wearing kept the hair from her eyes, but the wind teased the ends, dark tendrils dancing around her face like smoke from a forest campfire. She gave Bash a tug.

I blocked their path. 'I know Running Wild means a lot to you, but it's OK to take a break. Give yourself time to grieve.'

She gave me a long, disappointed look. 'I thought you'd understand what it's like. Being judged by people with no fucking clue what they're talking about.'

'People like your neighbors?' I hadn't heard the islanders condemn the Instagram account outright, but for people who liked peace and privacy, there were few benefits to sharing Running Pine with Sylvie and Cary.

'I'm talking about strangers,' she said, not missing a beat. 'They think they know me. Some think I owe them something, like they can say whatever they want online and I have to indulge them because it's my job to be nice. Running Wild doesn't *mean a lot to me*. It's not some fucking hobby. It's my *job*.'

Behind her, Kath's shivering husband cleared his throat. When Sylvie spoke again, she lowered her voice. 'I know things will be different now, with Cary gone. I'm not an idiot. But there's nothing waiting for me in Kingston. I have Dad's medical bills to pay, his credit cards . . .' She raised her gaze up to the sky, while my own lingered on her expensive outfit; only then did I realize much of what she was wearing probably came from a brand partner. 'That cabin and Running Wild are all I've got. I have to make this work.'

'There's no way that airboat is up to code, and with this wind it's even more dangerous.'

'I'll take my chances. I just want to go home and be alone.'

But you won't be alone. Tim had brought Ewan and Rich back to Running Pine already. The two men who'd last seen Cary alive would be minutes from Sylvie's cabin. *And you asked for my help*, I thought. *Begged Jane to bring me to the island.* What had changed between then and now?

Cary was no longer missing. He hadn't committed suicide, like Sylvie had suggested. He'd been murdered, probably long before she sent Jane to the mainland.

'Look, it's up to you,' I said. 'You're free to go if you think that's best.'

She nodded. It might have been the cold, but tears brimmed at the corners of her eyes and her nose was redder than it had been moments prior.

I braced myself against the stinging wind as Sylvie hurried down the dock. Burt helped her into the boat, where she bear-hugged Bash and buried her face in his fur. With a stutter, a roar, and a whoosh of air, the boat turned its bow toward Running Pine Island.

Sylvie didn't look back at me where I stood. Her gaze remained on the black mass of land across the river.

Back in my car, I took out my phone.

Today's Instagram post was of both Cary and Sylvie. They sat side by side on a log, looking out at the frozen St Lawrence. Sylvie's head nestled against Cary's shoulder, clad in the same red jacket that a rifle shot had shredded and soaked with blood. So Sylvie did have some content stored away. To anyone watching online, it would look like they were both still on the island, living their enviably cozy wilderness life.

She'd asked us to hold off on releasing Cary's name to the public, and we had. The missing person had initially been described as 'a Clayton man.' But the missing man was now a homicide victim, and Tim was probably sharing that information with the public right now.

If Sylvie was telling the truth, and needed to eke out every dollar from Running Wild while she had the chance, I couldn't fault her for going back. Hadn't I done something similar by strongarming Mac into taking me to O'Dwyer's? Sometimes, returning to the place that hurt you is the only way to move forward. I'd read a piece in the paper once about people who'd lost relatives on September 11, yet went back to Ground Zero to give guided tours. They told tourists from all over the world about the very horrors that befell their loved ones on that day. Crisis communication experts say facing things like that head-on can help us process traumatizing events. Maybe even help us heal. But Sylvie's trauma was an open wound with nerve endings exposed. Her leg had been torn clean off her body, and she was still too numb to feel it.

Or, she was a skilled actress who shot her partner in cold blood and was about to use his death to make a killing.

TWENTY-THREE

It was agony departing Clayton instead of following Sylvie to Running Pine, but I wanted to make another stop while I was out. Dori and Courtney lived twenty minutes from the Clayton dock, in a house I'd come to know well.

Since my first visit to their home, when Tim and I were still colleagues getting to know each other, I'd enjoyed Dori Wellington. She was a dynamo, the sort of woman who got things done not because it was expected of her but because she wanted to help. Having divorced when Tim was in grade school, Dori had raised him and his sister on her own for years before meeting Courtney and welcoming two stepsons into her life. Though I'd be seeing her later that night for dinner, I knew Dori would relish another chance to be close to her future grandchild.

In her colorful kitchen, she made two mugs of herbal tea while I flipped through one of Jane's books at the table. 'I saw the press conference. This must be hard for you,' Dori said, handing me a mug. 'Having to sit on the bench during a big game.'

I smiled at that. Tim's stepbrother, JC, played football at the University of Connecticut, and Dori delighted in annoying him with sports idioms. What had started as a joke over Thanksgiving had turned into a personal challenge. I considered telling my mother-in-law about the previous day's distraction, and decided against it. I wasn't sure how to explain the oddly pressing urge to revisit the East Village. 'I know Tim and Val have the case well in hand,' I said instead.

It was the truth. The homicide investigation was moving along under Tim's steadfast guidance. He and Val were searching Sylvie's cabin in an attempt to find the weapon used to kill Cary. They'd conduct additional interviews with the other islanders next. For the time being, at least, I wasn't needed.

But I could still be useful.

As a general rule, Tim and I kept work stuff from our families. Giving our parents a play-by-play on our open investigations wasn't good for their mental health. But Tim's mother had lived in town for decades, and her institutional knowledge had been useful to us in the past. I thought about that as I sipped from the steaming cup. The geography of violent crime was important. Not only did most offenders commit acts of violence close to home, but targets were often victimized in their own neighborhoods. Crime rates varied from place to place, of course, but a location's physical and social characteristics could factor into an offense. Just as communities near highways that crossed state lines were tempting targets for thieves looking to make a fast escape, those hit by hard times had higher instances of sexual violence. In the case of Cary Caufield, he'd been found in the river, not ten minutes from his home. The island, and its history, mattered.

'Dori,' I said, 'What can you tell me about Running Pine?'

The kitchen chair creaked when she leaned back, mug still in hand. 'It's a beautiful spot. I've spent some time out there. We took the kids camping once, when Tim was little. Lord knows what I was thinking, dragging a toddler on a camping trip! No doubt it was his father's idea.'

Dori had stayed cordial with Tim's dad after the divorce and throughout her union with Courtney. His move to the Tampa Bay area years prior probably helped with that. 'One thing I remember,' she went on, 'is that the island still had a one-room school house. Last in the state, I think. Running Pine used to be a happening place, both when it was settled back in the 1800s and for decades afterward. It looks densely wooded from the river, but it's really quite a pastoral landscape. Lots of farms out there. At least, there used to be.'

Dori explained that, over the years, the dairy farms had stopped producing milk. When the cheese factory closed and the lumber and granite mine work dried up, folks moved to the mainland. It was mostly part-timers now, she told me, who stayed close to the river. In summer, they arrived in droves and brought the community back to life.

'Not gonna lie, it feels like a ghost town right now,' I said.

'That might have something to do with the old buildings, too. When I visited,' said Dori, 'I remember thinking they should all be razed. It would be prettier that way. Meadows for miles. I guess there's too much history there. Those farms belonged to families once, some of which still have kin on the island.'

I'd seen the remnants of one of those farms on Running Wild.

Happy Cary and the snowman in front of that weather-beaten barn. The structure had looked like it was holdings its breath, one snowflake away from falling apart.

'I wonder why Jane Budd never wrote a book about Running Pine.' The question had been nagging. Jane's book on Prohibition in the Thousand Islands lay on the table now, but I'd been flipping through it. The others, too. She'd covered a lot of the area in her series, but the titles I'd purchased in Clayton didn't seem related to the island at all. 'With all her personal experience, family out there for a century or more, a book like that would practically write itself.'

'Maybe she's gearing up for her magnum opus. I would imagine the island means a lot to her. She may feel some pressure to get it right.'

'Maybe,' I said, but weren't people always telling would-be authors to *write what you know*? It was the path of least resistance, and positioning oneself as an expert on a subject was the faster route to publishing. The approach had worked for Adam Starkweather. But Jane had chosen to start with topics that were adjacent to her expertise, despite having access to a wealth of personal knowledge about her fascinating home. The whole thing struck me as odd.

'So,' said Dori. 'About tonight.'

'Ah.' It was hard to believe it was Friday already. 'Tim's back out there interviewing the islanders. I'm really not sure what time he'll be home tonight.'

'No problem,' she said, eyes crinkling as she smiled. 'We can play it by ear. We should monitor the weather anyway. They're calling for high winds and more snow.'

The Northeast did get blue skies in winter, but many days also brought a canopy of flat, boundless white. I'd once asked my father why that was, and still remembered his reply. It wasn't the sky that changed from blue to white, he'd told me. What I saw was wispy clouds of ice crystals scattering the sunlight and obscuring the blue. The white sky I saw through Dori's window could mean something else, too. There was a storm on the way. I could hear the wind shrieking outside the windows, searching for a way in. It would be twice as strong on the ice, which Tim would have to cross to get back.

'Hope you don't mind,' said Dori, 'but I invited Valerie too. With all that time spent on Running Pine this week, I figured she and Bobby could use a home-cooked meal. Listen.' She studied me for a moment. Leaned in close. 'Tim told me you've been a little preoccupied. Would it help if Courtney got Bobby home from school today? That way you could be around for the team if they need you. I can arrange it all with Val.'

Shit. It was *Friday*. I was expected at the school. 'Actually, that would be great,' I said, feeling a stab of affection for the woman's efficiency. 'I might call Sam too, see if he'd mind teaching solo for once.' It hadn't occurred to me sooner, but with an active homicide investigation, and Tim and Val still on the island, the odds that I'd be able to focus on karate were slim.

'What else can I do to help while Tim's away? Do you need any cooking done? Some cleaning, maybe? Seems a waste to have me in your corner and not use me when you're on the ropes.'

I laughed and gave the woman an affectionate smile. 'Really, we're fine.'

'Have you eaten lunch?'

'No, but—'

'Good,' she said. 'You go lie down for twenty minutes, and I'll make you some egg salad.'

What I really wanted was to get to the barracks and check in with Sol, but I knew better than to turn down a healthy meal when it was offered. 'Thanks. That sounds great.'

'Take JC's room. It smells so much better now that his jerseys aren't moldering in the corners.'

Grinning to myself, I walked down the hall to the room with the navy-blue walls. Plunked myself on the bed, and blew out a breath. It would take Dori at least fifteen minutes to make lunch. As tempting as it was to lie down and close my eyes, I clicked the bedroom door shut and took out my phone. Texted Sam to let him know I'd be skipping class, and did an online search for Jane Budd.

Google was replete with photos of Jane signing books on the grass outside the bookstore, presenting her work at the museum in A-Bay, and visiting libraries all the way from Cape Vincent to Morristown and Massena. She was popular with local readers, but she'd gotten some national news mentions too, including a feature on PBS. Still, there was no indication she'd ever written or spoken about Running Pine.

Once again, I pulled up Running Wild. Just a few miles from where Tim and I lived, a young couple had been building a media empire in what appeared to be an idyllic place. In the six months since Sylvie Lavoy and Cary Caufield launched the account, they'd worked every angle to monetize images of the island. Every second or third post was sponsored, the message one of cheering aspiration: *hey, look at our beautiful island life – and while you're at it, buy this three-hundred-dollar camp blanket so you can pretend you live it too.* Followers could take an extra 25 percent off their orders by using the code RUNNINGWILD. Even with the discount – plus free shipping, if you included the hashtag #runningwild4life – the designer blanket was out of my price range, but plenty of followers seemed excited to purchase Sylvie-and-Cary-endorsed wares. Most posts had thousands of likes, and comments that ran the gamut from gushing praise to strings of heart emojis in colors that matched Bash's bandanas.

The memory of Cary's belongings abandoned on the ice, what happened to him while he'd sat there fishing, hounded me. Someone had his watch and that fact, along with Sylvie's desire to get it back, raised suspicion. I trusted my team implicitly, and had been present when the victim was cut from the ice. None of our people had taken the field watch. And that left very few explanations.

I hadn't talked to Josie all week, so I wasn't surprised when my call triggered a lecture. We'd agreed to stay in contact about our pregnancies. My sister-in-law was getting close.

'You've got it so easy,' she told me now. 'Just wait until you get to the part where you can't tie your own boots.'

Laughing, I said, 'I hope Tim's prepared to be my on-call attendant. Listen, I've got a quick question for you. It's about social media.'

'Sure you don't want to talk to Hen?'

I would have loved nothing more, but Hen wouldn't be home from school for hours, and Josie had knowledge of her own, overseeing marketing efforts for a local outdoor gear and clothing brand. I explained what I could about the case without getting into details; a couple of social influencers, their union severed. An account that would now be run solo.

'Could it work?' I asked. 'If the account's been about both of them all this time?'

Josie said, 'Hard to say. It depends on who did the heavy lifting. But the account's potential for ongoing growth is about fan preference more than anything else. Her followers might embrace the change, especially if she plays up her independence. If she got dumped or cheated on, all the better – not for her, obviously, but it engenders sympathy.'

Sylvie would no doubt get plenty of that. 'What if there was a darker reason for the pivot? Like if something bad happened to her partner?'

'Oh. Well,' said Josie, 'I don't know how dark you're talking, but generally speaking, happy content and positivity gets more shares.'

I thanked her for her help, and promised to call again soon. The conversation had confirmed my suspicions that Running Wild would never be the same.

I didn't want to bother Tim and Val again, knowing they'd be busy hunting down a motive. But calling them wasn't the only way to get an update.

'Anything new?' I blurted when Jeremy Solomon answered the phone.

'This knack you have for sniffing out activity's uncanny.'

'Sounds like you've got something to tell me.'

'I do. There was no rifle found at Sylvie Lavoy's.'

'That's something, all right,' I said, though in reality it didn't provide the definitive answers we were looking for. The absence of a rifle could mean Sylvie didn't own one. It could also mean she *had* owned one and chucked it in the river after shooting her boyfriend in the chest. 'Anything else?' I asked.

'Actually, yes. A local man came in claiming to have a tip about Cary Caufield's murder. Guy by the name of Billy Bloom.'

I felt my brow furrow. *Bloom.* Tim had said Billy Bloom was a fixture in town, but hearing his name twice in three days was peculiar.

'How long ago was this, Sol?'

'About an hour.'

I tamped down a sigh. It was coming up on eleven thirty, hours since Val called to say Sylvie was returning to Running Pine and Tim and I chatted about the missing watch. I didn't expect a play-by-play, but being oblivious to a break in the case was sheer agony.

'What was the tip?' I asked.

'Bloom says he saw someone on the ice on Tuesday. A man he didn't recognize, crossing the river on foot around eleven a.m.'

A stranger, on his way to Running Pine. 'You're kidding,' I said, stupefied. 'Was he carrying a rifle?'

'Bloom was too far away to tell, but we can't rule it out.'

It was possible to walk across the frozen river. It was also highly dangerous, and a hell of an uncomfortable journey. So why had someone done it? Might there be something to our theory about an obsessive fan? Of all the slippery questions forming a slurry in my mind, that one was the hardest to grasp.

I probed Sol further, coaxing out every detail of his conversation with Bloom. By the time I was through, I was sure of two things. The first: When he'd engaged me in conversation at the diner, Billy Bloom had known something was wrong on Running Pine. If what he said was true, his tip changed the game. Getting to the island was one thing, but leaving undetected would require enormous luck. The attack on Cary Caufield had occurred sometime between ten a.m. and noon. Ewan and Rich and their wives were back home during that time, in cabins with windows that faced the bay, and might have noticed a stranger approaching. Once it was determined that Cary was missing, Jane crossed the river herself to alert us to his disappearance, after which our team raced out to launch a search.

Winter in the North Country was a sea of blinding white. I didn't know exactly how long it took to get from Clayton to the island on foot, but it had to be close to an hour. An hour on the river, with nowhere to hide. It would have taken a miracle for a man to get both on and off without alerting someone.

Which led me to the second point I was absolutely sure of.

Whoever they were, Cary's killer was still on Running Pine.

I wasted no time thanking Sol and placing a call to Tim. I needed to know he'd come to the same conclusion that I had. When the call went to voicemail, I tried Val. She didn't pick up either.

Jean-Christophe had a UConn football pennant on his wall, a gift from Tim when JC was accepted to the school. The team's mascot was a husky with teeth bared, its tongue bright red, and as I looked at it, an image of the coywolf with blood on its muzzle flashed to mind. I was stuck on the mainland, separated from my team by three miles of treacherous ice – but my afternoon was wide open. There had to be something I could do to help.

I'm here on the mainland, I thought once more. Closer to town than to the crime scene.

That might just work in my favor.

TWENTY-FOUR

That afternoon, I launched a search of my own, and it started at The Brig. I knew from the Tern Island case that Billy Bloom lived in A-Bay. It was only a little after twelve by the time Dori and I finished lunch, but there wasn't much trapping to be done in winter, when mink and beavers huddled in their dens and dams. I also knew Bloom used to frequent the Riverboat Pub, same as me and Tim. That place was gone now, but The Brig had the same gritty local flavor I suspected Bloom enjoyed. When I didn't find him among the handful of patrons washing down a deep-fried lunch with draft beer, I drove back to Clayton. Two of its three bars opened at five.

That just left Dillon's.

I parked my SUV in front of a well-loved mural, the blue river scene a wallop of color on a smoke-gray day. Clayton's most popular pub was on Webb Street, occupying the main floor of a mixed-use building across from the hotel. The sign out front boasted a late-night menu and live entertainment on weekends, some of which I'd already experienced first-hand. Mac had taken me there a few times on our girls' nights, swapping her sheriff's uniform for a V-neck blouse with actual sequins – her idea of dressing up (she'd paired the top with dark-wash jeans stiff as stretched canvas). On every occasion, Dillon's had been packed, every seat at the bar taken by patrons drinking five-buck cocktails in plastic cups and icy-cold bottles of Labatt beer.

The last time I'd come, I'd watched a cover band play The Cure's *Just Like Heaven* to a full house. There was a poster for that same band on the door now, three men and one woman with moody expressions. At noon on a Friday in February, just two barstools were filled, neither one by the man I was looking for.

'Get you something?' the bartender asked when I approached. She looked too young to be legal, too young even to be out of school, but the army haircut under a backwards cap and half-sleeve of tattoos suggested she might have put in time at Fort Drum.

'I'm looking for someone,' I said, eyes drifting to the wall-mounted photos of prize-winning fish. 'Do you happen to know Billy Bloom?'

'Old guy who reeks of bait? Billy's here,' she told me. 'He's in the john. He just ordered some food.'

'Thanks.' I settled onto a stool to wait.

A moment later I spotted him sauntering out of a door in the back, pants riding so low I feared he might lose them. Bloom had layered on multiple stretched-out t-shirts, the bottoms of which stuck out from beneath his gray hoodie like lewd, wagging tongues.

'Can I have a word, Mr Bloom?' I said as he reclaimed his seat. 'Not sure if you remember me. I'm a senior investigator with the New York State Police.'

'Thought you might come looking for me,' he said.

I hadn't been concerned that Bloom wouldn't want to talk; he'd had plenty to say in the diner, and his call to the barracks confirmed he was the chatty type. As the bartender slapped a plastic basket of fries on grease-soaked paper before him, I ordered Bloom another drink just in case.

'I understand you think you saw someone on Tuesday. Walking out to Running Pine.'

'Not think.' He snatched the beer from the girl working the bar and let it clink against his teeth. 'It was a man,' he said when I asked for a description. 'Dressed in dark gear with a snowmobile helmet. No Ski-Doo far as the eye could see.'

That explained why Bloom's report to Sol had been so sparse. Every member of my team wore dark winter gear too. If this person of interest had a helmet, there would be no way to gauge skin or hair color, especially at a distance. 'Where exactly did you see him?'

'Down river,' he said. 'He was coming around Calumet Island.'

'Calumet? Which side?'

'North. Straight shot from the hotel.'

The hotel that was across the street from Dillon's. I was willing to bet Bloom had been on his way to the bar when he saw the stranger. First customer of the day through the door.

The bartender, who'd been cutting lemons for non-existent customers, paused mid-slice to listen in.

'Let's take a table,' I told Billy, coaxing him out of his chair.

'That fella, he wasn't from town,' Bloom said once we had some privacy.

'How can you be sure?' I asked.

'On account of where he crossed. The locals all know what those trees are for. No sense in taking any other route to cross the river.'

If he was local, I thought while Billy Bloom guzzled beer, *he wouldn't have crossed on foot at all.*

'One more question.' My tone yanked the man's attention from his drink. 'What do you know about Sylvie Lavoy?'

Bloom stared at me for a long while before a spark of understanding glimmered in his eyes. 'You mean the internet star. Lavoy? Is that what she is?' Against the bottle mouth, his lips contorted.

'Does that name mean something to you?'

'Fits,' he said simply, chuckling to himself. 'Kane. Budd. Hamilton. Plum. Lavoy.'

'Are those—'

'A dozen or so in all. The first families, we call them. On the island for a century or more.'

'The first families,' I repeated. 'And the Lavoys were among them?'

'That girl's got deep roots out there. Funny,' he said with another self-satisfied snort.

'What's funny, Mr Bloom?'

Turning a watery gaze on me, he said, 'Must run in the blood. Old Roscoe and Tully were mixed up in their share of trouble, too.'

TWENTY-FIVE

New York City

Four Years Ago

'They're an indie rock band out of Brooklyn,' I told Dave at our desks. It was in talking to Adam – he was Adam to me now, an intimacy I wasn't sure I'd earned – about victims' hangouts and hobbies that I'd remembered the shirt Jane Doe was wearing when she was found, the words 'Wolves in the Woods' printed on black cotton in a curly font. I'd found the group with a single Google search, and learned that they were local. 'They only sell merch at their concerts,' I explained. 'The most recent of which was last week at a bar called Black Hall.'

A solemn nod. Dave said, 'That place serve lunch?'

I'd been hoping for a bit more enthusiasm, but the head bob would have to do.

Black Hall was near the Broadway Triangle on one of Brooklyn's least aesthetic streets, occupying the first floor of a seventies-era building of brown brick, brown trim, and brown-tinted glass. Green and gold Christmas garlands crisscrossed the road, swooping from lamppost to rooftop. It was nearly September; someone was either early or very late to take them down.

'Right behind you,' Dave said, pausing at the door to take out his phone. 'Me and the old lady had a knockdown fight last night. I need to check in.'

'I've never been married,' I told him, 'but the *old lady* stuff probably isn't helping.'

Dave's reply was a grunt. 'Thanks, Dr Phil. Give me five.'

I'd called ahead and arranged to meet Black Hall's manager, who swanned out of her office like she was on her way to Fashion Week in Bryant Park. Her tight black turtleneck was paired with gray high-waisted trousers and heels. I couldn't fathom the damage those pointy shoes were doing to her toes. Against the bar's vintage wood-paneling, she looked like a peacock in a trailer park.

At a table still tacky from last night's spilled drinks, I showed her our sketch. Jane Doe, the way she might have looked alive.

'We get fifty people in here most nights,' said the woman, 'but . . . there was a couple. I only noticed them because of her.'

Her. Eyes fastened to the sketch.

'The guy tried to pay for a shirt, but she wouldn't let him. He didn't like that.'

'This shirt?' I took out another photo.

'That's the one.'

'Did they argue?' I asked.

'They weren't happy, that's for sure. But there was something weird about how they interacted. I don't know,' she said. 'I got the sense they didn't know each other that well.'

'First date, maybe?'

The woman barked a laugh. 'If it was, and he'd pulled that shit with me, I'd have had his balls in a vise.'

'What did he say to her?' My shoulders had gone rigid.

'He told her she should be more grateful. Something like that.'

'Any chance you remember what the guy looked like?'

She shrugged. 'He had on a cap. I didn't really see his face.'

I gave her my card, told her to be in touch if she remembered anything else.

Outside, Dave was just getting off the phone. Before I had a chance to fill him in, a text message chimed in my pocket.

Not that I don't like drinking with you, but I was thinking this time we could do dinner. Give ourselves more time to dig into that case.

Heat rushed my cheeks as I looked up from my phone as if caught in a salacious act. I turned, giving Dave my back, and typed a quick reply.

'She's a ballbuster, I fucking swear. Anything?' my partner asked.

'Jane was here – and she may have had a boyfriend. A date, at the very least. But if there's a guy in her life,' I went on, 'why wouldn't he have contacted the police? She's been missing for almost a week now.'

'Who are you texting?' Dave asked when my phone chimed again. 'Why are you so *pink*?'

'It's ninety degrees out here,' I said, brushing the comment away. 'So, we know she had a date, and we know it was here. It's a start, right?'

Dave studied me once. 'Yeah. This asshole could actually be our guy.'

My phone dinged a third time.

'I get it now.' Dave's lips curved. 'It's you who's got the boyfriend.'

'What? No,' I said, but I knew Dave. He wasn't going to let this slide. As we walked to the car, I added, 'If you must know, I've been in touch with Adam Starkweather.'

He stopped, slip-on loafers squeaking on the concrete. 'What do you mean, *in touch with*?'

'Just that. I went to the guy's book signing. He's helping me get inside Jane's killer's head.'

Dave snorted. Stared at me in his squinty-eyed way, then snorted again.

'He's completely down to earth,' I said. 'He could be our ace in the hole.'

'Jesus Christ.'

'You're the one who called him a legend.'

'He's a legend, all right.' Dave rubbed the sweat from his bald patch with his palm. 'But not just for his work.'

It took longer than it should have for me to catch on. 'No,' I said. 'No way. You're wrong.'

'Nope. Guy's more of a playboy than Hugh fucking Hefner. Everyone knows this, Shana – ask around. If he's talking to you, there's only one reason. You can't trust guys like that. Honestly, you should know better.'

I refused to believe it. This man, a renowned criminal profiler, was not trying to bed me. The very idea of it was absurd. He had a young son, and while he hadn't mentioned a wife, I'd assumed he was married. Dave was out of his mind.

I was fairly confident in my abilities as an investigator. I was also realistic. I may not have been a veteran like Dave or luminary like Adam, but I caught things that others overlooked. My antenna for deception was finely tuned, my capacity for reading suspects scalpel-sharp. I had plenty attributes beyond my lady parts. The fact that Dave didn't see that riled me.

'I'll accept an apology when this leads to a break in the case,' I said coolly. 'Until then, I don't need a fucking sermon.'

The pockets under Dave's eyes deepened. Two empty sacks sagging from his pinched face.

'Don't say I didn't warn you, Shana.'

We were silent as we got into the car, both of us fuming. I kept my eyes on the road as Dave drove us back to the station. He'd been quick to dismiss my ability to protect myself, as if I hadn't already spent thirty years inside the body of a woman who sometimes attracted the attention of predatory men. I hated that he'd made me feel stupid and small.

But it was the pity in Dave's expression that hurt the most.

TWENTY-SIX

In a lot of ways, police work is a strategy game. To do it well, we need to play chess while our opponent plays checkers. Offenders think the goal's to clear the board, swiping away the evidence quick as can be. All the while, though, we're inching closer. Setting up our final move so they have no means of escape.

I thought about that as I stood behind Clayton's biggest hotel, snow swirling across the ice between me and Calumet Island.

Did you say north? I'd asked Bloom before leaving Dillon's. The man had confirmed it – and that was an interesting fact.

The route the islanders had marked with cast-off Christmas trees was south of Calumet, the little island close to Clayton where the town staged fireworks for Fourth of July. Looking at the ice now, I couldn't imagine why the traveler would have taken the long way to shore. How could he have known the ice was safe? On top of that, it left him even more exposed. The path Bloom had described was in full view of the hotel, and though bookings were low in the off-season, anyone could have watched the man cross the river. I'd been through the hotel already to ask workers and guests what they'd seen, including the delivery man with the handcart I found moving boxes to the hotel bar. They'd been filled with whisky, not the Frontenac brand once owned by Alan Nevil but a familiar label all the same, so popular that the bartender told me he'd already sold two bottles that week. No one had noticed the man in black, though. The stranger got lucky. Me, not so much.

The hotel's back patio had the air of an ice queen's courtyard, translucent eagles and anchors and snowmobiles scattered about the space. The ice sculptures had been part of Fire and Ice, an annual benefit to raise money for state troopers. Tim and I had attended in support of our friends, and I'd marveled at the evening's neon lights and colorful cocktails. With the festival behind us, the sculptures looked as forlorn to me as those frozen Narnia statues. Forgotten post-party, left to dissolve and trickle away. There had been a band the night of Fire and Ice, too. I could still picture them bundled in their winter coats while our fellow partygoers drank red and blue concoctions at the ice bar. Behind us, the sky above the river had been black as polished melanite.

I texted Dave as I walked back to my car.

Remember the Wolves in the Woods? That band Jane Doe watched a week before her murder?

Dave replied right away.

I remember.

Four years ago, the lead had gone nowhere. I'd tried to track down Jane Doe's date, first by interviewing the bar staff and regulars, then by reaching out to the band, but information had been in short supply. Now, though, I couldn't help but wonder if we'd been looking at it the wrong way.

We know they were on a date that night, I wrote, my fingers shiny-pink and numb with cold. I drew in a breath and typed, *What if she found him online?*

Dots. Silence.

Through a dating app. Like the kind Bram's victims used, wrote Dave.

Exactly. Could you try to get your hands on those old user records? See who else Bram was matched to in the weeks leading up to the murders, and if those women looked like Jane Doe?

On it, said Dave. *I'll keep you posted.*

Abe Skilton, my cousin, had liked to play games; not chess or checkers, but complex whodunits he'd cook up to keep me entertained. If his alter-ego Bram was involved in Jane Doe's murder, he would have planted clues for me to follow.

If my suspicion was correct, I might have just found one.

I stomped my boots before entering the barracks, and headed straight for Jeremy Solomon's desk. 'Tell me everything,' I pleaded. 'I feel like I've been in an isolation booth.'

'Sorry,' said Sol. 'Haven't heard from them in a couple of hours. They're probably getting ready to head back. The weather that's coming looks to be rough.'

I didn't need a reminder. 'Any chance you could do a quick search for me?'

'Sure thing. What do you need?'

'Everything you can turn up on a man named Tully Lavoy.'

As Sol's fingers clacked on the keyboard, I filled him in on my chat with Bloom and did some exploring of my own. Aside from one arrest for disorderly conduct the year before I moved to A-Bay, Billy Bloom was just what he appeared to be: a self-employed trapper with a weakness for liquor and gossip.

Tully Lavoy was an entirely different story.

Until Sol explained it, I hadn't realized there was a difference between bootlegging – smuggling illegal alcohol on land – and rum-running, which involved transporting it via water. Sylvie's great-grandfather, Tully Lavoy, had done the latter.

'That was pretty common in these parts,' Sol told me. 'Lots of smuggled liquor during Prohibition.'

I thought of Jane Budd's book – and something else, too. 'Isn't that how Whiskey Island got its name?' Mac had called her dog Whiskey after that place, so I knew the island's history.

Sol nodded. 'Whiskey was a big drop and run point. Farther north, up in Windsor, there was a Canadian who actually did deals with Al Capone, but it was plenty lucrative around here too. All the shoals made it a hard spot to police. Other stuff was smuggled too – horses, beef, you name it. That's what you get when you live on a border. People are always looking to make a fortune by slipping through the cracks.'

I said, 'But we're talking a century ago, right? Do people really care if this guy dealt in illegal liquor way back then?' The real question, I thought, was whether the islanders still cared enough about Tully's misdeeds to hold a grudge against Sylvie.

'Lavoy's chosen business is only the beginning. According to this, he was one of Canada's most notorious gangsters. Guy was a real nasty piece of work – there wasn't a Depression-era mob boss he didn't double-cross. He supplied huge amounts of liquor to Manhattan and Albany, but the feds could never prove it. It caught up with Lavoy in the end, though,' Sol added, scanning the screen. 'There were a bunch of raids in the summer of 1931, and they found his operation – a whole subterranean lair underneath an innocent-looking farmhouse. Care to guess where it was?'

I was pretty sure I knew. A notorious gangster had made Running Pine ground zero for his illegal liquor smuggling outfit. Set up shop smack in an idyllic community of farming families.

'No cash to be found,' Sol went on, 'but they seized loads of booze and brewing equipment. It was enough.'

'So Tully Lavoy went to prison?'

'Um, no. On the second day of his trial, he was shot and killed outside the courthouse by a rival gangster – right in front of his wife. And not a month later, his Running Pine farmhouse was found burned to the ground.'

'Someone wasn't happy with old Tully,' I said.

'Or a lot of someones,' Sol added with a nod.

'Any casualties?'

'No. Running Pine was just a hideout, on land that had been in his family for years. His wife and kids were in Kingston, safe and sound.'

I asked Sol to email me everything he'd found on Tully, and used my phone to click on each link in turn. The Lavoys were among the early settlers, with a presence on the island for a long time. They had just as much of a claim to the place as the other year-round residents. But in swept Sylvie, after years of not so much as visiting, to shine a spotlight on their secluded slice of paradise. I could see the situation spawning some resentment.

Again, I thought of Jane's book on Prohibition. I'd only had time to skim it, but I was certain I hadn't seen any mentions of Running Pine.

I dialed Tim to fill him in. He still wasn't answering his phone. But this time, finally, I got Val.

'So listen,' I said, 'I heard the tip from Billy Bloom about someone walking out to the island the morning that Cary was killed.'

Val sounded harried when she replied. 'Yeah. We're looking into that.'

'I just talked to Bloom myself,' I told her. 'Found him camped out at Dillon's, neck-deep in fries and beer. Maybe you already know this from his statement, but he told me the individual he saw didn't follow the marked route out to Running Pine. That's strange, don't you think? I mean, why take that risk? I don't think we're looking at a local. Anyone from around here would have stuck to the trees.'

'Interesting,' said Val. Was it me, or did she seem preoccupied?

'I'll say. Got some insight into Sylvie's great-grandfather too. The guy has a shady past that the islanders may take issue with. So what's next?' I asked.

After a beat, she said, 'We've launched a new search. Rescue personnel only.'

I knew what that meant. Val and Tim didn't want to put the islanders in danger, in case the stranger Bloom had seen was armed.

'Hey, is Tim close by right now?' I figured I'd save Val some time and explain what I'd learned directly with the added bonus of hearing his voice. Knowing for sure that he was OK.

'Umm . . .'

Dread, cold and viscous, leaked down my back. 'Val?'

'Tim's not here right now.'

'Where is he? Out searching?'

'He did go searching, yes.'

'Val,' I said. 'Tell me what's going on.'

She drew a breath. 'We lost contact, Shay. About an hour ago. But more searchers are on their way to help us look.'

'For *Tim*?' I braced myself against the edge of the desk to stop the room from spinning. I could feel Sol's eyes on me, his body tensed and ready to react should I sink to my knees right in front of him.

'We didn't want you to worry,' said Val. 'Odds are everything's fine. Cell service is spotty out here, especially with this wind.'

'But he's not responding? And it's been an hour?'

'Give or take. Hey, we'll find him,' she said. 'It'll be fine.'

I'd made a career out of tracking the lost. Following cryptic clues left by the missing to bring them home. I'd been missing myself once, and knew how it felt to be sequestered from the relative safety of civilization. Trapped between the darkness and the light.

The threats Tim faced now, in a different kind of limbo, were deadly. The fierce cold and wind, combined with the island's inaccessibility, made the situation dire. Val had downplayed the scene for my benefit, but if Tim had been MIA for an hour, my team would be in crisis mode. Teddy was already on the island, which meant I couldn't get there by airboat myself – but in crisis mode, we called for backup. Sometimes even to the sheriff's office in Watertown.

Through the window of the barracks, I could see the parking lot. The place where, just three days prior, Jane Budd had turned up to tell us Cary Caufield was gone.

'Listen to me, Val,' I said. 'From this moment on, I want you to call with every update that comes in. Report it all directly to me – OK?'

'But—'

'Don't stop looking,' I told her. 'I'm on my way.'

TWENTY-SEVEN

The snow was deep on Running Pine.

The cold was deeper.

My cheeks burned as I sat astride the snowmobile on the way to Emmeline's cabin. I'd called up Kath, the bookstore owner – not for the airboat, which terrified me to my core, but in the hope that her husband might have a snowmobile to lend. Burt had been happy to assist the State Police by loaning me his Ski-Doo. Now, Mac gripped me tighter as we roared along the runway of Christmas trees, lurching forward whenever we hit a divot of ice. Praying it would hold.

I wanted nothing more than to help with the search, but Val had insisted Mac and I wait for her at the cabin. In truth, I hoped not to see Val for a long time. When she arrived to brief us, there'd be one less person searching for Tim.

Under different circumstances, I might have worried about how he'd react when he realized I'd returned to the island. There had been times in our relationship when I'd made the unpopular choice. Pushed back against his far less controversial point of view, and had to defend my decisions. I'd worked hard to keep my head since then, as much for Tim's sake as for my own, because I knew my tendency to act on impulse scared him. I wanted him to understand he could trust me not to put myself in danger. But running to his aid was the only trajectory I could take. Days ago, Cary Caufield had lost his life in this treacherous place.

If Tim thought I'd wait at home when he was unaccounted for, he was out of his damn mind.

On the road outside Emmeline's cabin stood a man. The dark snowmobile suit, the helmet . . . it was him, the stranger Billy Bloom had seen. I was sure of it, about to warn Mac when I noticed the three-person snowmobile parked nearby. This was the Ski-Doo Ewan and Miranda had helped their neighbor buy when his machine went in the river.

This was Rich Samson, his beard frosted with ice.

I hadn't interacted with Rich much yet, but the man intrigued me. It took grit to cross the river almost daily, repeatedly making the dangerous trip so his neighbors could stay up to date on their magazines and bills. For months he'd been hauling waterproof boots and heavy camp blankets and portable fire pits to Cary and Sylvie's front door, and though this same job had almost killed him once already, when his snowmobile broke through the ice, that hadn't stopped him.

He was also a guy who'd gone bankrupt, for whom money might be very limited, and that couldn't be overlooked.

'You want us indoors,' Rich said as we advanced, no preamble at all. 'I know. I can't do it, though, not when there's a state cop out there. This wind is getting brutal. Power's already out on the mainland, and we're sure to be next.'

Mac caught my eye. We'd just come from the mainland. As of thirty minutes ago, the electricity had been working fine.

'National Grid power outage map,' Rich explained when he clocked our confusion. 'Believe me, out here we rely on that resource a lot.'

'We appreciate your willingness to help,' I said, 'but the situation's complicated. It's really better for you to go home.'

Rich was V-shaped, his wide shoulders and cinched waist summoning an image of a greyhound, but his bearded face lacked the breed's slick aristocracy. At the moment, his frustration made his fleshy smile read more like a sneer. 'I understand that, but my job takes me all over this island. Me and Jane have lived here longer than anyone else. Nobody knows Running Pine better. He's your husband, isn't he?' Rich said before I could reply.

I swallowed a mouthful of ash. 'He is.'

'Two men, missing in the same week.' Rich clucked his tongue and shook his head. 'Don't you worry, we'll find him. You want to follow me out to your team?'

He was speaking to Mac. 'You wait for Val at the cabin while I go see how I can help,' she told me. 'No reason for me to be lollygagging here when there's work to be done.'

Reluctantly, I agreed.

'Wait,' I said as Rich turned to go. I wasn't sure when I'd see him again, and didn't want to miss my chance. 'You spent a little time with Cary. Did he ever mention receiving any threats?'

Rich had swung back around, heels dug into the snow. 'What kind of threats?'

'The online kind,' I said. 'To anyone following Running Wild, it would look like Cary and Sylvie were living a pretty sweet life. I'm just wondering if some of their fans were jealous.' If Bloom had been right about the stranger not being from town, it was possible we were looking for a deranged fan after all. A bitter individual who couldn't stand watching Cary boast about his model life.

'Huh.' With so much of his face covered, it was hard to read Rich's reaction. At length, he said, 'Cary never talked to me about that stuff. We weren't close. Me and Sylvie either.'

'Ever feel like you're losing your mind out here?'

I hadn't meant to be so blunt, but the worrying and weather and sweat in my eyes had coalesced to test my patience. I added, 'Emmeline said the quiet can be overwhelming.'

He seemed taken aback by the question, and spent a moment blinking against the silvery light. 'Not for me. I like the seclusion. Not much of a people person, I guess.'

'Delivering mail out here's a pretty solitary practice.'

Rich grunted in reply, while Mac listened for what I'd say next.

'I've been wondering how all of this' – I swept my arm toward the endless drift of snow – 'affected Cary. You're a man who's used to isolation. Cary, not so much. Doesn't sound like the best fit to me.'

If he knew where I was going with my line of inquiry, Rich didn't show it. 'That man was out of his depth,' he said, more statement than opinion. 'He meant well, but he didn't have a clue. He should never have stayed on that ice alone. We tried to tell him.'

'Did you argue about it?'

'*He* did. Refused to listen to reason. And all because of a stupid photograph.'

'His phone was lost in the river.' We didn't know that for sure, but by all accounts, he'd intended to take photos for Running Wild. We had yet to locate his device, and our request to track it had been fruitless. Either the phone had been rendered useless by the icy water, or someone had powered it down. 'Do you know what kind of picture he was trying to take?'

'Just one of him fishing, I think. He had a way of setting it up with a timer. He didn't need our help.'

'I know he featured a lot of products. Any particular item he wanted to highlight that day?'

The helmet on his head, black and shiny, stayed perfectly still.

'I have no idea,' Rich said. 'Seems like a lot of nonsense to me, shilling for companies. Always pushing for a better, more original shot. Cary said he wanted the photo to look dangerous. Like he was living this hard, wild life.'

Dangerous. Hard, wild life. I was sure I'd picked up some resentment in Rich's voice.

'Hey,' I said as, once again, he turned to go. 'I'm sure you've been asked this already, but how easy would it be for someone to hide out here?'

'Hide out?' Rich's nostrils flared as he spoke, revealing nose hairs filmed with ice.

'Hide,' I corrected. 'From the islanders. From you.'

A gust of wind lifted snow from the ground, kicking up a flurry of sparkles. An eddy of glitter rained down around Rich, his own personal snow globe. 'Not hard at all,' he told me. 'Lots of land out there, and our group tends to stick close to home.'

'Thanks,' I said. 'One more thing. Do you have the time?'

He pushed up his sleeve to reveal a hairy wrist. 'It's just after two o'clock.'

The watch on his wrist was a Casio digital straight out of the eighties, its plasticky strap scratched and worn.

As Rich lumbered off, Mac hurried my way. 'He's a shifty one,' she muttered.

'Yeah.' Seeing Rich again, I couldn't help but think about Sylvie's reaction to the men at the airboat the day Cary's body was found. She'd been afraid. It was undeniable.

I said, 'We need to watch him closely. Of all the islanders, he has the strongest motive. He knew exactly how much stuff Cary and Sylvie were receiving, and he's had some money problems. Filed for bankruptcy a few years back. He's got motive and opportunity – plus, his wife was the one who reported Cary missing.' That hadn't occurred to me before, but it was worth consideration.

Rich Samson was stocky and strong and relied upon by this tiny community to deliver what it needed to survive. He'd rebuilt his life on an entirely different land mass from the one where he'd faced financial hardship and watched his reputation crumble. What was it like, delivering all those luxury products to Cary and Sylvie? Boxes and bins and crates of free stuff? It could take years to recover from a financial blow like the one Rich had experienced. And money could make people do desperate things.

'Coming!' McIntyre called when, from the snowmobile, Rich looked our way. 'I'll stick close,' she said. 'Watch for suspicious behavior.'

'Thanks. Watch your back, too,' I told her, reaching for her gloved hand.

Everyone on the team was assuming the person Billy Bloom had seen was a stranger. An out-of-towner, maybe. Possibly an angry fan. What did we really know about the man on the ice? He'd been wearing a snowmobile suit. Crossing where most people wouldn't dare to go.

Like Rich said: nobody knew the island better. He made regular runs to the mainland. I couldn't think of anyone better acquainted with the river in winter.

I wondered how Rich had felt on the day of the ice fishing trip when he saw Cary flashing his expensive watch, a watch he'd risked his life to put on the man's soft-skinned wrist.

Jealousy could be a motive for murder too. And not just for an unbalanced fan.

TWENTY-EIGHT

Emmeline's cabin was open. No locked doors here. Late the previous night, while we'd spooned under the covers far from the dangers of Running Pine, Tim had told me the woman had officially offered her home as a lead desk. A base close to the crime scene where our team could meet and grab something hot to eat when our energy flagged.

It reminded me of those warming huts you see along ski trails. The house smelled of simmering bone broth, which I traced to a stock pot on the stove. There were two loaves of homemade bread defrosting on the counter, each wrapped in a recycled grocery bag. With no one else around, the effect was apocalyptic, as if moments prior a family was flushed from their home by flesh-eating zombies. The kind of monsters who'd bloody the snow in their backyard.

Tim and Val had already made good use of the place. A sideboard had been cleared to accommodate stacks of notecards. Tim was nothing if not methodical; one card for each islander, including Imogen, noting facts like age and family lineage. Other cards mapped the timeline and locations relevant to the crime. At the barracks, he used a whiteboard and tacked up photographs, but resources were limited on Running Pine, and the cabin wasn't secure. We wouldn't want Emmeline to wander into her living room to discover her closest neighbors were murder suspects.

Back outside, I looked around me. To the south, the river was veiled in white. I could hardly see the mainland at all. The same was true of the road Rich and Mac had taken minutes before. I felt the change in weather like a hostile presence at my back, creeping ever closer. And still no sign of Val.

I'd been told there were two options for searching the island: by snowmobile, or on foot. But that was wrong. There was another way, and I couldn't believe my team hadn't thought of it sooner.

Cinching my hood tight around my face, I followed Rich's Ski-Doo tracks into the squall.

The Fowlers' cabin was a ten-minute walk from Emmeline's, and as I clomped along the wooded, snow-packed road, I willed myself not to picture Tim lost in a forest. With Gil Gasko's strategies for managing anxiety and many years of practice, I'd gotten pretty good at not jumping to morbid conclusions. Even so, I was concerned. It wasn't like Tim to be out of touch for long periods of time. If anything, he was the most communicative among us, always insisting on safety checks. His silence spoke of serious trouble – but I couldn't let that stun me into inactivity. Inertia could be fatal. Whatever had happened, initiative was what would bring Tim home.

I didn't see it at first, but as I rounded the far side of the Fowlers' house, the truck came into view. The one vehicle the islanders had access to in winter, used for plowing the roads. It was right where Teddy had said it would be.

At my knock, Miranda Fowler opened the door. 'You must be his wife,' she said, and those words almost did me in. There was a second state of emergency on Running Pine, and this time, it involved my husband.

'Ewan went out to help look. I know the police told us to stay indoors.' She looked abashed as she said it.

'I know. I spoke with your neighbor.' Though Rich hadn't mentioned Ewan's desire to pitch in at all.

'You must be freezing,' Miranda said. As she shepherded me into the cabin, I got my first look at the youngest islander. Imogen Fowler, this strange little community's only child.

The first thing I'd felt when Tim told me there was a kid on Running Pine was alarm. A young girl, living so far from medical help and other kids her age . . . I'd been concerned the child was being deprived of the life she deserved. But who was I to judge this family? I hadn't yet heard Imogen speak, but she looked healthy enough, not malnourished or unusually pale. North Country winters leached the color from us all, but the girl's cheeks were plump and rosy.

Both Miranda Fowler and her daughter had a sprite-like quality that I found appealing: pointed ears, pert noses, the white-gold hair of a Palomino in the summer sun. I'd always thought most young children looked like their fathers, but my recent readings had taught me the paternal-resemblance hypothesis doesn't carry the weight it once did. Imogen looked exactly like I imagined Miranda had at that age, with the exception of the hairstyle. Miranda wore a thick French braid while Imogen's hair was loose and fine, the static in the air lifting strands as if by magic.

Imogen sat at the table with a rickety house made of popsicle sticks. A Lego figurine was clutched tight in each hand. The fact that I'd found Miranda instead of Ewan wasn't ideal, but with any luck, she could give me what I needed.

'Can I borrow your truck?' I asked.

'The . . . I'm sorry, the *truck*?'

'I have to get to my team.' *I need to find Tim.*

'The truck is just for plowing.'

'I know,' I said. 'It's urgent.'

'You don't understand. It's for plowing our roads. The fuel trucks only come twice a year, and they won't be back until the spring. We need that plow ready to go at all times.'

There was a glint of genuine terror in the woman's eyes, and I could sense her imagining a life where the island's six surviving adults would have to resort to shoveling. A world where they were well and truly trapped, unable even to reach each other. I could sympathize. But I had bigger concerns.

'I'm pregnant.' My gaze flicked to her daughter, whose attention was still fixed on her toys. 'We're expecting our first child, he and I. Please, Mrs Fowler. I need the truck. I need to find him.'

The woman's expression softened. She seemed to be contemplating something. At length, she said, 'Ewan usually has the keys, but there's a chance he left them here. I'll look. OK?'

Flooded with gratitude, all I could muster was a quick nod.

She retreated into one of two bedrooms, assuring me everything would be fine. 'This happens out here,' she called through the open door. 'We had a man go missing just last year. Not a local, but he ended up on the island. The boys found him in no time.'

As she spoke, I felt a tug on my sleeve.

'They're going hunting.' Imogen had come to stand by my side, but now she took my hand and dragged me back to the table. Pulled me down into a chair, and brought her rosebud mouth close to my ear. 'See?' she said, picking up her figurines once more. 'See them going in?'

The child smelled of Ivory soap and cinnamon. With clumsy fingers, she pushed the Lego men through the popsicle stick house's door. 'I do,' I said. 'I see them. Are you going too?'

'I'm not allowed. Emmeline babysits. Sometimes we have popcorn.'

'Ah.' In the bedroom, Miranda was talking about the new batch of soup Emmeline had started. Explaining that, in her grandmother's time, the women made dumpling stew out of grated potatoes for the farm boys, which looked and tasted like wallpaper paste but stuck to your ribs like nothing else. 'They seem tired,' I told Imogen, gesturing at the two men lying flat on the floor of the house. 'Have they been walking long?' An image of Tim stumbling over the ice blinked like a distress signal in my mind.

'They go a lot,' she said. 'Mostly they ride.'

'Horses?' My niece Hen had liked horses when she was small. She had a collection of them, gifted to her by my mother. Tiny creatures of different breeds with felt-soft bodies and polished plastic hooves.

'There are no horses,' Imogen told me. 'Only wolfs.'

'Imogen.'

Miranda stood in the bedroom doorway, her gaze flicking between me and her daughter. There were no keys in her hand. But there was a cell phone.

'I'll check the kitchen,' she said slowly. 'Imogen, it's time to start making dessert. Can you clean up your play things?'

'They're not done,' the girl said. 'They—'

'I'll let you dip the ladyfingers. But only if you hurry.'

Though she looked disappointed, Imogen hopped off her chair and brought the house of sticks and Lego figures to the craft cart near the wall. The bottom shelf was piled with board games, many so new they were still sealed in plastic. Ticket to Ride. Catan. Clue.

In the open kitchen, Miranda had her back to me. My eyes roved the cabin. It was just as crowded as Sylvie's, only the Fowlers had chosen to fill their home with books rather than Instagram props. There were shelves in the sunroom addition too, but these were filled with food like Emmeline's, everything arranged grocery-store neat.

The combination living and dining room had the soft, lived-in feel of a well-loved summer house, but a few of the Fowlers' belongings clashed with the family's unassuming style. A colossal white candle in glittery glass that took up half the dented coffee table. A tawny-brown pillow that looked expensive. I crossed the room, sunk my fingers into its side. It was made of real fox fur, no question.

A clatter of dishes. I swung my gaze from the pillow to Miranda, who was stealing glances at me from the kitchen. There was an open bag of cookies in her paralyzed hands, and I saw that she'd brought out a mixing bowl. Was she really prioritizing dessert over the search for those keys?

'The truck,' I said. 'Mrs Fowler – Miranda – please, this is urgent. I need to get out there.'

'I'm sorry, but—'

'Hello!'

The sight of Ewan Fowler gave me a start. He came in so fast that the front door banged open, releasing a shower of snow from the header outside. The man was out of breath, but trying to hide it. Grinning like a maniac under that patchy black beard. Had Miranda texted him while in the bedroom? Had he come running when she told him I was after the truck?

It was the sight of her now, fingers pressed to pale lips as she stared at the fur pillow in my hands, that told me I was right.

TWENTY-NINE

'I wish we could have offered your team the Chevy,' Ewan said, 'but as I'm sure my wife explained, it's more effective to search by snowmobile so we don't have to stick to the main roads.'

Miranda hadn't said anything of the sort, and as I rode behind the man toward the forest, I had to wonder why the Fowlers were so intent on keeping the island's single truck for themselves. Instead of handing over the keys, Ewan insisted on bringing me by Ski-Doo to where the team was searching. He wouldn't take no for an answer.

Everything about his abrupt arrival at the cabin was unsettling. It felt as though my own unannounced appearance had upset Miranda. She'd been cagey with me, and quick to curtail my chat with her daughter. The experience reminded me of walking in on Jane and Emmeline at Emmeline's cabin on my first visit to the island. They'd been guarded when I caught them whispering, and had hurried out before I got a chance to ask more questions.

But I had questions for Ewan, too.

'How much farther?' I braced myself as the machine's cross-country tracks plowed through rutted snow. We were heading north, the steam from Ewan's breath streaming over his shoulder. His angled arms stayed rigid.

'If they're where I last saw them,' he called back, 'it's just a few minutes away.'

'Last saw them,' I repeated. 'Were you not with them?' Miranda had been very clear that Ewan was out helping with the search.

He was silent a moment before answering. 'Rich and I went our own way for a bit. He wanted to check one of the unplowed roads.'

While it didn't surprise me that Ewan and Rich had peeled off from the group, I wasn't keen to hear that the search crew had disbanded. Not with the weather starting to turn.

'Did you see any sign of Investigator Wellington? Anything at all?'

'Afraid not. But don't worry, we'll find him.'

Yeah, I thought. *I've heard that line before.*

Trees with long, bare trunks and branches that looked coated in vanilla frosting bordered both sides of the road, creating an illimitable corridor of snow. Already I was eager for the transition to open fields of white. I felt confined by the old oaks and walnuts looming over us. Trapped.

The woods stopped abruptly, and so did the road. It was as if someone had built a barricade to block our path; it was passable and then, all at once, it wasn't, which left exactly two options.

Turn back, or go on by foot.

'Maybe I should take you to Emmeline's,' Ewan said as he dismounted, eyeing the bulge beneath my coat. 'I was hoping we'd find them before we got this far, but . . . end of the road, I'm afraid.'

I climbed off the snowmobile too and took a few steps toward the wall of snow, eyes skimming the surface of the fields beyond. 'What's out here?' There were trees behind us, but nothing but farmland ahead. In the distance, through the blowing snow, an abandoned barn was barely visible on the horizon, the solitary structure bent and broken against a colorless sky.

'Not much, as you can see. Just a few old farms no longer in use.'

'Then why clear this far?' It was one thing to plow near the cabins, where the residents frequently traveled from one home to the next, but I saw no point in taking the path all the way to this empty field.

Ewan's eyes darted away from my face. 'This is just where I ran out of steam. Or maybe Rich plowed this route. I don't remember.'

'Tim!' I drew out the word till I ran out of breath, hands cupped around my mouth. '*Tim!*' My calls returned nothing but muffled silence. All around us lay a seamless mantle of snow.

'It would be too bad to lose this,' I said, turning to face Ewan.

He cocked his head. 'What do you mean?'

'This peace. The silence.' I forced a smile, though nothing about the island felt peaceful to me, not as long as it had Tim in its cold, curled hands. 'Running Wild might have brought in a lot more tourists, maybe even some who'd stay the winter next year. Still could, I guess, if Sylvie keeps it going.'

'Oh no, I'm sure she wouldn't do that. No,' he said, shaking his head. 'It would be in poor taste.'

'Thing is, she needs the money.'

'Is that right?' Ewan brushed a finger under his nose, pink and watery from the cold. 'Seems like they have plenty of sponsors.'

'Plenty of sponsors,' I told him. 'But also plenty of bills. Roscoe Lavoy was sick for a long time. Did they never talk about that with you?'

'No. Never.'

'Did they ever ask to feature you in a post? You or any of the other islanders?'

He laughed. 'We're not exactly Instagram types.'

'I know,' I said. 'I read your essay. *Psychology This Week*? Your take on how social media creates isolation was interesting. Isolation is something I imagine you know a lot about.'

'Because of the island,' he said.

'Because of your research. Didn't you say that's the reason you're here?'

'Yes. Yes, of course,' he said, holding my gaze.

The total lack of sound was unnerving. I couldn't hear the traffic from the Thousand Islands Bridge, or even the other snowmobiles. I couldn't even hear my team calling Tim's name. Wherever the search crew was looking for him, it wasn't anywhere near where Ewan had taken me. It was just me and him at the end of the road. Alone in a blistering whiteout.

'You wrote an article,' I said, 'about the dangers of social media three months after Cary Caufield put your beloved island online for the world to see.'

The man took a step toward me. 'I had nothing to do with what happened to Cary. I already told you that.'

This was a mistake. Ewan and I were miles from the others. He'd brought me to a place so remote I could scream until the act shredded my throat and still fail to summon help. There was no way I could outrun him, whether he chased me down by Ski-Doo or on foot.

I brought a hand to my holster and felt the solid comfort of my sidearm.

Since talking with Billy Bloom at Dillon's bar about the stranger headed out to Running Pine, I'd been thinking about the logistics of vanishing on the island. Wherever Tim had gone, wherever he was now, he would have created visible tracks. We'd had countless snowfalls since the inevitable deep freeze that locked in our winter fate, layers upon layers of the stuff that would only take on more mass until it began to melt in spring. There was a name for this phenomenon; we called it snowpack, each layer boasting its own unique texture. Over time, the older snow got crusty in the deep cold, and when that happened, it cracked easily under the weight of an animal. A fallen branch. A winter boot. The wind was strong enough to move the surface snow a little, but until the current snowfall started piling up, a foot trail would remain visible. Finding Tim was a matter of finding that trail, and catching up with him.

The same was true of an interloper. If Bloom was telling the truth, a stranger might have killed Cary, intending to hide on the island until he could escape unseen. He would leave tracks too. But so far, our search team hadn't found any such trail.

Now, standing with Ewan Fowler at what felt like the edge of the world, I wondered if we had it wrong. Maybe we weren't looking for a stranger at all, but someone who didn't need to hide out on the island. Someone who could commit a murder and walk back to the comfort of their own home.

Ewan was watching me, his eyes gone dark. 'I didn't—'

When my phone rang inside my pocket, the device felt like a bomb in my hand.

'We've got him.' It was Val, and she was breathless on the line. 'Tim's OK. We found him.'

'Oh thank God.' All the questions plaguing me about his whereabouts and safety dissolved like snow by the fire. Tim had been recovered. He was alive. I wanted nothing more than to surrender to my relief, but something sharp and hard was still lodged in my chest.

'Great news,' said Ewan, his voice ruler-flat. 'Tell me where they are and I'll take you there.'

He didn't blink as he said it, his eyes hard as ice.

THIRTY

'Jesus, Tim. You scared the hell out of me.'

My knees almost gave out when I saw him. Tim stood between Val and Raymond, a state trooper and member of the search crew, with a silver emergency blanket draped over his back. His lips were as colorless as his skin. I'd been hoping for one of his crooked smiles of reassurance. Instead, his eyes rolled back in his head, white and phantasmal as he groaned.

Ewan had known right where to go when Val explained they were on an old farm near the island's center, where the main road forked north. 'There are dozens of those ancient properties around here,' he told me. Moments before, at the field, I had implied he was a killer, but Ewan's voice was breezy now, as if we were old friends. 'Some buildings are more than a century old, left behind by the island's early settlers.' One of those buildings was before us, and it set my hands to shaking.

'The barn *collapsed on him*?' I repeated as Val filled me in. It hadn't been huge, just large enough for a few head of cattle. So weathered and decayed it was hard to imagine what it had looked like when newly built. Its windows were punched out, one exterior wall torn clean away. And in its gable roof, a gaping maw.

The cold had drained Tim's phone battery down to nothing. Teddy had heard him screaming, and tracked the cries to the barn.

Tim had been lucky to make it out alive.

'Thanks for bringing her here.' Val fixed Ewan with a convivial smile. Then, with a nod at Tim, 'We need to get him warm. Can you take him back to Emmeline's cabin? We'll be right behind you.'

Ewan nodded – *right, of course* – and helped Tim onto the snowmobile. A moment later, they were heading off down the road.

I wanted to go along, but Val's forehead was puckered, her jaw clenched.

'You need to see this,' she said, taking me by the arm.

As I followed her toward the barn, she explained what she knew. When the team got Bloom's tip, they'd started looking at other houses on the island – the ones closed for winter. Places someone could break into to hide undetected. Newer homes with electric heat. During the search, though, Tim had found tracks in the snow, and followed them to the old barn.

The structure did nothing to defend against the cold. There was snow and debris all over the floor, that hole in the roof like an enucleated eye providing a clear view of the white sky above. My gaze trailed to the place where Tim must have been. Heaps of wood lay in piles in the old cattle pen. Val pointed out a huge galvanized wash tub, and told me Tim had managed to take cover beneath it when the roof caved in. Its underside was mangled, scarred with dents as big as my head caused by hunks of falling wood. 'My God,' I whispered, stomach churning.

I took another look around. What remained of the barn's siding was split and cracked, the gaps between the boards wide enough in places to swallow my arm to the shoulder. The barn looked as though it was made of popsicle sticks. Like Imogen's craft project on her mother's kitchen table.

It was an eerie place to be, long since drained of life. Not all life, though. Under pieces of the caved-in roof, there was something charred and ashy. I toed the wood with my boot. It was the remains of a campfire. Beside it, a collection of open cans: tuna, peas, the brown bread my English father liked to eat with baked beans. The edges weren't rusted. What was left of the food looked fresh.

'Someone's been squatting in here.'

Val nodded slowly. 'And recently, too. Smell that? The fire might have been going as early as this morning.'

That was it, then. There was no doubt anymore that Bloom's account had been accurate. The day of Cary Caufield's death, an outsider had come to the island, and stayed. Hidden himself in this abandoned barn miles from the islanders. Waiting for the chance to escape back to shore.

I said, 'Well, shit. Did Tim see anyone?'

'No. But whoever's been in here came prepared. He knew he'd be stuck while we searched. Probably counted on the fact that we wouldn't find Cary's body, and figured we'd give up and look again after the thaw. That means this was premeditated.'

'The rifle.' I swung my head around to scan the barn once more. It would take hours to sift through all that rubble.

'No sign of it yet,' said Val, 'and we're not sure it's safe to keep searching. What's left of this place could collapse any second. But Tim did find something, right before the roof fell in.'

With some difficulty, she reached a gloved hand into her pocket. What she withdrew made my breath catch in my throat.

There it was: Cary's field watch. The same one I'd seen on Instagram.

'It was hanging from the wall on a rusty old nail. Someone *put* it there,' said Val. 'Almost like they wanted it to be found.'

'Are you saying it was a trap?' I took the watch from her. Turned it over in my gloved hand.

'It's possible whoever left it knew the barn was unstable. That this was bait to lure us in so they could make their escape.'

'Then why choose this place to hide out in?' I asked. 'Why risk the barn collapsing on *them*?'

'Yeah.' Val sighed. 'It doesn't entirely add up.'

'This watch is worth a lot of money. If the offender has any sense at all that we're looking for him, wouldn't the tracks in the snow be bait enough? It's a strange move, giving up something as valuable as this.' I examined the watch more closely. It was in perfect condition, not so much as a scratch on its gleaming face.

Val said, 'Whatever he was thinking, at least we know we're looking for a new person of interest. This guy came in from the mainland, loaded his rifle, and set up shop until he got his chance to take Cary down. Probably stalked him and saw an opening when Rich and Ewan went home after fishing. It fits.'

It did. We had an eyewitness sighting of an unidentified man crossing the ice on Tuesday, evidence of a squatter, and the lost watch, which Sylvie believed Cary had worn on the day he died.

All we were missing was our killer.

We arrived at Emmeline's cabin fifteen minutes after Tim, and immediately sent Ewan home. The decision was made to get the search crew back to the mainland too, with the exception of Mac, who'd ride later on with us. Teddy didn't want to risk an overcrowded vessel with visibility so poor, and I appreciated his caution. He'd be back for our group once he dropped off the others.

In the meantime, I couldn't wait to talk to Tim.

'Val, can you make some tea?' I asked as I hurried over. Tim was nestled on the couch by the fire, still in his winter gear with teeth clacking. We needed to warm him up slowly.

'On it.' Val set to filling the kettle at the kitchen sink.

'I knew the minute I got inside the place was bad news,' Tim said. 'The interior walls were completely torn apart. Some of the flooring, too. It's a miracle it was still standing.'

I said, 'It's a miracle you're still alive.'

'Well, I am.' There it was at last, the puckish smile I'd come to love.

'And you're sure you're OK?' I asked. 'No frostbitten fingers or puncture wounds from rusty nails?'

'Not that I'm aware of.' In a whisper, he added, 'But I'd accept a full-body check when we get home.'

I rolled my eyes. Tim was clearly fine.

'Sol called while we were searching,' said Val. 'Thousands of homes have already lost power on the mainland, and this wind? It's just the beginning. They're calling for lake-effect levels of accumulation. The first snow band should be here in a couple of hours.' Her tone had grown incrementally bleaker with every word.

Tim turned to face the window behind him, and darkness clouded his face.

'Then let's make sure we're out of here by then,' I said. Being snowed in by a blizzard didn't faze any of us, but we'd be foolish not to take reports of rough weather seriously. 'We should make sure everyone's aware. The islanders, I mean. Check that they have enough supplies and firewood in case they lose power here too. Not you,' I said sternly, nudging Tim back down as he tried to rise from the couch. 'How are we doing with that tea?'

'Coming up,' said Val. 'Where the heck are the tea bags?'

'I'll help.' Emmeline had made me tea on my first visit to her cabin, and though the shelves were crammed with boxes and jars, I thought I remembered where she kept it.

'It's moments like these when I wonder what they were thinking,' said Val.

'The islanders?' I asked.

'Yeah, but mostly Cary and Sylvie. I know social media doesn't tell the whole story, but people so young and full of energy . . . it's one thing to move out here when you're retired, or to teach your kid the joys of living offline, but the more time I spend on the island, the more I feel like I'm in a disaster movie. Cut off from the world by another ice age. Maybe it's the divorcee in me talking,' she went on, 'but if me and my ex had to live this way when we were dating, even for a few weeks, I'd be seasoning his eggs with rat poison.'

'Easy now,' I said as I sifted through the items on the shelf. I knew Val well enough to understand that she was joking, but a man was dead and the comment had landed like a lead balloon. 'In Clayton this morning, Sylvie told me she and Cary were hard up for money. Sounds like she has some medical bills and credit card debt, which is weird,' I said as my fingers tripped over the dry goods, 'because she and Cary gave up their jobs and leases to come out here. It can't be that easy to launch a successful Instagram account, can it? Or that fast to attract enough followers that luxury brands bang down your door? Here we go.' I extracted a silver bullet-shaped tin from the shelf. I'd spotted the words 'oolong tea,' but the rest of the text was in a form of Chinese I couldn't begin to grasp. 'Val,' I said, 'would you Google the name of this stuff to check for caffeine?'

Val took out her phone.

'Sylvie inherited the cabin from her dad,' I went on, returning to Tim's side, 'but Emmeline made a point of saying that living out here isn't cheap. If Sylvie's in debt, she likely doesn't have much in savings. With no immediate source of income, how did they plan to make enough money to pay their bills?'

'What bugs me most,' said Tim, 'is that we still don't have a motive. That theory about an obsessed fan is paper-thin. Sylvie claims someone sent threatening messages to the account, but she hasn't been able to produce a single one, and Sol hasn't found any menacing messages either.'

'Shana.'

I looked at Val. The woman's eyes were plates.

'That tea,' she said. 'It costs two hundred dollars a tin. Look!' She closed the space between us and showed me her phone. 'It's some kind of specialty brand, like for connoisseurs.'

The sleek tin in my hands felt nearly weightless. 'Why would Emmeline have this?' I asked, but I already knew. We all did. 'Val—'

'Already there.' For a moment we were silent, waiting for her to scroll through Running Wild. Waiting for the account to spill yet more secrets. 'Here it is,' she said, holding up her phone. 'October thirteenth of last year. Cary posted about this same tea.'

'I went to the Fowlers' cabin, while everyone was searching,' I told them as I squinted at the screen: winter sunlight glinting off the tin of tea, a mug steaming in Cary's strong hand. 'I was hoping to borrow their truck to help search, but Miranda refused.'

As Val kept scrolling, Tim said, 'We asked about the truck too, when we first got here. Ewan said gas was hard to come by.'

'Miranda too. But while I was there, I got a good look at the cabin. The Fowlers have a stack of brand-new, shrink-wrapped board games. An expensive-looking candle. A pillow made of real fox fur.'

Val said, 'Was it square? Tan in color?'

'That's right.'

'November nineteenth.' She handed me her phone now, and there it was. The same pillow I'd seen in Miranda's house had started off in Sylvie and Cary's cabin, where Sylvie had pressed the fur to her rosy cheek.

'They've been giving their stuff to the neighbors,' said Tim, his eyebrows inching higher. 'After they shoot photos of it for Running Wild.'

'Stuff that's outrageously expensive,' I put in, thinking of Emmeline's cashmere scarf. 'To people who, by all accounts, aren't their friends.'

'They can't possibly need everything they get from brands, though, and that cabin is tiny,' said Val. 'But yeah, it's a little weird since everyone claims they didn't hang out.'

'What's weirder,' I said, 'is that they didn't choose to sell those things to make some extra cash.' Josie had once told me that was frowned upon – most brands didn't like influencers profiting from gifted items – but if Sylvie was desperate for money, it was an easy way to make some.

Chewing on what I knew, I said, 'They didn't hang out . . . but it wasn't always that way. Emmeline said they'd been inviting Sylvie and Cary to their monthly dinners, but that they only came a few times. Those posts about the tea and pillow were from late last year. There was a candle at the Fowler house too – and Emmeline has a green scarf.'

Val's phone was in my hand. I scrolled some more. 'Look, they're here too. The scarf and candle were from September. They posted about the pillow in early December.'

'And the watch?' asked Tim.

'He wore it a few different times, but the spotlight post is from a few weeks ago.'

From his place on the couch, Tim held out his hand, and I passed him Val's iPhone. 'There's a ton of other stuff on the account,' he remarked. 'Winter gloves and anti-fog goggles and cookware – all from more recently. Any of this look familiar?'

Val and I shook our heads. Val said, 'It's possible we just haven't seen it, but it is a little strange that all the stuff we *have* seen was promoted in the fall.'

Tim said, 'So maybe something happened. Everything was good out of the gate, when they first got to the island. Sylvie and Cary shared the wealth to make friends. And then . . . what, they had some kind of falling out?'

'They stopped coming to Supper Club,' I said. 'After a few months of attending. Emmeline claims they started making excuses and stayed home.' I brushed my thumb across the tea's smooth tin again, and looked at the window behind us. 'How long did you say we've got, Val?'

'Teddy should be back within the hour, at which point we need to hit the road.' Tim had pulled up the weather app on Val's phone. The satellite map was royal blue, a solid swath of color that meant we could be looking at up to thirty inches of accumulation. 'Personally,' said Val, 'I don't want to be riding in that airboat with zero visibility and a hellish wind at our backs.'

'That makes two of us,' said Tim, giving me a pointed look.

'An hour.' I tapped my chin. 'We need to make sure the islanders know about the storm – Sylvie especially. If anyone's likely to be clueless about the weather situation, it's her.'

Tim's lips, still tinted blue, were tight as a denim seam.

I said, 'That means we've got less than sixty minutes to find out what caused a rift between Sylvie and Cary and the islanders.'

THIRTY-ONE

Rich Samson and Jane Budd's cabin was the only home belonging to a long-time islander that I had yet to see, and it was the one I was most eager to visit. We'd called a meeting with all the residents apart from Sylvie Lavoy, whom Tim, Val, and I agreed shouldn't be present. We wanted to find out whatever we could about the gifts first. After that, we'd go to Sylvie's to make sure she was OK before departing for the mainland. In and out; that was the plan. It was almost three o'clock. I hoped we'd all be tucked in our beds beneath down-filled blankets by the time the snow got heavy.

Mac finally caught up with us as Tim was about to knock on the door.

'Got some things to report,' she said, breathing like she'd just run a mile. 'Fill you in on the boat.'

I knew Maureen McIntyre well. She could annihilate a perp with a single caustic word, but brushed her Maltipoo's Tic-Tac sized teeth with the tenderness of a new adoptive mother. She had dance moves to rival Mick Jagger's and thought sweet pickles were sacrilege – and when she cracked a case, she was useless at hiding her glee. Her swoopy blonde bangs were plastered to her forehead, held in place by a bright orange wool hat. The eyes behind them flashed with anticipation.

'You sure it can wait?' I asked, a knob of anxiety wedged behind my ribs.

'You do your thing. I'll wait at Emmeline's. Meet you at the river,' she called over her shoulder as she stomped back off toward the road.

The cabin was the shabbiest of the four by far. Bald patches on the rugs, sun-faded curtains freckled with dust and darker spots that might have been mold. A desk by the window held an old Dell computer, piles of books and papers, and three stained mugs, two of which still contained a few inches of cold, sludgy coffee. In the fireplace, flames danced high. With so many bodies and me, Tim, and Val still in our winter gear, the heat of the cabin was stifling.

The islanders were seated in the living room, which – like the other cabins I'd seen – was oriented around a large picture window. The scent of toasted nuts filled the air, and there were muffins on a platter surrounded by the fixings for afternoon tea. Imogen was present too, napping on her mother's chest, her bird-boned back rising and falling with every soft breath. In spite of the convivial setup, all five adults sported purple eye circles and waxy complexions. Their condition was deteriorating by the day.

'We're so glad you're OK.' Jane flashed Tim a smile. 'What a horrible thing to have happened.'

'We should have warned you,' added Ewan. 'Those old abandoned buildings are awfully unstable. We locals all know to steer clear.'

'They're an accident waiting to happen, if you ask me,' said Val. 'Some of those things look a hundred years old.'

'Most are much older than that.' Jane pushed her dark hair behind her ears as she spoke, the pieces curling like commas. 'We would have knocked them down long ago, if we weren't so smitten with the island's history.'

I studied Jane's face. She'd put in years of painstaking effort to preserve the culture of the Thousand Islands in her books. Not this island, though. Not Running Pine.

My gaze flitted from Jane to her husband, whose dark eyes were fixed on the tabletop. Rich hadn't said a word. The mugs and cups spread out before the group were mostly empty, the area closest to Imogen scattered with crumbs, and it was dawning on me that the islanders hadn't gathered here because we'd asked them to. They'd come to this house of their own accord. There had been a murder in their midst. No doubt these people had some things to talk about.

I caught Tim's eye and said, 'Jane, can I have a quick word alone?'

The woman blinked. Slowly, she nodded.

As Jane led me to the bedroom, I heard Miranda's voice. 'What matters is that everyone's safe.'

Not everyone, I thought as I closed the door behind me.

'Am I in some kind of trouble?'

In the bedroom – fifties-style mint-green walls and curtains, pinkish-beige door and trim, hand-stitched quilt draped over a pillow-laden bed – Jane had backed herself into a corner, and she didn't seem to know what to do with her hands. After wiping her palms on her pant legs, she tucked her fingers into the pockets of her jeans.

'I wanted to ask you a question,' I said. 'Since you seem to be the historian of the bunch.'

'Oh.' Her attempt at a laugh came out warbly. 'I don't know about that.'

'Don't sell yourself short. I picked up your books at the store in Clayton. Kath's a big fan.'

The woman's smile was genuine when she said, 'Kath's been so supportive. I dedicated my last book to her, actually – the one about Gilded Age mansions? She put me in touch with some property owners, even helped me arrange tours.'

'That's terrific. What I'm wondering, though, is why you've never written about Running Pine. From what I hear, this place was quite a hotspot during the Prohibition Era.'

A flush crawled up Jane's neck to reach her cheeks, which were suddenly blotchy. 'You aren't the first one to ask that. To be honest, it's a little close to home.'

'How so?'

'I grew up here,' Jane said. 'I know everyone, and they know me. I would be too afraid of making a mistake. Getting something wrong, or hurting someone's feelings.'

'Huh,' I said, inclining my head. 'It's just, here's Sylvie Lavoy, living not ten minutes from your cabin for an entire year, and you're an author who specializes in recounting the history of the area. As I understand it, the Lavoys are a big part of this very island's history. Seems like a missed opportunity, not talking to her. Doing your best to keep your distance.'

'I don't *keep my distance*,' she said. 'I'm friendly. I have been from the start.'

'We know you spend very little time together. What I want to know is why. Because I'll tell you, it's suspicious.' I gave her a pointed look. 'We're investigating the homicidal death of Sylvie's boyfriend. Suspicious behavior is something we take very seriously.'

Jane's face wasn't splotchy anymore. She looked so sickly white I worried she might pass out.

The woman steeled herself, and drew a breath. 'I have nothing against that girl. But she comes from a family of criminals. Everyone knows her father's guilty of killing that man in Kingston. But he lived his whole life free and clear with no repercussions.

'I met Alan Nevil's son once, at a book signing. Imagine losing your father to such a brutal act of violence and never getting justice. As for Tully Lavoy,' she went on, 'he and his gang of crooks terrorized the people of this island. Put kind, hard-working families at risk. I've heard all the stories, horrible things, things you can't even imagine that happened right here. His wife and kid lived at some fancy home in Kingston, oblivious, while Tully and his goons made Running Pine their den of sin, just running wild.' Jane paused then. Gave a small shake of her head before going on. 'There were rumors of what they'd get up to at night with the local girls. Children, really, just fourteen or fifteen years old. Walking home from the dance hall thinking they were safe. One of those girls was my grandmother.'

Her words settled over the room like a shower of snow, still and cold. This was the reason Jane had never written a book on Running Pine. To talk about the place's history, she'd need to address its settlers. The families who'd preserved the land throughout the years. The Lavoys included.

'I have nothing against her,' Jane repeated, 'or Cary, either. But I'm not interested in giving the Lavoys any more attention than they've already had.'

I scrutinized the woman where she stood. She sounded sincere. Jane's loyalty was to the island, and the family that came before her. Despite her insistence that she had no beef with Sylvie, I had to wonder what it was like for the woman to share her long-time home with a descendant of a man she looked ready to gut and skin like a dead buck, carcass dangling.

Tim was talking about the storm when we rejoined the others, explaining that the weather was expected to turn even nastier – and soon. 'We wanted to make sure you were aware.'

Rich and Ewan exchanged a look and chased it with a chuckle. 'It's not our first rodeo,' Ewan said. 'We've all got enough firewood to last for weeks.'

'I made a supply run recently,' said Rich. 'If we lose power . . . well, that's the nice thing about North Country winters. You stick your food outside in nature's fridge.'

'It's good to know that you're prepared,' Tim said, 'but the storm's not the only thing to be concerned about. There's no need to panic' – in his calming way, he raised both his hands – 'but we need you to know we found evidence of an intruder. In an old barn about a mile north.' He didn't mention the watch.

Jane traded an anxious look with her husband.

'What kind of evidence?' asked Rich.

'Open cans of food. Signs of a recent campfire.'

Ewan said, 'I see.'

'A man from Clayton witnessed someone crossing the ice on Tuesday morning,' Tim went on. 'We want you to be aware of the possibility that you're not alone out here.'

Rich shifted in his seat. If the evidence of a squatter surprised the islanders, news of a trespasser left them stunned.

'Hold on,' said Miranda, her voice harsh and low. 'What exactly are you saying? Do you think we're in *danger*?' The way she stroked her daughter's head, an act both rhythmic and relentless, reminded me of Sylvie petting Bash.

Tim said, 'There's no reason to think that, but it wouldn't hurt to lock your doors tonight.'

'Oh God.' Miranda's gaze bounced from her husband to Emmeline and Jane before landing back on her daughter. 'I wouldn't have a clue where to look for our key.'

'I don't think I've ever locked my door,' said Emmeline. 'Not once in all the years I've lived here.'

'They did this.' Ewan's voice was a growl. 'They brought this . . . this *violence* here.' His nostrils flared as he spoke. 'They made a spectacle of themselves on the internet, and attracted the attention of some deranged killer. And now we're all sitting ducks.'

Miranda reached for her husband's hand.

'I'm sorry,' Ewan said, drawing a steadying breath. 'This place, it's our home, and here you are telling us to stay behind locked doors like prisoners.'

'We'll be careful,' Jane assured us, running her hands up Rich's arm to grip his bicep. 'We'll barricade our doors tonight. Like you said.'

'I wish I knew him better,' said Miranda, stroking Imogen's head once more. Wearing the same faraway look I'd seen on Sylvie when we first met. 'I wish that more than anything.'

The contrast between her words and her husband's was jarring. 'We all do,' said Emmeline then. 'It's just so horrible. He came here thinking this would be a fun adventure, and now . . .' Her gaze swung to the nearest window, and she shook her head.

Dropping his shoulders, Rich said, 'We shouldn't have left him alone out there.'

'I was concerned about them when they moved here,' added Ewan. 'But I never expected this.'

'No one did,' said Rich. 'Nothing remotely like this has ever happened out here. Not until she arrived.'

She. I was pretty sure the group hadn't used Sylvie's name once since we walked through the door.

'Guess you'll be heading back to the mainland, then,' said Ewan. 'Now that you've got all your people again.'

'Right after we check on Sylvie,' said Tim.

That, they weren't expecting. I felt the shock of Tim's words surge through the room, crackling like a damaged wire. Bringing each of them to full attention.

Miranda said, 'We didn't realize she was back.'

Emmeline brought a crepey hand to her lips. 'Is that right? She's here? I thought she was staying in Clayton.'

'She was,' I said. 'But she wanted to come back. She caught a ride with a local a few hours ago.'

'She wanted to come *here*?' Ewan was looking increasingly distressed.

Tim said, 'For the moment, it's still her home.'

'Sure, sure. It's just a little strange. I wouldn't think she'd be comfortable here, after what happened.'

I couldn't deny that Ewan had a point. Two days ago, Sylvie learned her boyfriend had died a violent death not half a mile from her cabin, yet she'd been so desperate to return that she'd paid a stranger with a rough-and-ready airboat, climbed aboard with her Golden Retriever in tow, and made the treacherous journey back to Running Pine.

The islanders' energy filled the room now, that nervous current I'd picked up more intense than ever. I said, 'What are you not telling us, Mr Fowler?'

All eyes went to Ewan.

'We've been meaning to ask you,' Tim said. 'Did you all have some sort of falling out? Sometime in late fall, maybe?'

'Why would you think that?' asked Ewan.

Tim gave me a nod. I said, 'With investigations like this, we look at timelines. Of the events leading up to the crime, but also of the victim's relationships with those in his community. How they began. How they evolved.'

I could hear Adam Starkweather's voice in my head, his words urging me onward.

'We noticed something,' I went on. 'It looks as though Cary and Sylvie gave you some gifts. Things they received from brands for Running Wild. Is that right?'

Their gazes ping-ponged around the room. At length, Emmeline said, 'Is that a crime?'

'They were very generous,' Miranda added quickly.

'Were,' said Val. 'When was the last time you received a gift from Sylvie or Cary?'

Another thinly veiled collective panic. 'November,' said Miranda. 'No, December.'

'November for us,' said Rich, to which Jane nodded.

'Sometime in the fall,' Emmeline put in. 'I couldn't possibly remember exactly when.'

I said, 'Do they not get packages anymore?'

Rich said, 'No, they do. Those never stop coming.'

'Then why are they no longer giving them to you?'

Silence.

'We should tell them.'

Jane's voice held steady as she spoke. She locked eyes with Ewan, who nodded.

He said, 'We – all of us – worry that Sylvie's not cut out for this life.'

We'd heard this line before. It was Ewan himself who'd told Tim that Imogen was better equipped to survive in the wild than Sylvie Lavoy. I said, 'Can you be more specific?'

Ewan's jaw hardened. 'Specifically, we observed some behavior that made us wary.'

'Wary.'

'Afraid,' said Miranda, pulling her child close.

'Afraid of what?' asked Tim.

'Afraid,' Ewan said, 'of Sylvie. I don't like to make assumptions, but as a person with some psychiatric training, I have . . . concerns. About her mental health.'

Though it was Ewan who suggested Sylvie couldn't hack life on the island, it was Emmeline who'd told us living out here could make someone loopy. If that was true, and the islanders didn't trust Sylvie, it would explain a lot. That alone might have been enough to convince them they should steer clear of the couple. Now that Cary had turned up dead, they had all the more reason to be unsettled.

Online, the woman was a star with the power to convince others to buy into her beautiful life. Out here, where she was outnumbered six to one, it seemed she possessed a different kind of sway. I looked to Tim and Val, whose expressions told me they were just as alarmed as I was.

Sylvie scared her neighbors.

The islanders didn't trust her.

'Isolation can have a profound effect on people,' Ewan said. 'There's plenty of research on this, including studies conducted on prisoners placed in solitary confinement. Even just a few hours of complete seclusion can lead to increased levels of anxiety, paranoia, even hallucinations. There have been times when Sylvie has behaved strangely,' he went on, and before I could ask for more details, he raised his hand. Chalk it up to his profession, but Ewan had a way of commanding the room that reminded me of Adam. When he spoke, listeners were captivated. Clinging to his every word.

'Sylvie's moods are unpredictable,' Ewan explained. 'You can ask Emmeline about that.'

'It's true. I heard them arguing, many times,' she said. 'I'm ashamed to say I snuck a peek through the window. I was worried. Sylvie's shouting . . . it often sounded frantic.'

'Did Cary shout back?' Tim asked, mouth twisting like a screw.

Emmeline gave a sad shake of her head. 'From what I saw, he would just stand there, looking down at the ground. Taking the barrage of insults, the poor dear. Some of what she said was just awful. It was difficult to watch.'

'Why didn't you mention this before?'

More silence, this time weighted with shame. It was Jane who spoke next.

'I think we all believed that Cary would come home. We were certain he'd left of his own accord. That he needed a break from her, and seized his chance.'

While he was out fishing, I thought. *Away from Sylvie for hours.*

Rich said, 'We thought he was spending a few days in Clayton, or maybe A-Bay, and that he'd come back home. But we couldn't be sure, could we? We needed help searching.'

'It was just speculation,' said Ewan. 'We had no proof that he'd left on his own.'

'Suspicions like that are crucial to investigations,' said Tim.

Next to Ewan on the sofa, Miranda stroked and stroked her daughter's wispy hair, burnished from the oils of her palm.

Days after Cary disappeared, here were the islanders – five of them, all seemingly sensible adults – telling us Sylvie Lavoy was psychologically imbalanced. Suggesting she and Cary often fought, loudly enough that their arguments could be heard from Emmeline's cabin. They'd implied that Sylvie was so difficult to live with that Cary might take his chances crossing the river rather than return home. What did that mean to our investigation?

Val cleared her throat, and flashed me her watch. We needed to go, quick as we could.

'Stay indoors tonight,' Tim reiterated as we bundled ourselves back toward the door. 'We'll be back first thing tomorrow.'

THIRTY-TWO

There was heaviness to the air outside already, as though the atmosphere was bulking up. Rich had insisted we take his snowmobile, which he'd retrieved from the bay, and as we thundered toward Sylvie's cabin I tipped my head up to where the sun, choked out by clouds, should have been. It felt like we were sitting in a small, white room. Like the walls and ceiling were closing in.

'I can't believe it,' Tim shouted over the grumble of the machine. 'They lied to us. They've *been* lying for days. Every one of them thought there was a chance Cary left of his own volition, and they didn't say a word until now.'

'That excuse about not being sure was bullshit.' Val's voice was so loud it made me wince. I was sandwiched between them on the three seats, Tim in front and Val behind me. 'Yeah,' she yelled again, setting my ears to ringing, 'we would have searched for him either way, but why withhold that information? How did that benefit Cary – or them?'

'It doesn't add up,' I agreed, hugging Tim's back. 'If they thought Sylvie was that volatile, you'd think they would have told us for her safety – and theirs.'

'Sylvie did leave the island when we found Cary's body,' said Tim. 'Maybe the others didn't think she'd come back.'

I said, 'Did you notice their faces when they found out she had? They definitely didn't see that coming.'

'They want her gone,' said Val. 'Which makes you wonder if they wanted Cary gone too.'

With the cabin in view, quaint as a Swiss postcard in the swirling snow, Tim slowed to a stop.

'I think this is the first time I've heard Bash bark,' Val said as the three of us crunched up the cabin path. 'He's usually the strong silent type.'

'Right now, I wish they all had dogs,' I said. 'No keys to lock their doors? What's that about?'

Tim's knuckles were encased in layers of fabric, his knock

unintentionally subdued. When Sylvie didn't answer, he yanked off the glove with his teeth and tried again.

'Think she's in the bathroom?' I asked. There were few places to hide in the small cabin. Between the postage-stamp square footage and the plate glass window that faced the woods, nearly every inch of the place was visible from the outside. It was that window Val peered through as Tim knocked harder.

'I don't see her, or Bash either. They must be in the bedroom. She has to realize we're here, though,' Val said, 'even if she was sleeping. The dog's barking his head off in there.'

Tim shook his head. 'I don't like this. Val's right, this is unusual behavior for Bash.' When another minute passed without response, he said, 'I think we need to make sure she's OK.'

In our region, a part of the state with both a scattered population and limited police resources, the line between law enforcement and community assistance often blurred. Our ultimate goal was to ensure safety, so I'd done numerous wellness checks on citizens presumed to be in danger. In service to the community, everyone pitched in.

It was the islanders' claims that living on the island could mess with your head that compelled me to reach for the door handle. That, and the memory of Cary frozen underneath the ice.

'It's locked.' The other islanders had all lost their keys, but here was newcomer Sylvie, boarding herself in for the night.

'Let's check around back,' said Tim.

Tentatively, Val and I followed.

It was clear from the moment we'd arrived on the island that Sylvie was the outsider here. What we hadn't grasped was just how isolated she must have felt. People in small communities band together. Share priorities and values. Lift each other up. Running Pine was a microcosm of the mainland, but the islanders' bond was stronger because, unlike the residents of Clayton and beyond, they relied on each other to survive. They needed Rich to connect them to the broader world by delivering food, supplies, the mail. Emmeline, the self-appointed matriarch of a highly self-contained group, cared for them much like she did her fifteen grandkids, even cooking soup for our team to eat while they moved from one search quadrant to the next. She was caring for us in other ways, too, by opening her home.

Jane and Miranda were lifelong friends. Imogen no doubt lit up the group with her toothy smile. Everyone here had a purpose – and what had Cary and Sylvie brought to this place? Publicity. Unwanted attention.

Violence.

I had to wonder if the aura of solitude I perceived around Sylvie was about her neighbors. She and Cary had deliberately detached themselves from life with the locals, turning down dinner invitations and keeping to themselves. With very few options for company and conversation, they'd chosen an insular life, fulfilled their needs for socialization by talking to strangers online. And now, Sylvie was truly alone, with only Bash – who continued to bark – for companionship.

There were no lamps on in the cabin, and while the picture window in front had provided enough daylight to see inside, the windows at the back – smaller and high off the ground – returned only a wedge of darkness. Tim wrenched off his glove once more, this time to reach for his flashlight. Behind him, Val and I waited while he stood on tiptoe, directing a beam of light into the room.

'Jesus Christ.' With an intake of breath, he stumbled back on to his heels. 'She's in there,' he said, his eyes wide.

I was nearly as tall as Tim, with half a foot on Valerie Ott. Tim handed me the flashlight, and I took his place at the window. Leaned against the cabin's exterior wall, and peered inside.

Sylvie's bedroom looked like a teenager's closet, shoes and towels and items of clothing cast across the floor. There were storage bins in this room too. More props. The blankets on the bed were bunched and twisted. Sylvie sat at the foot of it. No sign of Bash.

I was mere feet away from her, my face visible in her window, but her eyes remained fixed on the closed bedroom door. As I stared at her profile, she didn't so much as twitch. Wearing a haunted, unblinking expression, the woman looked possessed. But that's not what summoned the wave of fear that was spreading hot and fast through my limbs.

What scared me was that Sylvie Lavoy, who that very morning had clawed her way back to this tiny community in her stylish tartan skirt, held a rusted splitting axe across her lap.

As I watched, her head slowly swiveled, and her blank green eyes met mine.

THIRTY-THREE

'Well, that answers that,' Val muttered. 'The others were right. This woman's off her gourd.'

Huddled by the trees behind Sylvie's cabin, Val, Tim, and I considered what we'd seen. Sylvie in her bedroom, clutching a corroded axe. The look in her eyes had been petrifying.

I was starting to think Ewan's diagnosis of Sylvie Lavoy had been right.

'How do we play this?' Tim asked as he shivered beside me. He hadn't had much time to warm up since escaping the barn. More concerning still, our window of opportunity for leaving the island was closing.

'She's scared of something – or someone,' I said. 'That much is obvious.'

'Scared,' Val asked with a sarcastic snort, 'or homicidal?'

Tim said, 'She locked herself in. She's hiding in the bedroom with her dog. That sure reads as scared to me.'

'Could she know about the trespasser?' I asked.

'We didn't tell her. And after what the others said about her,' Tim added, 'I doubt they'd have called to fill her in.'

'If she doesn't know there's a stranger out here, then who is she afraid of?' asked Val.

It was the question that bothered me most.

'Given what we just saw in there, and what the neighbors told us about her behavior, I think we need to bring her back with us,' I said. 'She needs to see a counselor. She won't want to come, but we can't leave her alone like this.'

With Tim and Val both in agreement, Tim faced the window once more.

'Sylvie? Sylvie, it's Tim Wellington with the police. Please come to the front door. We need to speak with you.'

Bash's barks came loud and fast now, and seemed to move closer toward the cabin's back wall.

'We're coming around to the front,' Tim called. 'Please open the door for us, Sylvie.'

After a moment, I peeked inside. The bedroom was empty. Sylvie was gone.

I held my breath while Val placed a hand on her weapon, and we backtracked to the front.

The door flew open, and there stood Sylvie and Bash.

'Hi. I thought I heard you calling. You're back,' she said to me. 'How are you feeling?'

The air wafting from the cottage was warm, the parts we could see from the door golden-bright. Sylvie had flicked on the lights. Gone was the haunted expression we'd seen when she thought she was alone. The woman's cheeks were pink, her eyes bright. The change in her appearance was startling. There was no axe in sight.

'I'm fine, thanks,' I told her, though it was a lie. I'd managed to ignore the aches from my fall for most of the day, but after hours spent outside my bones throbbed like a struck bell, every movement sending a fresh bolt of pain zinging up my battered side. 'We're just checking in. Everything OK?'

'As OK as possible. You were right,' she said. 'It's hard, being back here without him. But it's also good to be home.' She reached down to ruffle the fur on Bash's wide, golden head.

'We were worried,' Tim said, shrugging snow off his shoulders. 'Bash was barking. You didn't answer the door.'

'Oh. He was hiding under the bed, so I went in there with him.'

'Hiding?' said Val. 'From what?'

'The storm, I think. He can sense it.'

We all can, I thought, shivering in my coat.

Tim said, 'We have to ask, Sylvie. Have you got a weapon in here?'

'What?' Her eyes went a shade darker. 'You searched the cabin. You tell me.'

'I don't mean a gun,' he replied. 'I'm talking about an axe.'

Sylvie may not have seen Tim looking through the window, but she'd sure seen me. Did she really think she could fool us?

'I don't know what you mean? Yeah, I have an axe,' she said. 'We make a fire every day. We use the axe to split the wood. It's not a *weapon*.'

'Do you make a habit of keeping it in your bedroom?'

'You've seen this place. With all the props we need for Running Wild, stuff ends up all over.'

I noted her use of the word *we*. Maybe Val was right. Nothing about Sylvie's behavior indicated she was OK. Grief disorders could take many forms, from PTSD to poor long-term sleep. Cary's death was fresh. For the second time, I felt an urgent need to get her some help.

'Listen,' I said, 'with this storm blowing in, why don't you come back to the mainland with us? Not sure if you've been through one of these yet, but it isn't uncommon for homes to lose power. Electricity's out on the mainland already – but the hotel has a generator. This isn't the best place to be in rough weather.'

Sylvie chewed her lower lip. 'What about the others?'

'Your neighbors? They're staying.'

Sylvie looked down at Bash. 'Then we're staying too.'

'Sylvie,' Tim said, 'it's not safe out here. No offense, but you're still new to this life. It isn't like Kingston or Cape Vincent, where you can hunker down with Netflix and wait for city workers to clear the roads. Your pipes could freeze. You could run out of food.'

'You told the reporters his name,' she said, staring hard at Tim. 'In that press conference. I saw it online. You told everyone Cary's dead.'

He exhaled through his nose. It was one thing to withhold the name of a missing person, but Cary had been identified, his next of kin notified of his death. This was all standard procedure, and we couldn't allow the fact that the victim was Instagram famous to stand in our way.

At the same time, I had concerns about what this would do to Sylvie. A suspicious death in the Thousand Islands was a big deal – and this one involved a minor celebrity. What was currently local news could balloon into a national story in no time, and here was Sylvie, back on Running Pine. Trying to keep Running Wild's weak heart beating as long as she could before the media made the connection, because who knew what would happen after that? Even if she was capable of maintaining the account on her own, a cowl of darkness had been pulled over her and Cary both. Sylvie couldn't continue to pose and smile in designer sweaters when the world knew her dreamy boyfriend had died a gruesome death in their wilderness paradise.

I had a fair amount of experience living in the public eye as an adjunct to violent crime. Sylvie's own life was about to be forever changed. Her instincts may have told her she needed to stay, stick to the calendar and fulfill her duty to her partner brands, but she was delaying the inevitable. And the inevitable wouldn't fail to turn up at her door.

'We can't force you to come,' Tim said even as the three of us stared her down, a united front in Gore-Tex. 'But we strongly advise it. It'll be negative ten out here tonight, and feel even colder with the wind chill. This storm is no joke.'

'Perfect time for a party,' she said with a derisive snort.

Tim frowned. 'I'm sorry?'

'It's the third Friday of the month.' Sylvie's tone was impassive. 'Supper Club.'

Emmeline had mentioned this. A monthly dinner party to keep the islanders sane. Surely they didn't intend to have it now, days after Cary had been found dead?

'They never miss a date,' Sylvie said when I voiced my doubt. 'Trust me. It's happening.'

'Were you not invited?' I asked, though I was certain I already knew the answer.

'They're all related,' she said dully. 'Did you know that? By blood or by marriage. They chose to live a mile or less from each other, and they hardly see anyone else all winter.'

'They must be very close,' I said.

'Yeah, well. You couldn't pay me to live that close to family. You should probably hustle if you want to make it back. It'll be dark soon.' She nudged Bash behind her, gaze drifting in the direction of the bay.

'Listen,' said Tim, 'if you need anything—'

'I'll call. Safe travels.'

She closed the door.

As far as Sylvie Lavoy was concerned, we couldn't get off the island soon enough.

THIRTY-FOUR

By the time we trudged down to the river the snow was flying sidewise, merciless ice pellets stinging bare skin. Had Rich not lent us his three-seater, it might have taken half an hour of slogging to reach the shore. Instead, we made it in five minutes.

My cheeks felt like hamburger straight from the fridge.

'I'm starting to think we wrote Sylvie off too fast,' Val said as we walked the short distance to the bay. The river was completely obscured now, the world gone fuzzy and white. I couldn't even see the airboat. 'I don't know about you, but that woman gives me the willies.'

'I don't know what to think,' I told her. 'The islanders make a convincing argument. Let's look at the timeline. Initially, Sylvie wanted us to believe Cary could be suicidal. After we recovered his body, and it was clear that wasn't the case, she floated the idea of a crazed fan. That jives with what Billy Bloom saw the morning Cary was killed – but if we're really dealing with a stalker, why would Sylvie want to stay at the cabin alone? When I talked to her in Clayton, she seemed cagey. She wanted to come back, made all the arrangements herself, but she kept looking around like she expected an armed shooter to jump out from behind a tree. It was weird.'

'Very weird,' Tim agreed. As we neared the icy shore, he took my elbow and held me close. 'Let's not forget her frantic search for that watch in Watertown. It's feeling more and more like that's the only reason she agreed to leave the island in the first place. As soon as she got her answer from Art, she hightailed it back to Running Pine.'

'The question, though,' said Val, 'is whether she's dangerous.'

Tim said, 'I'm not convinced. No means, and no motive – right? So they argued. Who doesn't? I don't see how Running Wild can survive this, and with no murder weapon, there's nothing to suggest she's guilty. I think what we saw in there is a woman who escaped her grief long enough to realize her boyfriend was killed by an unknown perp who's still on the loose. There's Mac.'

My heart dropped as she came into view. Normally, I'd be thrilled to see Maureen McIntyre. Trouble was, she was alone.

'What took you so long?' she asked through clacking teeth. 'As you may have noticed, the boat's not here. And my guess is it isn't coming.'

'What? You can't be serious,' said Val. 'I have a kid at home.'

Mac's expression softened. 'I know you do, hon, but we missed our window. There's zero visibility out there.'

'But Teddy was supposed to come back for us.'

'I'm sure he tried,' Mac told her, 'but look around. That wind's going forty miles an hour. It's just too dangerous. We're stuck here, I'm afraid.'

'You mean for a couple of hours,' said Val.

Mac's thin lips went taut. 'I mean for the night.'

'But what about Bobby?' Val's phone was out now, her expression careening toward full-fledged panic. 'I need to get back there tonight. I need—'

'That's the other thing,' said Mac when Val's head snapped up and she fixed all three of us with a horror-struck stare. 'Cell service is out.'

I reached for my own phone. Thirty minutes ago, service had been strong, but Mac was right; where I usually saw a series of bars there were now three tiny letters: SOS. Equally distressing was what I saw at the top of the screen. I swiped down to check my battery life. I was down to 18 percent. And Tim's phone was already dead from his time in the cold.

Val said, 'What are we supposed to do?'

When no one answered, Tim looked behind him. 'What are the chances Emmeline will let us crash on her floor tonight?'

There were countless reasons why I didn't want us to sleep on Running Pine, starting with family back in A-Bay. It was nearly four, which meant Courtney would have brought Bobby home long ago. She and Dori would happily take the girl in, but we had no way to reach them to explain that we were stranded. When Tim and I failed to follow up about dinner, and Bobby couldn't contact her mom, all three of them would be frantic.

Emmeline would invite us to use her cabin for the night – about that much, I was sure. Even so, the thought unnerved me. An unidentified suspect was roaming Running Pine, and the islanders had been fleecing us from the moment we made landfall.

The image that occupied my mind as we prepared to return to the cabin, though, was Sylvie Lavoy, and the look on her face as she clutched that heavy, rusted axe in her trembling hands.

'I'm heating some stew for your dinner, and there's bottled water and blankets, too. Just make yourselves at home.'

Rich and Jane had offered Emmeline their couch, she explained, so our team could camp out in her cabin. She waved at us as she left, directing one final smile our way. When the door finally closed behind her, a frisson skipped down my spine.

Funny how a change of circumstance can make you reassess. Two days ago, Emmeline Plum's cabin had felt like a godsend, as bright and unfussy as the woman herself. I'd welcomed her tea and saltine crackers, and felt a swell of gratitude when she insisted I put up my feet. While I was thankful we'd be warm and fed tonight, especially considering what could have happened if Teddy tried to come back for us, the place had lost its shine. An improperly ventilated fireplace could fill the cabin with carbon monoxide. The wind that was causing the roof to creak and rattling the panes could sever a branch from a tree like a necrotic limb. We were miles from home – miles from help – with no means of communication. We were on the islanders' turf now, well and trapped. And nothing about that felt safe to me.

Tim, Val, Mac, and I had shed our winter gear to stand in a huddle by the fire, and though the intense heat prickled the backs of my thighs, I didn't dare abandon the flames. 'If we had any doubt about their opinion of Sylvie, I think we can put it to rest,' I said of our visit to the islanders. 'Even tonight, with this monster storm, they're together while she's alone.'

Mac said, 'Sylvie must be wrong about that. Throw a party in this weather? No way. Did Emmeline say something about stew?' Slapping the backs of her thighs, which the fire had done its best to blister, she followed her nose to the kitchen.

'Try not to worry,' I told Val as she took out her phone yet again, willing the signal bars to appear. 'Bobby's smart. When you don't come home and she can't reach you, she'll know what to do. She'll probably call me, and when she can't get me either, she'll figure out it's because of the weather. Same goes for Tim's moms.'

'The power's out in town already,' she replied. 'I keep picturing her alone in the dark.'

'Dori and Courtney will be too. They'll get Bobby to their place. It'll be OK.'

'It'll be more than OK,' added Tim. 'That lucky kid'll get to eat the onion dip I've been craving all week.'

Mac had ladled out bowls of stew for everyone. I lifted the spoon to my lips. It was piled with soft gnocchi in a creamy broth of shredded chicken, vegetables, and thyme. My mouth watered at the scent. As hard as Tim was trying to lighten the mood, I was pretty sure he felt as uneasy as I did. I'd heard him whispering with Mac about losing power in the cabin. That seemed inevitable in this weather, and though we'd still have the fire to keep us warm if the electricity failed, the lack of hot water and a working toilet – not to mention an oven to heat our meals – made getting back to shore a priority.

When the wind howled outside the windows, Mac said, 'Well, I'll tell you one thing. Whoever's hiding on the island is in for one hell of a night.'

Stirring her soup and licking the hot, clouded back of her spoon, Val said, 'The barn was empty when Tim found it, and there's been no sign of the guy since. Is it possible he's long gone?'

'Those tracks were fresh,' said Tim. 'The fire too. As of this afternoon, he was definitely here.'

'Then he's still here now.' Mac wiped a dribble of broth from her chin. 'Crossing the river back to Clayton on foot today would be a kamikaze mission. You'd have no idea which way you were walking. Picture a massive sandstorm in a desert, only in deadly temps. Even here on the island, where the trees help block the wind, the snow can be blinding.'

We listened as she told us about the winter of '76, which McIntyre had heard about from her father. Back then, most children from, Running Pine attended school in Clayton, which meant someone had to get them back and forth across the ice. That winter, a friend of Mac's dad had been escorting half a dozen kids of various ages when a blizzard hit. The white-out rendered their snowmobiles useless, and they had to finish the journey on foot, the man orienting himself only by the direction of the westerly wind.

I forced a lump of gnocchi down my throat, which had closed up like a pinched straw.

I said, 'There are lots of other properties our man could hide in, right?'

'Sure,' said Tim. 'Smarter to switch locations than stay in one place. But leaving that watch felt intentional.'

'You think he wanted us to find it,' Val said through a mouthful of potato dumplings.

'Us,' said Tim, 'or someone else.' He paused as he stirred the stew in his bowl. 'The islanders made it sound like everyone knows the barns are dangerous.'

'Do you need further proof? That barn tried to kill you,' I said.

'Yeah. And the way the islanders described them, I got the impression that everyone steered clear. But there were tracks leading inside, and whoever they belonged to had to fight their way through knee-deep snow. You don't do something like that without a reason.'

'I'm a little late to the game,' said Mac, 'but are you sure this isn't a team effort? Because I'll tell you one thing. At least a couple of these people are keeping secrets.'

It was only then I remembered that Mac said she had something to report. 'You've been holding out on us.'

She waggled her eyebrows, playing coy. 'I saw misters Samson and Fowler acting shifty when they thought no one was looking.'

She'd been helping the search crew find Tim when she noticed them, the two men wading side by side through the snow.

'They left the group during the grid search. It was privacy they were after. Whatever their huddle was about, they talked for about five minutes and looked mighty worried when they came back – and not about Tim's whereabouts.'

'Sounds like a strategy session,' I said. 'What could Rich and Ewan have needed to talk about?'

'That's the question,' said Tim.

It was certainly a question that had occupied space in my mind. 'Ewan's adamant that he's innocent,' I said, 'but his stance on social media is clear. Here's what I don't get, though. If one – or more – of the islanders killed Cary for the watch and the rest of their riches, they'd still have to face Sylvie. This isn't Manhattan, with an unlimited number of suspects. Sylvie was sure to notice that the watch, supplied by a brand partner, was missing. She would know the band took some effort to unclip. And there's nobody here but these five adults and a preschooler.'

'But would *they* know that she was that sharp?' Tim asked. 'The other adults out here?'

I thought back to the conversation we'd had that afternoon. 'Sylvie said they all have deep roots on the island. Two couples plus a senior citizen, all from families that have owned property out here for decades, all of whom are related or close friends. And here comes Cary and Sylvie, young and beautiful and out of their depth. If you were one of these year-rounders, what's the first thing you would do?'

'Check out Running Wild. Probably often.'

'Exactly. Which means they'd know about the new watch, and that Sylvie would miss it if it disappeared.'

'They're fish in a barrel,' said Tim. 'Nowhere to hide. If the watch vanished, she had to know it was taken by one of them.'

'Except they aren't alone out here now. Maybe Ewan and Rich knew that before we told them they had company.'

'I love you,' Tim said, 'but this thing you do where you talk in circles? It's not my favorite, hon.'

'If it ain't broke.' This was how we'd always worked: kicking theories to see if they'd hold their shape or burst open like powdery snowballs, nothing left but crumbs of ice. I knew what Tim meant, though. Cases with no clear access point got under my skin, too.

Which was why we needed to find an in.

I reached for my phone. It had occurred to me that the others may not have had a chance to see what Sol found on Tully Lavoy. If the site content I'd viewed at the barracks was cached, I could access it again without an active internet connection. I would need to work fast to conserve battery life. Emmeline Plum's cabin had a lot of things, but an iPhone charger was not one of them.

A new email caught my eye, with a time stamp that read 2:43. The message must have downloaded when I was with Ewan, searching the island for Tim. *You were right about the dating app*, it said, and I could almost hear Dave's breathless voice reciting the words. *I found her, Shana.*

'What is it?' asked Tim. 'What's wrong?'

He was close at my side, watching me. Dave had done it. After all this time, he'd managed to ID our victim.

Our Jane Doe had a name.

And so did her killer.

The problem with instincts is that we don't always trust ourselves enough to acknowledge them. My mother had wisely listened to hers when she was pregnant with Doug, and I'd managed to do the same plenty of times in my own life. Instinct was what had led me to the Thousand Islands, and out of my relationship with Carson, and to Tim – but not before I shunned every hunch, got engaged to the wrong man, and told Tim I couldn't risk pursuing my feelings for fear that he'd become Bram's next target. And before all of that, even before I left New York, I'd ignored the growing sense of disquiet I had while working Jane Doe's case.

Now, as I stared at the words on my phone screen, I finally understood how crucial it was to trust myself.

And just how much worse everything could have been.

THIRTY-FIVE

New York City

Four Years Ago

'The problem with instincts,' Adam said as we strolled side by side down Avenue A, 'is that they require the suspension of disbelief. You have to trust them even if they go against logic, and have confidence enough in yourself to accept that, gut-tug notwithstanding, they might be wrong.'

We were eating shaved ice, cherry for Adam and coconut for me, scooping tiny spoonfuls of syrup-soaked crystals into our mouths. Adam's shoulder was close to mine as we passed a drycleaner, a wall of bubble art graffiti, the discount liquor store. It was late, after eleven, just a trickle of pedestrian traffic and a light, ghostly mist in the air. It felt as if we'd stuck a flag in some faraway city, claiming it for ourselves.

Dave's warnings had been hounding me, unrelenting. Even now, when my mind conjured my partner's face, I had to breathe through my nostrils to keep calm. I'd kept waiting for him to apologize, so sure he'd picked up on my irritation, but he hadn't brought Adam up again. And when I packed up for the day, telling him I had plans with a friend, he'd merely nodded and returned to his paperwork. I couldn't believe he didn't realize how deeply he'd offended me. It felt as though I didn't know the man at all.

'Maybe there's a difference between instinct and a hunch,' I told Adam, scraping the last of the ice from my cup and letting it melt on my tongue. 'Hunches always seem tenuous, but instincts? Those are serious stuff.'

'For a profiler especially,' he said. 'So much of what we do is guesswork. It's all based in facts and data, yes, but you've still gotta know which trail to follow. Which thread to tug on next.'

'Every one of our threads leads to a dead end.'

'That just means you haven't found the right one yet. When Vincent was six,' Adam went on, 'he wanted to have a party with his whole class. Now, his birthday's in December, and it was absolutely Baltic that year, so we had to come up with some indoor games. My wife turned the entire living room into a spider web. It was amazing – all these multicolored strings weaving this way and that, around table legs and doorknobs and potted plants. Crossing over each other and doubling back on themselves. There was a string for each kid, and they had to follow the trail wherever it took them. All the way to the prize.'

'Sounds like an elaborate game of Twister.' I tried to imagine twenty first-graders bound up in colored string.

'Oh, it was hilarious,' he said with a chuckle. 'Took them an hour to get through it. But to this day, Vince will tell you it was his favorite birthday yet. You and your partner are all tangled up,' he said, stopping next to a trash can and tossing his empty cup and spoon inside. 'But you'll find the right thread. I have faith in you.'

We'd turned the corner onto East 4th Street. The side of the liquor store was all orange brick, just one narrow doorway punched into the wall. Adam took a step toward me.

'Don't take this the wrong way,' he said, 'but I don't think your partner appreciates you.'

All the tiny hairs on the back of my neck lifted at once. 'Dave's a good guy.' I said it slowly. 'You should meet him sometime.'

'It may seem that way, Shana, but I've heard the way you talk about him. He dismisses your instincts. Like the one you have about that cut. Guys like him are all about asserting their authority. They're easily threatened. Guys like him get off on keeping women like you down.'

He took another step forward, and started to raise his hands. The blood rushed from my head so fast I felt dizzy. *No.* Adam was a colleague. More than that, he was a friend. Our time together was about mutual respect, and it meant something to me. This couldn't be happening. Dave couldn't be right about him. About *this*.

'Adam, no,' I said, jerking back. 'I like you, I really do, but we can't do this. I'm sorry.'

Silence. Neither one of us moved. Adam looked down at the hand I'd splayed against his chest. His confusion was so pure it almost buckled my knees.

Ever so gently, he took the empty shaved ice cup from my other hand and dropped it in the trash. Disappointment writ large on his face.

Fuck. Dave *wasn't* right. Adam was going for the trash. And I'd just humiliated myself in the most spectacular way.

I was mortified, so caught up in my shame that I didn't hear the shuffle of shoes on asphalt until they were right beside us. There wasn't even time enough for Adam to turn around – which meant I had a clear view of his face when it happened. A front-row seat to the horror show.

The first blow, angled at his right kneecap, sent him listing sideways, his mouth yanked wide with shock and pain. The second hit his back with the nauseating crack of an axe on a log. Crying out, Adam Starkweather crumpled in my arms. I scanned the street, frantic, but his attacker was already down the block, the wooden baseball bat still clutched in his hands as he ran.

His face, I didn't see.

Adam's, I would never forget.

THIRTY-SIX

So much time spent searching. So many dead ends. Tug on the right thread, though, and secrets unstitch like old sweaters until they're just a pile of yarn in your hands.

The people at the dating app were reluctant to hand over user records, Dave explained in his email to me, but when he told them about the murder and my suspicions that Bram could be involved, they'd acquiesced. Four years ago, news that a homicidal man was using the app as a hunting ground had nearly sunk them. Though executives weren't keen to relive that experience, they also knew that failing to cooperate would only make things worse.

According to Dave, a woman fitting Jane's description had been matched to Bram on the app.

Not one week after they'd connected online, we'd pulled her body from the East River.

'Her name is Cleo,' I said as Tim, Val, and Mac crowded around me to listen. 'Cleo Salazar.' All she had in the way of family, Dave wrote, was an estranged sister named Liz who lived in Ellijay, Georgia. That explained why Liz hadn't noticed Cleo was missing. Cleo had been more than two decades younger than her sister, the product of a second marriage for a father who would now be in his eighties, and a woman who'd long since left him for a realtor in Augusta. Cleo had been well and truly alone when she was taken, with only me and Dave to avenge her death.

In his email, Dave had also said he owed me an apology. *You sensed something was up with that cut of hers back then, but I dismissed it. You were right, and I stood in your way, and if I hadn't, maybe we would have found her sooner.*

I couldn't be sure of that. There was too much else I'd failed to see.

'I didn't want to believe it,' I said as my husband and friends watched me in stunned silence. 'But there's no question. The mutual connection between Cleo and Bram's other victims is undeniable. Three weeks before he killed Becca Wolkwitz, the woman we'd always assumed was Bram's first victim, he murdered Cleo Salazar blocks from my precinct, and left a postmortem mark on her body.' A message meant only for me.

The fire spluttered, splashing the room with orange light. 'He wanted me to know,' I went on, my voice thin. In a torrent, countless moments from that time in my life rushed in. The man outside One Police Plaza, wishing me Happy Thanksgiving with crumbs in his tatty beard. The persistent sense that I was being followed. That conspicuous cut. I suspected it was Bram who'd attacked Adam too, jealous over my new friendship. 'Bram had already found me. He knew where I worked, and what neighborhoods I covered. He used Cleo to get to me. Only I missed the signs, and he kept on killing.'

I hadn't seen my cousin in fifteen years by the time I caught the Jane Doe homicide, had done a bang-up job of banishing him from my conscience until a man who'd been walking his dog spotted her body in the East River. But no. That wasn't entirely true. Part of me *had* wondered if, somehow, he'd returned. All my talks with Adam had summoned him like a dark spell. The problem was that I didn't believe my own eyes. How could he have tracked me down in New York? Why would he want to? I had gotten so good at convincing myself I was finally safe that I'd miscalculated his tenacity.

As a child, I often spoke of wanting to join law enforcement. I'd tipped Abe off to my career path in high school, long before we went our separate ways. And he'd orchestrated an elaborate game in an effort to flush me out. Bram gave me every opportunity to see what was right in front of me, but my guard had been down. And that had cost far too many people their lives.

This was the very darkness I'd been trying to vanquish before my kid arrived. But who was I kidding? There was always another sin to atone for, always more guilt to allay. Bram's evil ran deep as the river, and I was forever stranded, feet planted on a sheet of ice about to crack. Even in death, he still reached for me. A hand clutching at my ankle. Pulling me down with him.

They were muttering sympathies and assurances, Tim, Val, and Mac, but I'd heard those before. There was only one way for me to feel better.

As the four of us sat there, the lights flickered once and went out, pitching us into darkness.

Until morning, maybe longer, we were stuck in Emmeline Plum's oppressive cabin while Cary's killer roamed free.

If there was one thing my mistakes had taught me, though, it was resolve.

'Enough of this,' I said, tapping my phone awake. With a stone in my gut, I realized I'd forgotten to power it down while we talked. Still, what I wanted to show the others was worth the strain on my dying device.

Returning to the web pages Sol had shared with me, I cleared the thickness from my throat and said, 'We've got work to do.'

THIRTY-SEVEN

New York City

Four Years Ago

Word about the attack on Adam Starkweather traveled fast. What interested people most wasn't the seemingly random assault or the magnitude of the violence, but that I'd been with him that night. A renowned criminal profiler and a female homicide detective, walking together in the dark.

The rumors spread like a lightning fire, hot and bright.

The next time Dave met me outside the precinct, he came empty-handed, trading our usual breakfast sandwiches for a tight expression and disgruntled attitude.

'Everyone's talking about it,' he muttered when he saw me. 'It's fucking embarrassing.'

'Yes,' I said flatly. 'It fucking is.' What had happened to Adam was horrible, but my presence made it even worse. I wanted to be known for my solves. Respected by my peers. Instead, I'd be remembered as the detective who stood idly by while the illustrious Adam Starkweather got the shit kicked out of him on the street.

The corners of Dave's mouth twitched. 'You know everyone thinks you're fucking, right? You and Starkweather? And that includes his wife.'

'We were talking about work!' I shouted. 'The man was attacked by a stranger!'

'Hell of a job Starkweather did protecting you. Some boyfriend he is.' Dave capped the comment with a sneer.

From the corner of my eye, I could see a couple patrol cops approaching the building, eyeing us as they walked. We were making a scene.

'I don't know what gave you the impression that I can't take care of myself,' I said, 'but you couldn't be more wrong.'

'Yeah, yeah, the big bad martial artist. Please don't hurt me, lady!'

That stung. Had I reacted more quickly, I might have been able to help Adam, or at least chase the guy off before he got in that second blow. As it was, Adam lay in the hospital with a scapula fracture and busted kneecap. The asshole hadn't even tried to take his wallet.

'Could we just get to work?' I said, fed up to my back teeth with being ridiculed. 'Where the hell do we stand with that Facebook page?' I'd sent the data to Dave days ago. What was taking his alleged 'buddy with the cyber task force' so damn long to help? 'If we can get it live and get some shares—'

'You're wasting your time, and mine. It's been two weeks, Shana. We're not finding this girl's killer.'

'Wow.' I took a step back. Shook my head. 'I really read you wrong. Don't you know how this works? A seemingly trivial detail cracks open a door. That's all we need, Dave. Just an *in*.'

How could I explain to him that I felt a kinship with this woman? A personal responsibility to get her the justice she deserved?

I couldn't, because the fact I'd been denying was staring me right in the face. Dave had already given up.

On Jane Doe.

On me.

THIRTY-EIGHT

Six o'clock now, and the sky was black as soot.

My mind had never felt brighter.

'This case has always been about two things,' I said, tucking my feet under me on the couch. 'The victim, and the island. Cary Caufield wasn't murdered back in Kingston while working an office job. It was only when he got here, halfway through his year of Running Wild, that he became a target. What we need to ask ourselves is why.'

After polishing off the gnocchi stew and piling the dishes in the sink, our small group had grown pensive, all of us soaking up the room's warmth while the wind yowled and snuffled outside. We'd lost power an hour prior, but Tim had dug up some candles and was back at the sideboard, studying our collection of suspects.

Until we knew who we were looking for, or stumbled on to them in the snow, the island's supposed stranger remained a question mark. But we had other persons of interest to consider, too.

Ewan Fowler. The apparent leader of the tight group, he was a man who inspired confidence and trust. He'd been fishing with Cary the day of his death, and was familiar with the bay – well enough that he'd be aware of soft spots in the ice he could use to hide a body. He claimed he didn't own a rifle, but that could be a lie. He'd lied to us before. Though his wife had accepted gifts from Sylvie and Cary, Ewan wasn't happy about Running Wild or the idea of the couple exploiting his long-time home for financial gain.

Rich Samson. He knew what it was like to need money, and risked his life for what little he made now. He might have resented Sylvie and Cary's windfall. We'd never witnessed Cary interacting with the islanders, and didn't know how he treated them. The fact that he chose not to socialize suggested his relationship with Rich and Ewan may have been strained. Rich, too, could be lying – hadn't Jane said something about leading hunting parties? If he owned a second gun, he could have shot Cary and plunged the weapon into the bay. Above all else, his wife loathed Tully Lavoy, and possibly also the idea of sharing her island with his great-granddaughter.

That led us to Sylvie. Sylvie Lavoy may not have wanted Cary dead, especially if it meant she might lose Running Wild, but it was possible her time in isolation had led to a cognitive breakdown. I'd seen her acting highly strung several times; maybe she'd grown confused and perceived Cary as a threat. She knew where Cary was fishing that day. She might have seen Rich and Ewan coming home alone. There were any number of possibilities that would explain how she ended up in her cabin with an axe in her lap, but sitting there, with her back like a staff and her eyes unblinking, she'd looked to me like she could take down a bear and skin the thing in the same breath.

And then there was the stranger Billy Bloom had witnessed crossing the ice. A disturbed fan, perhaps, though we couldn't be sure.

'Did you know they used to hold square dances here?'

Antsy over the distance between her and Bobby, Val had picked up a lit candle and taken to wandering the room. There was a lot to see. Emmeline kept a meticulous home, but she was a collector. The dining room wall was decorated with old printers' trays filled with minuscule perfume bottles, glass animals, antique rings. What Val had found, though, was on one of the bookshelves. A slim volume with a familiar land mass on the cover.

'There was an actual dance hall at the church,' she told us. 'Looks like it was the place to be on Friday nights. I guess this explains why Jane wrote about other things. There are already a bunch of books about the history of Running Pine.'

I recalled what Jane had said about Tully's men and the girls of the island, and fought off a wave of revulsion. 'That's possible,' I told Val. 'But let's not forget Jane's got other reasons to steer clear of this place's history. Where are you off to?'

Tim was pulling on his jacket and boots. 'Nature calls. With the power out, we need to think about plumbing. It's a lot easier for me to go outside than all of you.'

'I've never known true chivalry until this moment,' Val said through a laugh.

'Ditto,' I put in. 'Just don't go too far.'

'No chance of that.' As he opened the door, a blast of cold air rushed the room. With a full-body shiver, Tim shouldered his way into the storm.

In the meantime, I joined Val at the bookshelf. She'd been right;

Emmeline had everything from a memoir written by a one-time resident who looked to be at least ninety, to a book about the geology of the island.

'There are some pictures in here,' Val said, returning her attention to the book in her hand. 'These ones look personal.'

'Let's have a look,' said Mac, and the three of us convened on the sofa.

The first photo was dated 1929, and captured a man on a small boat filled with barrels.

'If I didn't know any better,' said Mac, 'I'd say someone's ancestor was a rum-runner.'

'I think that might be Tully.' I recognized him from the pictures online. I'd already explained to Tim, Val, and Mac what Sol and I had grubbed up on the man, and that Jane's hatred for Sylvie's great-grandfather seemed to know no bounds. It struck me as odd that Emmeline would have kept Tully's photograph. 'Let me see that map?' If I squinted, I could just make out a name. 'This looks like a list of the early settlers,' I told them. 'R. Plum. See?'

'And there's Budd. It's a distribution of property,' said Val. 'These must be the island's first farms.'

I took the book in my hands. Each farm had been marked with a name, several of which were familiar: Plum. Budd. Lavoy. The book had been published in the 1950s, but the map dated back to 1864. And one of the properties was circled twice in black ink.

'Val. Remind me where the barn was where you found Tim?' I didn't know the island well enough to orient myself, but Val and Tim would have seen maps during the search.

'About two miles from here, just north of Split Road.' Val pointed at a spot on the page, and her eyes met mine. 'Jesus. That property belonged to the *Lavoys*?'

Sure enough, it was the Lavoy name sprawled across the page, and someone – presumably Emmeline – had made a point of circling it. 'Sylvie's cabin is newer – built by her father in the fifties, Emmeline said. That barn, though . . .' I thought once more of my talk with Jane. 'Is it possible that's what's left of Tully Lavoy's distillery?'

Sol had found out a lot about the Lavoys' operation on Running Pine. There had been a raid. The man was arrested. Shot outside the courthouse. Not long afterward, his island home was burned to the ground.

Seeing the Lavoy name on the very spot where Tim found the watch in the barn conjured a memory, and I snatched up my phone from the table. The battery life was down to 10 percent, but I needed to confirm a suspicion. See it one more time to make sure I was right.

I'd taken screenshots of the more interesting posts on Running Wild: Bash in the luxury SUV, Cary and the snowman. Squinting down at my screen, though, left me feeling puzzled. I'd suspected the barn in the photo with Cary and his mug of champagne was the same barn that collapsed on Tim – the very barn that once belonged to Sylvie's gangster great-grandfather.

I was wrong.

'I don't get it,' I said, looking up. 'I really thought this barn might be the missing link.'

With a shrug, Val said, 'Cary probably thought it made a cool backdrop for Instagram. Nothing more meaningful than that.'

'There are dozens of old barns on the island,' Mac put in. 'What we should focus on is the fact that someone chose to hide the watch in the one that once belonged to a Lavoy.'

'You're right – and you know what I think?' I said. 'That watch wasn't meant for us. It was left in Tully Lavoy's old barn. That watch was a warning for Sylvie.'

Up until that moment, I hadn't really trusted Sylvie Lavoy. There had been times when I felt sympathetic, yes. She had no source of income beyond the unorthodox business she now ran solo. Sylvie must have known that Running Wild's days were numbered, but she was making a go of it anyway, all while grieving the loss of her partner alone. Now, when I thought of the woman in the cabin up the road, all I felt was fear. Between the threatening messages she claimed to have received and Tim's discovery of the watch in her ancestors' barn, it was looking more and more like Sylvie was the killer's next target.

'Cary died a violent death,' I said, drumming my fingers on my thigh. 'A rifle shot at close range. Why? He was already out on the ice. Let's say one of the islanders did this, someone Cary already knew. They could have lured Cary farther on to the river with the promise of a great pic for his post, and led him right to a current or the mouth of a creek. Somewhere he could have broken through and sunk like a stone. Simple. Clean. Instead, they shot him in the chest, even knowing the sound might carry.'

'That's an act of hatred,' said Mac.

'And incredibly messy. If it wasn't for that light snowfall on Wednesday morning, Cary's blood would have been all over the place just like that turkey behind Rich and Jane's cabin. Fresh blood in the snow, out in the open? You might as well send up a flare.'

Mac was listening intently, nodding along as I spoke. Now, she said, 'The timing was tricky too. Wait for Rich and Ewan to leave, blast Cary in the chest, and hope the snowfall covers the tracks? Weather reports aren't always reliable.'

I said, 'It's feeling more and more like the killer didn't think it through. The blood spatter, the sound of the gun.'

'So maybe it was premeditated,' said Val, 'but it was also about seizing their chance. What were they after?'

I shook my head. I had no idea.

'Guys?'

I felt the cold before I saw Tim at the open door. How long had Val, Mac, and I been talking? It suddenly felt like he'd been gone for ages. 'Can you all come out here a sec?'

Exchanging looks, the three of us rose to our feet.

At first, after suiting up and meeting Tim in the yard, all I could hear was the wind. It was the kind with no clear direction, flogging us from all sides. Couple that with the snow, and the island was reduced to black and white, all memory of color and warmth stripped clean away.

But after a moment . . .

'There.' Tim sucked in a breath and strained to listen. I did the same – and then I heard it too, arriving in a reverent hush.

Emmeline had talked to me about the island's silence. Its *total absence of sound*. Ewan had mentioned it too – but now, in the snow squall and wintertide night, it wasn't silence we heard, but music. The rootless peal of a woman's bluesy voice over the plinking of piano keys. An old-timey jazz song, silky smooth against the storm's doleful moan.

'What is it?' Val whispered, looking shaken.

'It's *Cheek to Cheek*,' said Tim. 'Louis Armstrong and Ella Fitzgerald.'

'But where is it *coming from*?' I asked. This far north, the only reliable radio station played French country and western music and the occasional Canadian pop song.

'Supper Club. By God,' said Tim, 'they're really doing it. Just like Sylvie said.'

I could scarcely believe it. A few houses away, a voice sang of heaven and dancing while a man from Running Pine lay on a morgue slab. Killed in cold blood.

When she'd told us the event wouldn't be canceled, in spite of the death and the storm, I had written Sylvie off. It added up, though. Earlier, Emmeline had gone to Miranda's to help clean the house, and I'd heard Miranda talk to Imogen about making dessert. Tiramisu, if the ladyfingers were any indication. A party dish.

'I don't know what to make of this,' I admitted.

'Talk about cold,' said Val. 'How can they throw a party at a time like this?'

She and I both looked to Tim for an answer. But it was Mac who spoke.

'I don't really know them,' she said, and paused. The music had stopped too, the song ended. A moment later, Ella Fitzgerald's voice started up anew, unfurling across the island like a bolt of velvet. *Someone to Watch Over Me*. 'These people – the kind of people who can live like this, all winter long – they're different from us. Practical. Hardy.'

Val said, 'You mean heartless.'

'No,' said Mac. 'Not heartless. Just well-acquainted with death. Islanders are like farmers that way. They have these intimate experiences with mortality. Birth and illness, among animals and within their own communities. Killings, too.'

Tim was nodding. 'We saw their reaction when Cary went missing. They jumped into action to help find him, put their own lives at risk out there to try and get him home. His death was unnatural, but I'll bet that has only brought them closer together. They're in there now because they have to be. Because it's what feels safe. Mac's right – these people aren't soft,' he said. 'But that doesn't make them cold.'

As we shuffled back inside, Fitzgerald's ethereal voice echoing around us, I thought about what Mac and Tim had said. I didn't doubt their theory was sound; banding together to continue a tradition that infused their world with good cheer and light made sense, especially now.

That didn't change the fact that they continued to shut Sylvie out. The group had written her off as a threat. Closed ranks. And they'd done it even knowing that, out here, solitude could kill.

THIRTY-NINE

They're going hunting.
 They go a lot.
 Mostly they ride.

I bolted upright with a gasp, blood rushing to my head, and found myself in a stranger's bed.

We had agreed to sleep in shifts, Tim, Val, Mac, and I, and I'd had to fight for the opportunity to pull my weight. What I hadn't argued about was a spot on the mattress. Tim lay beside me, doing that thing he did where each breath released a tiny puff of air – not snoring so much as issuing secrets into the night. I was pretty sure it was Val's turn to keep watch, but when I got up, I found her and Mac curled on opposite ends of the couch, wrists folded against their chins. I reached for my phone, which I'd left on the coffee table. Twelve a.m. Still not a bar to be found.

We'd packed it in at eleven, which meant I'd only been sleeping an hour. I didn't have to pee yet. So what had woken me up? As I stood there, trapped steam burst from a log with a crack. *The fire.* Must have been the sound of the flames that I'd heard in my sleep.

I went to the kitchen. Flicked a switch on and off, though I knew it was unlikely that the power was back on. I pulled open the door – unlocked, because none of the islanders seemed to own keys – and a fresh drift of snow tumbled onto my socked feet, swept in by a vicious rush of wind.

I snapped the door shut with a shiver.

'Shit.'

A thick whisper. Val was rubbing her eyes on the couch.

'You OK?' I asked. 'I'm sorry I woke you. I was trying to be quiet.'

'I have a kid,' Val replied. 'I haven't slept soundly in twelve years. You've got that to look forward to.'

A kid. 'Imogen,' I said, blinking fast. 'I think I had a dream about her.'

My conversation with the island's only child had been on my

mind, to the point where it seeped into my subconscious. I explained this to Val as we sat on the braided rug and pulled a plaid blanket over our laps. 'Miranda seemed nervous the whole time I was in her house. She tried to silence Imogen. Distract her from talking to me.'

'Think the kid knows something?' Val asked. 'It would be hard to keep her in the dark in a place like this, in a cabin so small. What did you two talk about?'

'She said her Lego figurines were going hunting.' I told her about the toys. *Only wolfs.*

'There was that coywolf at Rich and Jane's place,' Val noted.

'Which the islanders are aware of. Maybe her parents warned her about it so she didn't wander off on her own. That might explain the mention of wolves.'

'You don't sound convinced.'

I heaved a sigh. 'It could be nothing. A five-year-old's active imagination. Some of what she said, though, it was oddly specific. She told me she wasn't allowed to go hunting. That Emmeline babysat her, and they made popcorn. Does that sound like something a preschooler would make up to you?'

My own knowledge of children was limited. Though my time with Henrietta had put me on a fast track to parenthood, little kids like Ewan and Miranda's daughter were mostly a mystery. But I knew witnesses. That when asked for statements, they often made connections in their minds that led them to remember the kinds of details we were looking for. I'd once watched a woman asked about a suspect's car talk herself from her childhood home in Minnesota, to the backseat of her granddad's Cutlass, to the vintage Jaguar that had killed a young man on Third Avenue. I'd seen Imogen make similar connections, her mind drawing parallels between her toys and what had seemed to me like a true-life memory. I had no idea what she'd meant when she said there were wolves on the island, but if her universe didn't include horses, there was only one explanation for what the people she'd referred to had been riding – and that was snowmobiles.

'Here's what I know about kids that age,' said Val. 'They have very limited knowledge of the world. What they do know, what they talk about, it comes from their home life or books and TV. They talk about friends too, but Imogen doesn't have any of those – at least not her own age. I think it's likely whatever she told you is grounded in truth.'

'Yeah,' I said, chewing my lower lip. 'I think you're right. Which means when she said *they*, she meant the islanders.'

Val pushed her sleek, dark hair back from her face. 'So what have they been hunting for?'

'I don't know. She was playing with this little building made of popsicle sticks, though. When Miranda caught her showing it to me, she shut the conversation down.'

'Did it look like a cabin?' Val asked. 'Like someone's house?'

'No,' I said. 'It looked like the barn that fell on Tim.'

I'd seen Imogen tuck her figurines into a building that looked just like the tumbledown structures scattered all across the island.

The ones Jane said the locals loved enough to preserve in spite of the dangers they posed.

'Do you remember me telling you about the search?' asked Val. 'On the first day, I went out looking for Cary with Jane. I thought I saw movement in an old barn.'

'I remember.' Val had filled me in on that while we were walking Buckhead Bay. 'The barn was empty. Jane said it was a bird.'

'That barn wasn't just empty,' Val said. 'It was torn apart. Most of the walls were exposed beams to begin with, but someone had pried the boards off the others. Same goes for the floor. The place looked ransacked.'

'Like the barn Tim was in?'

'Exactly.'

'Could someone have needed that wood?' I asked. 'For fires, or some kind of construction project?'

'That's the thing,' said Val, her cheeks pink in the firelight. 'The wood was all still there.'

'You're saying the barn looked like it had been searched.'

'That's what I'm saying.'

I believed it. The barn that still stood on Tully Lavoy's land had looked that way too. But why? 'What would anyone want with an old barn?' I asked.

'I have no id—*fuck!*'

Val's nails dug into my wrist like claws. We'd been sitting close, her to my left, me with the picture window at my back, and she gaped at it now, her eyes wide with fear.

'There's someone out there.' Her words were unmoored, her voice monotone.

'Outside?' I could scarcely believe it. As Mac started to stir on the couch, I struggled to my feet and hurried to the window. The only face I saw reflected was my own.

'What's going on?' Tim stood in the bedroom doorway, at once disheveled and keenly alert. For her part, Mac looked as if she'd just awoken from a drug-induced coma.

'Val thinks she saw someone outside.'

'There was someone there,' Val insisted. 'They were wearing a snowmobile helmet. The visor was down so I couldn't see their face.' Her own face was wan between panels of dark hair, both hands pressed to her diaphragm.

'What time is it?' Tim patted down his pockets in search of his phone.

'Just after midnight. It's got to be one of the islanders,' I said. 'Everyone out here has a snowmobile suit except for Sylvie.'

'You know who else has a snowmobile suit.'

Mac had been sitting quietly by, rubbing the sleep from her eyes, and for a moment I was back at her house in Watertown, where I'd lived for a few weeks after breaking off my engagement to Carson. Me and McIntyre, drinking wine by the fire while she assured me my life would be better post-controlling fiancé. Her advice had always been sound. Now, she'd listened to us work through explanations for what Val had seen, and had arrived at a new conclusion.

The peeping Tom could be the suspect we'd been looking for.

Tim went to the window. Cupped his hands around his eyes, and pressed his nose to the frost-splashed glass. 'I'm going out there,' he said, leaving a halo of condensation when he pulled away. 'If Val's right, there'll be tracks.'

Val made a wet noise deep in her throat and croaked, 'I'm coming with you.'

'You're sure about this?' I asked. Any amount of time spent outside in this weather was asking for trouble.

'Positive,' Val replied as she and Tim suited up. 'Why would someone be watching us?'

'To keep tabs, maybe. If they're making a run for it.'

There was another possibility, I knew.

To make sure we didn't see what they planned to do next.

A gust of icy air rushed the room as Tim and Val closed the door.

At the window, I stared at the gleam of my reflection, and of

Mac's beside it, while the room quivered in the firelight. 'Where are they?' I said it through my teeth. If they were checking for footprints outside the cabin, they should have been visible, exposed like the figure in that insulated suit. But still, I saw nothing.

'Whoever it was, I bet they're long gone,' said Mac, laying a hand on my arm.

A moment later, Tim and Val came into view. When Tim turned his head in our direction, studying the outside of the window, he wore an expression of concern.

'There was somebody out there, all right,' he said when, a few minutes later, they came back inside. 'Fresh prints in the drift outside the window. They go all the way around the house.'

'Snowmobile tracks?' I asked.

Tim shook his head. 'Whoever was here, they came on foot along the road.'

'Where do the foot tracks lead?'

Tim swallowed.

'Toward Sylvie's.'

FORTY

It took about three minutes for the panic to set in. It pinballed through my body. Knocked against my bones. Three minutes of knowing that Tim, who'd already nearly lost his life on this island, had set out by snowmobile with Val to check on Sylvie Lavoy in weather conditions more dangerous than ever. If the watch had been left as some kind of threat, Sylvie could be the killer's next target.

If she was, and Tim and Val showed up, that made them targets too.

'How long has it been?' I asked Mac.

'Half an hour, maybe? It only takes five to ride over to Sylvie's. But visibility's poor.'

I got up from the couch and did another tour of the room. There wasn't nearly enough space to pace effectively as I went over scenarios in my mind. Seeking a feasible explanation for what was going on here.

'Let's talk about something else,' Mac said as I scuffled around in circles. 'To get our mind off things.'

'Like what?' I asked.

Mac said, 'Talk to me about Cleo Salazar.'

I focused in on my friend's familiar face. 'I think on some level I already knew. That cut on her cheek, it was too similar to mine to be a coincidence.'

'Doesn't make it any easier,' said Mac.

'No, it doesn't. As soon as we have service again, I'm going to track down that sister in Georgia. Close or not, I'm sure she'd appreciate some answers.' I would call up De La Cruz, my old sergeant, too, and see about DNA testing. It was Bram who'd murdered her – we knew that now – but the woman's family deserved a definitive truth.

'It kills me,' I said, 'that we didn't follow the right trail.'

'You know what they say about hindsight. That's the thing about reopening a cold case, though,' she said. 'You've got a whole new breadth of experience. Other investigations to draw from, and new capabilities to tap. Every case you work becomes a wealth of knowledge you can exploit down the line.'

'If that's true, then technically, you and I have never been sharper.' 'So let's figure out what the hell's happening on this island?'

With a small smile, I said, 'My thoughts exactly. If our unidentified suspect is actually after Sylvie, we need to find out why.'

'It sounds to me like you don't think this is about Running Wild.'

I shook my head. 'Cary's murder ended that outright. The account will never be the same. That's not reason enough to target Sylvie now, not when the stakes are so high.'

Running Pine wasn't the same place it had been on Tuesday morning, when the land and ice were almost deserted and no one suspected a man would be shot. Our numbers had dwindled, our team down to four, but our presence on the island was well-known. No, if someone planned to kill Sylvie tonight, that was about something else.

'Let's go over what we know,' said Mac.

I massaged my lower back through my sweatshirt, and nodded. 'One. Something happened between the fall and now, something significant enough that Sylvie and Cary both stopped attending Supper Club and giving the islanders gifts.'

'A rift in their relationship,' said Mac.

'Right. I wondered if it could have something to do with her great-grandfather, Tully Lavoy – but the islanders would have known who Sylvie was the minute she moved into that cabin. If they're holding a grudge solely because of Tully's shady reputation, why wouldn't they have shut the couple out from the start?

'Two,' I went on, 'the island's history means something to these people. Jane said as much earlier today, when she warned us about the unstable barns.' We'd been sitting on the couch, but now I went back to the shelf where Val had found the books about the island. All appeared to be self-published, with decades-old photographs for cover art. Instead of selecting the same book Val had shown us, I picked up the memoir, flipping pages as I spoke.

I'd never been deeply attached to a home before. Swanton held some fond memories, but Abe had shown me its unpleasant side too, cracking open a cabinet of curiosities that brimmed with corruption and sin. 'I guess it means a lot when your ancestors all lived on the same land,' I said.

'Especially if someone sullies its name.'

Though I agreed with Mac, it was surprising how much information Emmeline had collected on the island. Had I not known Jane Budd to be the author of the bunch, I might have thought it was Emmeline Plum who was researching a book.

As I thought about the books in the cabin, and Tully Lavoy, and Cary Caufield, Mac's message rang in my ears.

Every case you work becomes a wealth of knowledge.

'Think they found him?' she asked, head turned toward the falling snow.

Him. We still didn't know who we were looking for, did we? Whether *he* was an obsessive fan, or a local jealous of the couple's attention, or one of the islanders who, not an hour before, had been eating and dancing at their monthly Supper Club. What we did know was that someone had stolen Cary's watch and left it hanging in the barn as some kind of threat or sick taunt, and they were armed, and Tim and Val were out there with them.

There was pounding on the door then, and the outline of a figure behind the veiled glass. In the fraction of a second before I pushed the curtain aside, I swore I saw Bram, his hair dark and stringy. Crooked teeth glinting like screws in a jar. My cousin had worn many masks, but his true look was keen-eyed and forbidding. Blood rushed my ears, a reaction to the fear that had been growing for hours. It had metastasized; I felt it through every part of my body now. Terror. I knew it well.

'Avon calling.'

I gave my head a shake to clear it.

I was looking at Steady Teddy.

'Oh my God,' I said, exhaling hard when I spotted Tim and Val behind him. 'I've never been so happy to see anyone in my life.'

'I'd take offense to that,' said Tim as the three of them stomped their boots on the porch, 'if I hadn't almost dropped to my knees to kiss the man's feet myself.'

Teddy brushed the snow from his knit hat and laughed. 'I'm happy to see you guys too. I was a little worried I'd have to sleep outside tonight.'

'How the heck did you get here?' asked Mac. 'You must have been driving completely blind!'

'Pretty much. It is *not* a good scene on that ice. But I wouldn't be very good at my job if I left you stranded out here, would I? At least this way I can get you back home as soon as there's a break in the weather.'

'Now that's dedication,' Val said with a laugh. 'You're making me look bad, kid.'

'You must be freezing.' I ushered Teddy inside, draping a blanket over his shoulders as I steered him toward the fire. Snow dripped from the ends of his chin-length hair, darkening the front of his flannel shirt.

'We found him on our way to Sylvie's,' Tim explained. 'But we've got a problem. Her cabin's empty, and wherever she went, she left Bash behind.'

Our group fell silent. It was one thing to learn Sylvie had ventured out into the storm, but the woman didn't go anywhere without that dog. 'Where could she have gone in this weather?' I asked.

'Not back to the mainland,' said Teddy, 'that's for sure.'

'Agreed. She doesn't have access to a snowmobile,' said Tim, 'or any way to reach Burt and his makeshift airboat.'

'Could she be with the other islanders?' After everything we'd learned about the community, it seemed unlikely that Sylvie would turn to them now. But where else could she have gone in this hellish winterscape?

'Honestly?' said Val. 'I hope she is.'

'No sign of the stranger?' I asked, my tone growing serious.

Tim shook his head. 'But the tracks we were following led straight to her door.'

'Then we need to alert the others. We'll come with you – you need us,' I said before Tim could object. 'And I'm done feeling like a sitting duck.' I couldn't imagine staying behind in the cabin without knowing Sylvie was safe. Not now.

'We stick together,' said Tim.

'Deal.' I had no intention of getting lost in the storm.

Mac and I suited up, I gave the fire one long last glance, and together, the five of us set off for the Fowlers' cabin.

FORTY-ONE

Gone were the gentle flurries of that afternoon. As we hiked down the road, the beams from our collective flashlights bouncing before us, the snow looked frenzied, flying every which way but down.

There wasn't room enough for all of us on the snowmobile, so we left it behind. It was a short walk from Emmeline's to Ewan and Miranda Fowler's house, but every time I looked at Teddy I longed for the hard aluminum seats of the airboat and ached to make the journey home. The jaunty music we'd heard earlier had been muzzled, replaced by the roaring wind and occasional crack of a tree branch somewhere in the distance. Our boots squeaked and shuffled on the snow as we followed the plow's path into the night.

What I hoped to see when we got to our destination was all of the island's remaining residents sharing tiramisu by the fire. I had my doubts about such a convivial scene. The energy between Sylvie and the others had never been positive, but in recent days it had shifted, the chasm widening. Sylvie's reaction to Rich and Ewan at the airboat, and the perceived need to defend herself with an axe, were undeniable indications of fear. I had yet to see Jane or Miranda offer their condolences, or even a word of comfort. Only Emmeline went out of her way to show Sylvie any kindness – but Miranda was Emmeline's niece, and she'd known the islanders for decades. Her allegiance lay with them.

Through the trees, the cabin emerged like a beacon in the storm. Butter-yellow light poured from its windows, blue chimney smoke perfuming the air with the scent of kiln-dried hardwood and something else, too.

'Is that . . . turkey?' Teddy remarked.

I said, 'Roasted with rosemary, if I had to guess.'

'Wow.' He shook his head in disbelief. 'Hell of a time for Thanksgiving dinner.'

There was a single snowmobile sitting outside the cabin, which I recognized as Ewan's. Since Rich had lent us his three-seater, currently back at Emmeline's, I wondered if he and Jane had been using Emmeline's machine and whether it was now parked at their place. Their cabin was a short distance from the Fowlers', but I couldn't fathom why they'd choose to walk it.

It was Tim who knocked on the door, tossing me a look of deep concern at the lack of movement behind the glass. Through the curtain that covered the window, I could only make out one figure in the living room.

'Oh,' Emmeline said when she opened the door. 'Well. Isn't this a surprise.' Despite the evening's hearty meal and heat from the fire, her complexion was as pale as milk-soaked Wonder Bread. Nearly one o'clock in the morning, and here she was. Wide awake.

'Just doing the rounds to check on everyone.' Tim said it with a jaunty grin. 'Everyone OK in here?'

'Fine, just fine. I was cleaning up. We had our dinner tonight – I wish I could say there were leftovers, but the men make short work of those.'

She spoke without pause, stringing the words together like beads on a cord.

'Where are the men?' I asked over Tim's shoulder.

Her bottom lip drooped. 'We were getting low on firewood.'

'We didn't see them outside,' I said.

'May we come in?' Tim gave the door a nudge, and it swung open in slow motion. Spotless kitchen. Turkey carcass in a roasting pan. A bottle of whisky, the same brand I'd seen being unloaded at the hotel, sat half-empty on the counter.

On the sofa, Imogen Fowler was curled beneath a blanket.

On the craft cart, her house of popsicle sticks shuddered in the breeze from the door.

Where the hell were the others? Rich and Jane, Miranda and Ewan, even Sylvie, weren't where we'd expected them to be. In the Fowlers' cabin, alive with music earlier, only Emmeline and Imogen remained while all the rest had scattered like wild turkeys in the night. Before following the team inside, I took a few steps back toward the road that led to Rich and Jane's, the same route Val and I had taken when we discovered the coywolf eating bloody snow. There were no fresh footsteps that I could see. No recent snowmobile tracks either. But I did see something of note.

My stomach dropped like a stone in the river as I rushed to the opposite side of the house.

The truck. The snow plow that the islanders cherished.

It was gone.

FORTY-TWO

If Emmeline was anything, it was loyal. For a full five minutes she evaded us, scratching at her short white hair as she tilted her head in response to our questions, feigning confusion and innocence. When she tried to convince us she'd fallen asleep and awoken to find the others missing, Tim threw up his hands and said, 'We're wasting time, ma'am. If you don't tell us what you know, we'll just get the snowmobiles and follow their tracks.'

'Please don't do that,' Emmeline said. 'Everyone's fine, I promise you.'

'Even Sylvie?'

The woman's mouth dipped into a frown. 'Sylvie's at her cabin.'

'No,' Tim said briskly. 'She's not. And if I had to guess, that has something to do with your neighbors.'

Emmeline's shoulders slumped. When Imogen stirred at her side, she put a hand on the girl's back to still her.

Without hesitation, I dropped to my knees by the little girl's side. 'Imogen,' I said softly. 'Honey, wake up.'

Emmeline looked stunned. 'What are you doing? You can't—'

'If you won't tell us what's going on,' I said, 'you leave us no choice.'

At length, the child blinked and came around. Five unexpected visitors in bulky winter gear, looming over her like a tactical unit. Her eyes went wide.

'Imogen,' I said again, calling her attention away from my team. 'Remember me? I came to visit you this afternoon. You showed me your toys at the table.'

Slowly, the girl mustered a nod.

'Your mom and dad aren't here right now, and we really need to find them. Can you tell me where they went?'

Imogen glanced at Emmeline, whose eyes seemed to be sinking deeper into their sockets. When the woman opened her mouth to speak, Val put a firm hand on her shoulder.

'Earlier today, you told me they liked to go hunting,' I pressed. 'Is that where they are now?'

Imogen rubbed her small nose. 'They have to get there first.'
'Where?' I asked.
'The axe.'
'The axe?' I looked to the others for help, but even Emmeline seemed baffled. Was Imogen talking about *Sylvie's* axe? I couldn't parse her meaning.

'We can't let the wolfs find the axe,' she said, sitting up a little. 'So Mamma and Daddy are looking extra hard.'

It was the second time Imogen had mentioned wolves that day, but I didn't think she was talking about island wildlife. No, I was quite sure the wolves she was referring to were Sylvie and Cary.

'The axe,' I repeated. 'Where is it?'
'In the barn. They don't know which one. But axe marks the spot.'

I froze. Behind me, my team stood stock-still.
'What are they hunting for, Imogen?'
The girl's eyes sparked and glittered as she purred the word.
'Treasure.'

FORTY-THREE

'The barns. They've been searching the barns on the island,' I said as we all convened outside the cabin. 'Cary and Sylvie. The islanders.'

And I had a good idea of what they were after.

It was Sylvie herself who'd tipped me off to her family's tarnished reputation. Her father had been accused of homicide – but long before that, he'd been born into a legacy of crime. Had Tully Lavoy's unlawful rum-running and ill-gotten gains made it easier for Roscoe to do what he'd done? I'd spent quite a lot of time thinking about Alan Nevil, the Frontenac County Distillery owner shot and killed inside his home.

What I should have been thinking about was old Tully, who'd amassed a fortune smuggling Prohibition liquor.

Money that had never been found.

'The truck gives them a huge advantage,' said Tim. 'No wonder the Fowlers didn't want to let us use it. They can travel all over the island in half the time, and transport the money when they find it.'

'With access to a snowmobile, though,' said Val, 'Sylvie had a head start.'

Emmeline had given us that, at least. After telling her we'd witnessed a stranger lurking outside and instructing her to stay indoors with Imogen, she'd confessed that Sylvie had taken her snowmobile from outside the cabin while the islanders were eating dinner. The fact that Sylvie had walked all the way from her place to snatch the machine out from under her neighbors concerned me. It was an act of desperation. The behavior of a woman who was running out of time.

'We'll split up,' said Tim, our plan to stick together abandoned already. 'Mac, Teddy – the three of us will go back to Emmeline's for the three-seater.'

'Val and I will take Ewan's Ski-Doo,' I said, 'and follow those truck tracks.'

Tim only regarded me for a moment before giving a nod. We didn't understand why this night, of all nights, found Sylvie, the

Fowlers, Rich Samson, and Jane Budd on a frantic hunt for a hidden fortune, but the urgency smacked of danger. If we'd found the truck tracks, so could our unidentified suspect in the snowmobile suit.

'You honestly think there's treasure out there?' said Teddy. 'The kid couldn't be confused or something?'

'Sounds crazy, I know,' I said, 'but it fits. That barn Tim got trapped in had been taken apart from the inside-out. Same goes for the one Val saw on her first visit to the island. There's no question about it. Those properties were searched.'

There was a lot about the situation we still couldn't fathom, but certain facts were slotting into place. Sylvie had inherited the cabin from her father, whose family had owned property on Running Pine for more than a century. Shortly after his death, she and Cary had abandoned their lives on the mainland to move out to the island. That might have seemed suspicious to their loved ones, and even other locals – two young people, opting to hole up in a secluded cabin – but Running Wild gave them an excuse to stay. I wondered if they'd been surprised by its success. If the account's purpose was simply to provide cover while they searched the island for the fortune Tully Lavoy left behind, Sylvie and Cary hadn't needed Running Wild to take off. The fact that it did hadn't stopped them from searching for the real prize.

That told us we were looking at a lot of loot.

'There have to be dozens of barns out there,' said Teddy, waving at the road that disappeared into a stand of tall trees as he huffed white clouds of breath.

'Yes,' I said, 'but I bet Sylvie and Cary already eliminated quite a few. They've been on the island for six months.'

'Do you think Cary found it?' asked Teddy, eyes large.

'I don't know, but we're going to find out. All we have to do now is follow the hunters' tracks.'

We broke off then, Tim, Teddy, and Mac thumping off down the road while Val and I started the snowmobile's engine.

'Ready?' I asked from the driver's seat.

'As I'll ever be,' said Val.

With a twist of the handlebars, we were off.

The wind burned my ears as we rode through the night, following the truck tracks over the snow. The trail took us north, past the waterfront summer homes and deep into the forest. We rode for nearly ten minutes before the tree line started to thin, then stopped completely. Only when the road intersected with a second, narrower one did I realize where the islanders were headed. A few moments later, I skidded to a stop mere feet from the truck that had materialized out of the snowy darkness. It was right next to Emmeline's snowmobile. The storm obscured my view of the field, but I already knew what lay ahead.

'Ewan took me here,' I told Val. 'Earlier today. There's an abandoned barn up on the hill.'

'Were there tracks in the snow?' she asked.

Was that what Ewan had been looking for too? Why he'd brought me out here to this desolate place? I had tried to check for footprints, but the wind had been blowing hard by then. I told Val I couldn't be sure.

'Well,' she replied, 'there are now.'

Multiple tracks, in fact, the prints extending from the road into the field. No sign of Rich and Jane or the Fowlers.

'What do you think?' said Val. 'By the looks of things, they're all in there.'

It was hard to imagine. Between the distance and snow, I saw no flashlight beams flickering through gaps in the old siding – only gusts of blinding white. Tim, Mac, and Teddy would be right behind us, ten minutes away at most. I opened my mouth to tell Val we should wait and approach all together.

I snapped it shut when I heard the scream.

It sounded animal in nature, high and shrill, and the anguish of it lifted the hair on the back of my neck. It could have been a vixen, crying out in the night.

The second sound confirmed the cry belonged to a woman, and that she was in trouble.

'Come on,' I said, setting off through the snow.

Even when sticking to the existing tracks it was slow going, like wading through water in a ballgown. The crisp middle layers of snow snapped and gave way with every step we took, sinking us deeper. Val wore a snowmobile suit, but my coat was down to my knees. It dragged as I walked, sweeping a channel in the powder that continued to fall.

Before long I was out of breath and panting, my forehead slicked with sweat. As we urged our bodies onward, I thought about Cary. Up until that moment, we'd imagined we might be searching for someone far removed from the island. An autonomous force with an axe to grind. A fan, maybe, who didn't want to see Cary succeed. But a fan couldn't know about a lost fortune. Even if he'd been hiding on the island for days, or weeks, following Sylvie and the islanders from one abandoned property to another, he wouldn't have information enough to suspect the real reason Sylvie and Cary came here.

So why were they still on the island? Who had Val seen outside Emmeline's cabin?

The barn stood in front of us now, ugly and menacing. 'Val.' As I looked up at it, I dragged my tongue across chapped lips. My mouth had gone sticky with exertion. 'It's the barn from Cary's post. He took a picture out here.'

Val lifted a gloved finger to her mouth. We could hear voices now. Flashlight beams sparked behind the barn's kindling walls and my skin prickled, at once itchy and tight. I turned to face her, and we both reached for our sidearms. Held them close as we peered through the gaps in the wall.

The scene inside was otherworldly. A large LED lantern illuminated the gaping space and Sylvie stood next to it, Rich close at her side. He had a tight grip on her right arm. She wasn't struggling. Rich's dark eyes shone like the pearls of melted snow caught in his beard. I couldn't see the others where they were across the barn, but I could hear them. Urgent muttering. The squeak and screech of rusted nails pried loose with the claw of a hammer, century-old boards being tossed on a pile nearby. I kept listening for Tim, Mac, and Teddy. Nothing.

'Come on,' I told Val, voice low. With a hand on the wood to steady myself, I moved along the barn wall, peering between crooked boards as I went. Val followed, doing her best to maintain her balance. Leaning into the groaning structure, even just for a moment, could give us away, and we weren't ready for that.

The entrance to the barn was all the way at the other end of the building, but as we rounded the corner, I saw the gap. A tear in the north-facing wall like a gaping wound, the space between the warped boards aglow.

Together we moved closer, and looked inside.

Every farming tool and piece of machinery the barn ever held had long since been stripped away, leaving behind a hollow cavern. There wasn't so much as a ladder to reach the hay loft, the floor of which appeared to have collapsed. The walls and rafters were all the same weathered shade of gray, bleached and beaten by the elements like stones on a far-flung beach. Ewan, Miranda, and Jane were hard at work peeling back floorboards. Exposing the dark, frozen earth underneath.

It was true then. Imogen had been right. There was treasure here, something left behind by Sylvie's relatives. Hidden for decades while the barn made its gradual descent into ruin. I could hardly believe it. Was this really it? The reason for Sylvie and Cary's presence on the island, and the motive for his murder? The explanation for it all?

'Shana.' I followed Val's gaze to where Rich stood. His back was to us now, and there was something dark strapped to him. Days ago, Val had confiscated his shotgun. She and Tim had searched Sylvie's home for a weapon, and found nothing. And yet, another gun had materialized on Rich's body. A rifle like the one we believed had killed Cary.

All I did was shift my weight, but it was movement enough for the snow to creak under my feet. He'd been frozen in place next to Sylvie, watching the others search, but at the sound, Rich turned. Blotchy skin, beard like a snarl of gray wires against his barrel chest. His mouth was a grim line.

Rich's gaze alighted on us, and stayed there.

FORTY-FOUR

'The gun's not mine.' Rich said it in a rush of words, immediately relinquishing the weapon to Val. 'It was here in the barn. I didn't kill Cary, I swear it.'

I'd heard every manner of excuse from criminals caught red-handed. *I found it on the street. I'm holding it for a friend.* Rich's was no more original – but when Sylvie broke away from him, she grabbed my arm.

'He's telling the truth,' she insisted, looking from me to Val and back again. '*I* found the rifle, lying right here on the floor. Rich took it away from me.'

The scream. Rich had disarmed her, likely wrestling the gun from Sylvie's hands. These people were lucky no one had been killed.

The group had been surprised to see us, no question about that. For all they knew we were fast asleep in Emmeline's cabin, oblivious to the frantic late-night search playing out not two miles away. Something had happened between these people tonight, something we didn't fully understand, but one thing was clear: Sylvie and the islanders were afraid. I scanned the space once more, and this time my gaze alighted on a charred patch on the floor. Just like the barn that had swallowed Tim, someone had been hiding here. Someone with the same kind of gun that killed Cary.

'There's someone else out here,' Sylvie confirmed. 'They know what we're looking for. They want it too.'

'Who?' I asked. Who could be left?

Sylvie swallowed once, and said no more.

'She's right,' Ewan told us from where he stood with Miranda and Jane. 'And so were you. The man who killed Cary, he's here, on the island. And we think he's dangerous.'

It was Jane who spoke next. 'Our families used to own this land – neighboring parcels that went from here all the way north and south to the river. It belonged to the Budds and the Plums – my family, Miranda's, and Emmeline's husband's. They gave it to the conservation society a long time ago, in exchange for property down on the water. But before that, my great-grandparents used to live here. On a farm right in this very spot. This barn?' She swept her arm around the vast, tumbledown space. 'It was mine.'

'That money belonged to *my* great-grandfather,' Sylvie said. 'It's my rightful inheritance. If anyone should have it, it's me.'

It made sense to me now, why the islanders felt they had a claim to whatever hid in these walls. At some point since Sylvie and Cary's arrival, most likely in the fall, Jane and the others had clued into what was going on. Somehow, Tully had stashed a fortune in rum-running money behind the walls of an abandoned barn, only to bleed out on a courthouse sidewalk before he could retrieve it. I reached for everything I knew about the Lavoys. It was possible Tully had told his wife about the money before he was killed, and that she'd relayed the story of his wild, cursed life to her children, who passed it along to Roscoe. Legends had a way of surviving time, especially the kind that involved hidden treasure.

If I had to guess, Roscoe had searched himself – until his own brush with the law drove him from the island. Based on Jane's account, there was no love lost between the locals and the Lavoys. But now here was Sylvie, a new generation, trying to find out once and for all how much of what she'd heard about her great-grandfather was true. She'd come up with a perfect excuse for moving back to Running Pine, buying herself an entire year to search for what remained of Tully's riches. And she'd brought her boyfriend along for the ride.

What I still didn't understand was who killed Cary, and who was still roaming the island in the storm.

'We thought we had it figured out,' said Jane.

'It was *Cary* who did that,' spat Sylvie. 'All you did was follow him around like a pack of wolves.'

I surveyed the room once more. Either tonight, in the days prior, or some combination of both, the barn had been taken down to the studs. If something was hiding in here, though, I sure as hell didn't see it.

At the creak of a floorboard, Sylvie swung around. Tim, Mac, and Teddy cast long shadows across the barn floor. The cavalry, arrived at last. But something wasn't right. Sylvie was looking at them like they were demons come to tear her limb from limb.

Like she'd looked at Rich and Ewan by the airboat.

The realization gripped me like a hammy fist as I watched all the color drain from Sylvie's face. It hadn't been Rich and Ewan Sylvie was afraid of that day.

It hadn't been them at all.

He was on Val before she could draw a breath, snatching the rifle and shoving her down. Time seemed to slow as the weapon swung in my direction, stopping only when Steady Teddy, the sweet young man who'd kept us all safe, cocked the rifle with a metallic click.

'*No.*' Tim's voice was a croak. From the corner of my eye, I could see he and Mac had both drawn their sidearms. But already Teddy had me in his sights.

'This wasn't how I planned it,' he said. 'But sometimes you have to improvise. Oh, hey, sis,' Teddy added with a sneer as his gaze flicked to Sylvie.

Next to me, Sylvie Lavoy let out a single, wretched sob.

FORTY-FIVE

We were frozen, all of us unmoving in that frigid barn. Tim and Mac with their sidearms trained on Teddy, and Teddy with the rifle aimed squarely at me. My hands were up, though I wanted nothing more than to cradle my stomach. The pull was agonizing, a magnetic force, but I didn't dare move. With this same rifle, he'd killed Cary Caufield. The cold glint in his eye told me he wouldn't hesitate to fire again.

Teddy. He'd been right in front of us, the trespasser part of our very own team. Sylvie's half-brother from Northern Ontario. A tour guide, Tim had told me on the day Cary disappeared. A wilderness expert, if I had to guess. Neither Tim nor Val had mentioned Roscoe's son's name, but if they had, I wouldn't have given it a second thought. No doubt Steady Teddy used his mother's last name, which he kept under wraps by adopting a cutesy nickname – and what possible cause could we have for suspecting a half-brother of murdering Sylvie's boyfriend when we hadn't known the real reason for Sylvie and Cary's move to Running Pine? Northern Ontario abutted Hudson Bay. Lots of water in those parts. Teddy's skill at driving a boat had come in handy when he'd decided to go treasure hunting on the St Lawrence. He was well-acquainted with outdoor survival. Far more than Sylvie or Cary had ever been.

Across the barn, huddled like a litter of coywolf pups, the islanders looked stunned. Not Sylvie, though. She'd known. At some point, she'd realized Teddy was in the area, and that he might be responsible for Cary's violent death. It was possible she'd only seen him once before, when he took us to the mainland after we'd confirmed Cary was murdered, but even then, she'd said nothing. And Teddy had continued to help with the search, masquerading as a concerned rescue worker. Pretending to be one of us, even as he hunted for the fortune he felt he was entitled to.

It was why he'd come. Roscoe Lavoy had two children. He'd been closest with Sylvie, whom he'd raised after her mother passed away. Sylvie had lived near her father her whole life, first in Cape Vincent and, later, in Kingston. She'd stayed with him throughout his illness. Teddy was the result of a romance, an on-again, off-again relationship that had produced a child. But Teddy was still a Lavoy, and the Lavoys were sitting on a hidden fortune.

'Put it down,' Tim said, his voice like flint. 'Teddy, *now*.'

The man only smiled.

'Please, Ted,' begged Sylvie.

'Sorry,' he replied, 'but she's collateral until I get what I came for.'

Sylvie's face hardened then. 'Haven't you taken enough? I loved Cary, and you killed him. You killed him!'

Teddy flinched, but simply said, 'I gave him a chance. All he had to do was tell me what he knew. I've been watching you, following that stupid Instagram account since the day you got here. I knew you had to be close. I was right.'

Rich sucked in a breath. 'You know where the money is?'

Teddy said, 'Cary sure did. Didn't he, Sylvie?'

Sylvie's lips trembled as she spoke, and a tear slipped down her wind-chapped cheek. 'We used to always go together,' she said, 'but then Cary started searching on his own. He was obsessed with finding it, even more than me. That picture he posted . . . I think he wanted to surprise me.'

Cary's wide, toothy grin. The champagne in his hand. The photo I'd seen on Instagram had been a celebration post. Taken outside this very barn.

'He knew I'd see it when I woke up. He had already left for the bay. We'd been fighting a little.' She made a move to swat the tear from her face, thought better of it, and showed Teddy her palms again. 'I was . . . frustrated. I wanted to start selling some of the gifts we got from brands, in case it all went sideways and we ended up with nothing. We'd been searching for months. We were running out of time.'

I didn't need Sylvie to tell me Cary's field watch was among the items she planned to sell. The woman had a contingency plan. After Cary was killed, and she'd learned Teddy was after the money too, she knew the odds of getting it were slimmer than ever.

'When he didn't come home that day,' Sylvie went on, 'I was afraid there'd been an accident on the ice, or that he went back to the barn and got lost or trapped or something. I didn't know where to look and I couldn't tell anyone, because they might find what Cary did and take it for themselves.'

'You told us you suspected he was suicidal.' I didn't move my body as I spoke, keeping my full attention on Teddy and his rifle.

'I had to so you would look all over the island, and not just on the ice. I thought I could convince you.' She was talking directly to me now. 'That maybe you'd feel bad for me, because you've been through so much too.'

It had been a calculated plan, devised to get me to the island and manipulate my emotions. And the entire time my team was out searching for Cary, Sylvie and the others had been looking for something else.

'When did you know?' I asked the islanders. 'About Tully Lavoy's hidden fortune?' I kept a close eye on Teddy as I spoke. He was twitchy, an invisible thread tugging at the skin above his left eye, but talk of the money had preoccupied him. As long as he was listening, he wasn't shooting.

It was Jane who replied. 'Everyone knows the stories. There was never any cash found in the raid on his operation. We used to look for it as kids, digging all over for buried treasure.'

I could picture it: Jane and Miranda, friends since birth, borrowing rusted spades from their parents' tool sheds and playing at being marauders.

'Most islanders thought that his wife – Sylvie's great-grandmother – hid the money in Kingston,' said Miranda, her eyes still on Teddy. 'We didn't really believe it was here. Not until Sylvie moved into the cabin.'

'It was at Supper Club where we found out,' said Rich. 'Cary had too much to drink. He told Imogen he was a pirate looking for a chest of gold.'

X marks the spot.

'They stayed away from us after that,' said Ewan. 'Kept to themselves. Stopped giving us gifts. That was how we knew it was true. And then we started looking too.'

'For *my* family's fortune,' Teddy spat. 'I should kill every one of you right now.'

'Then you'll never find it,' said Sylvie. 'I know Cary. If anyone can figure out where he hid it, it's me.'

With a smug twist of his mouth, Teddy said, 'Who's to say I don't already know?'

I could feel Tim's eyes on me, alarm radiating from him in waves, but I suspected that Teddy was bluffing. *Until I get what I came for*, he'd said. If Teddy had Tully's riches, or even a sense of where they were, he wouldn't be here, waiting for Sylvie and the islanders to clue him in. But he was here. Cary had refused to tell him anything, which meant Teddy was back to following the others. But he couldn't leave Cary alive to tip them off about the rogue huntsman.

If that was all true, though, there was only one reason for him to be here now.

To make sure none of us survived the night.

Tim said, 'Teddy, listen to me. Do you know what happens when you kill a cop? It's a capital felony. Look around. There's no way out of this for you.'

'It's you who should look around,' Teddy said, finger twitching on the trigger as he nodded at the snow-silent island. 'No one's coming to arrest me. Not now, not ever.'

'Ted.' Tears coursed down Sylvie's face. 'Please. She's *pregnant.*'

A wave of nausea rolled over me, and I swayed where I stood. All at once my knees felt weak, my face unbearably hot. Tim and Sylvie's voices were both far away and impossibly close, like I was inside Oscar's anechoic chamber. Smothered by the sounds of my own bone-deep fear.

There was another sound, though, on the outskirts of my consciousness. A noise both familiar and hard to comprehend. It was quickly growing louder.

The others heard it too.

'What the fu—'

Teddy swiveled his head to look behind him.

In an explosion of noise, the corner of the barn buckled, its rickety walls folding in on themselves like a house of cards. It was the opening Tim and Mac needed – but it was Rich who got there first, tackling Teddy and pinning him to the ground. Behind them, in the driver's seat of the truck she'd plowed straight through a field of snow, I could see Emmeline. I couldn't hear her, but the shape of her mouth was unmistakable, the word she'd uttered impossible to miss.

It was the same word I spoke to kids at the school while teaching them karate, the advice I always gave them.

Run.

The groan that the barn released into the night sent a bolt of terror straight through me. All around us, boards popped and cracked.

Already the islanders were running for the gap in the wall, Jane and Miranda clasping hands while Ewan yanked Rich off Teddy and pulled him to safety. Val was screaming something I couldn't understand, towing Mac toward the exit too, but Teddy was free now. On his knees. Reaching for the rifle. Tim shouted at him to stay down as Teddy's fingers found the pistol grip. Tim's eyes met mine then, desperate and alive, and I knew. He wanted me out. We had seconds, maybe less. He couldn't let Teddy get that gun.

More boards snapped and split above my head, the racket like gunfire. I had almost forgotten about Sylvie until her nails dug into my arm. 'Go,' she gasped, and then she was airborne, her small body flying as if from a springboard as she lunged. She collided with Teddy at the same moment that I felt myself flying too. The same moment that the roof finally let go.

The last thing I saw was the barn crashing down in a crush of wreckage and dust. But it wasn't a torrent of splintered wood I felt on my face.

It was snow.

FORTY-SIX

New York City

Four Years Ago

It was Friday, not yet late but dark-skyed from the impending rain that threatened to fall on Tompkins Square Park. The park wasn't quiet, far from it; women in work clothes and sneakers, joggers, and dog-walkers all hustled to get indoors. I felt a sense of urgency too, an electric zap that made my feet move faster, though unlike them, I wasn't headed for home.

Jane Doe was no longer my principal case. I'd been working a hit-and-run when, out of nowhere, De La Cruz told me about Blake Bram. The series of murders tied to a dating app, and a man whose profile claimed he was from tiny Swanton, Vermont. My hometown of not quite six-and-a-half thousand.

That Friday night, my destination was the construction site where Bram had dumped Jess Lowenthal's body. She'd been found draped over a pile of gravel with bits of rock glittering in her hair. Jess had been stabbed like the others: Becca Wolkwitz, and Lanie Miner. The connection was obvious: all three victims had found Bram on the same dating app – or, more likely, Bram had found them. Apart from understanding how he'd managed to transport his victims to their final resting place, something I suspected I'd never know, my team and I had a good handle on the *how* of the crime.

It was the *who* and *why* that plagued me now. All my time spent with Adam had made me realize that Bram, whoever he was, might have sought attention. Adam maintained some killers wanted to be caught out, knew what they were doing was wrong and felt that deeply, but couldn't trust themselves to keep their violent tendencies in check. I wondered if that described Blake Bram, and whether his tie to Swanton was genuine.

It could have been a lie. Everything else about his dating profile was likely fabricated, from eye and hair color to interests and line of work. According to the app administrators, he'd updated his data multiple times, most likely in an effort to lure the right type of target. But no matter what he listed as his favorite movie or book, one detail stayed the same: Bram said he was from Swanton. A town that meant nothing to anyone in Manhattan but me.

As I followed the cracked asphalt path past mature trees whose canopies made the evening feel even darker, it struck me that there was another explanation. A reason why Bram had included a detail that might expose his identity to the police. I was the only detective in my precinct, my name and face on our website. Bram's latest victim had been found in my jurisdiction.

That night, as I spotted a pub called O'Dwyer's and gave myself permission to get off my feet and have a pint, I wondered if Adam had been wrong about Bram. Maybe he wasn't looking to get caught.

Maybe he was looking for me.

FORTY-SEVEN

March brought another dump of snow so heavy and dense that, for the first time ever, Tim sprung for a plow service. I'd watched the truck from the living room window, and though there was a man behind the wheel, it was Emmeline Plum I saw there. Slicing through the barn like a knife in pound cake. Come to save us all.

It was nearly twenty-four more hours before we got back to the mainland, most of which I spent in her cabin. Mac explained what had happened after my cheek hit the snow and the smell of old wood filled my nostrils. None of us would ever know what Sylvie was thinking when she dove at her brother, giving me and Tim a chance to escape before the roof twisted and the barn came down. I suspected, though, that she was thinking of Cary. Teddy had already taken one life. Sylvie wasn't going to let him take ours too.

In the end, she sacrificed both herself and her half-brother to the barnwood and snow, the last of the Lavoys ending their lives in the place where their family's black legacy started: on Running Pine Island.

'Hell of a story,' Dave Johansson said from across my dining room table. I still couldn't believe he was right in front of me. It had been his idea to drive up for the weekend, one he'd floated after I replied to his email with an update on my current case. 'I wasn't there for you the last time you almost bought the farm,' he said, causing my eyes to prickle even as I smiled. 'I'm not making that mistake again.' Dave was staying with us through Sunday, and along with Mac, we were kicking off his weekend in the Thousand Islands with an activity tailor-made for the season: takeout Caesar salads topped with fried calamari, eaten hearthside. There was Dori and Courtney's onion dip, too, a vat of which currently sat in our fridge. I suspected they'd be spoiling us for a long time.

'Bowl of ice?' Tim offered when he got up to fetch Dave another beer. At my feet, Bash stirred and lifted his head. A sign, no doubt, that we'd been giving our adopted pet too many treats. I stroked his muzzle as I shook my head.

'That craving has sailed,' I said. 'I'm pretty sure I've had enough ice to last me a lifetime.'

We knew more now about the crimes on Running Pine, but there were some things we'd never understand. A nurse at the cancer center in Kingston told us she'd overheard several odd conversations between Roscoe Lavoy and his daughter – including one in which he broke down and confessed to killing Alan Nevil. He'd told Sylvie about Tully, too. The treasure chest just waiting to be found. Roscoe blamed his own immorality for his failure to recover it. Bad karma for killing an innocent man. But he insisted that Sylvie stood a chance, and told her to search the farms. Knowing, perhaps, that Tully would have used an unsuspecting islander to his advantage.

That was how Sylvie and Cary's adventure on Running Pine began.

Over dinner, we explained to Dave that the islanders were none the wiser until Sylvie and Cary's third Supper Club. They'd become friends by then, the couple going out of their way to give them gifts and ingratiate themselves with the community. They couldn't allow the islanders to get suspicious. Prior to that night, they'd done a good job. But then Cary had too much whisky, and struck up a conversation with young Imogen. Talk of treasure-hunting is something kids aren't likely to forget.

The islanders noticed a change after that. The couple started to keep their distance. The gift-giving dried up. Sylvie and Cary turned down every invitation – right up until Rich and Ewan suggested ice fishing. That had been Jane's idea. She wanted the men to mine for more information. For his part, Cary still needed content to distract the outside world from the couple's true purpose.

Fresh off his victory that morning, no doubt devising a plan for how and when he and Sylvie could collect what he'd found, Cary had been guarded but chatty. By the time Rich and Ewan packed up and went home, they were certain their theory about Tully's hidden cash was sound. It wasn't until Cary disappeared and Jane rode out to the State Police barracks for help that the islanders saw his Instagram post.

'They thought it was over,' I told Dave. 'Figured Cary had found the fortune, only to suffer an ill-timed accident on the ice. But when Sylvie was reluctant to leave Running Pine, and came back to the island quick as she could, they started to wonder if they still stood a chance.'

What no one knew, apart from that observant hospital nurse, was that while Roscoe was dying, he'd called up Teddy, and made the same confession to his son. Teddy hadn't taken offense when Roscoe left Sylvie his cabin – what did Teddy want with a thousand-square-foot shack in the woods? – but the cash the feds had never managed to seize during that Prohibition raid was something altogether different. Teddy moved to Clayton, and started plotting a way to search the island. Taking a job with the fire department gave him access to a boat, and he spent as much time as he could crossing the river to Running Pine. With his mother's surname, Teddy didn't need to worry about being recognized as a Lavoy. When he realized that Sylvie and Cary were already on the island, he knew why. And Teddy had no interest in sharing his family's fortune with Sylvie's boyfriend, or anyone else.

For days at a time, he'd squatted in old barns all over the island waiting for Cary and Sylvie to do the legwork so he could make his move. By the morning of the fishing excursion, he was back on the mainland. It was Cary's Instagram post that made Teddy decide to confront him.

'We had a witness who saw a man crossing the ice. We thought it was our killer,' I said, 'but Rich admitted it was him. He'd gone to get the mail on foot since all the snowmobiles were in use, and picked up some whisky for the party in the process. He took the most direct route to the hotel.'

'Meanwhile,' said Mac, 'back at the bay, Teddy was with Cary on the ice.'

'We don't think Sylvie knew Teddy was here until she saw him at the airboat,' Tim added. 'She would have been searching for the barn from Cary's post by then. Hoping to get there before someone else did.'

It had been right in front of us, in the post Cary put up the day of his death. A smile like a cloudless sickle moon, the champagne already flowing. By the time Sylvie saw it, and realized Cary had found the right barn, he was already dead.

By then, Teddy had seen it too.

'So this stupid cow knew her brother killed Cary,' Dave said, 'and she didn't tell you?'

I flinched. Dave's words had landed like a slap, and I sensed both Tim and Mac stiffen. The lack of respect in Dave's tone rankled me. Had he always been this crude?

'We believe she suspected it,' I said, thinking it best to ignore the comment. Dave was our guest, after all. 'But tipping us off to what was going on wasn't an option. If Sylvie told us the truth about the situation, she'd never get a chance to retrieve the money.'

'You're killing me here.' Dave paused to toss back the dregs of his fourth beer, and reached for the fresh bottle Tim had delivered. 'Yeah, they all wanted the gangster's fortune. Yeah, Sylvie and Teddy died without ever getting their hands on the loot. So where the fuck is it?'

'That's what we'd like to know.' Tim's mouth was arranged in a polite smile, but I saw through it. Tim didn't like Dave – and it was only Friday. He said, 'Cary took that secret to his grave.'

'So what now?' said Mac, looking from Dave to me.

'What now? Well,' I said, 'I guess I stoke the fire and we get out a deck of cards. Anyone for a game of Gin rummy?'

Mac laughed and shook her feathery blonde head. 'I was talking about your cold case.'

'Ah.' I turned back to Dave. 'I was thinking of calling the sister down in Georgia, but now I'm wondering if it's better to wait for the DNA results.'

'DNA results?' The corners of Dave's mouth dipped downward.

I was pretty sure I'd mentioned the hunt for Bram's other victims when Dave and I reconnected a few weeks ago, but now I said, 'The FBI's been working to match Bram to unsolved homicides in and around Manhattan. Now that we have evidence of a link between Cleo and Bram, we can have DNA forensics confirm it.'

Dave swiveled his beer bottle on the table, twisting it back and forth. 'That's not gonna be easy. With Bram dead, why would anyone want to waste resources confirming what we already know?'

'It isn't a waste of resources. We need to know beyond a doubt that he killed her.'

'We *do*. The dating app is the link. Look, it's not my place to say it, but it might be time to move on from this. Focus on your life, and that kid on the way. For your own mental health, Shana, I think it's time to let it go.'

Let it go. Like the woman's murder was a distasteful jab or inappropriate comment I should let roll off my back. Next to Dave, Mac's jaw had hardened. I could sense the tension in Tim's shoulders too. Dave wore a lazy smile, pity writ large on his face. I felt belittled, but more than that, I was pissed. If he thought I was backing down now, when we were so close to closing this case, he was out of his mind.

Dave's behavior puzzled me. He had seemed optimistic when I broached the idea of reopening the case, but recalling moments from our original investigation had made me realize just how strange that was. He hadn't had high hopes for Jane Doe's plight four years ago. In fact, it seemed like he'd been convinced of our defeat all along.

'It's crazy that we even got to this point,' I said now, forcing a smile. 'The first time around, there were obstacles at every turn.'

'Some cases are like that,' said Dave with a shrug. 'Sometimes it feels like you're cursed.'

I nodded. Flashed him another smile. Dave was wrong, though. It hadn't felt like we were cursed.

The obstacles we'd faced felt more like sabotage.

With a spark of clarity, I saw Teddy standing in the barn sneering at his half-sister. The image reignited a fuse that had long since grown cold. In the case of Cary Caufield's homicide, we'd been duped, the killer shoulder to shoulder with us every boot stomp of the way. Teddy was a member of the Clayton Fire Company, and a participant in the search and rescue effort. *One of us.* So, we'd conducted our investigation like we always did, never realizing the man had distracted us with carefully planted nuggets of truth. Never once thinking to look for signs of deception. He'd leveraged our implicit trust to his cruel advantage. Played the part of the good guy until the bloody end.

In New York, Dave and I had failed to identify Jane Doe. We'd missed our chance to disseminate her image to the press. The Facebook page I wanted to create had gone nowhere. The same was true of the promising lead linked to her t-shirt. In the meantime, my relationship with Dave had soured – but not because the case proved exceedingly difficult. It was Adam Starkweather who'd come between us. A man Dave hardly even knew.

Bile, sour and fizzy, inched its way up my throat.

'You don't look so good,' Mac said from across the table.

Slowly, I got to my feet.

'God, when am I gonna learn that I need to avoid rich food?' I laughed lightly as I said it, not meeting Dave's curious gaze. 'That fried squid did me in. Back in a few.'

With a squeeze of Tim's arm, I retreated to the staircase.

When we first moved into our old house on the water, Tim and I had used the small room closest to the stairs as a study. We'd been told by the realtor it was made to be a nursery, and now the space – connected to our master bedroom – had been returned to its original form. We were going for a woodland theme: creamy white walls with forest-green accents, little pine trees on the bedding. I hadn't gotten to the point where I could picture the child who'd sleep beneath our mobile of falling leaves – even now, the pregnancy felt surreal – but I liked to sit in the plush glider and try.

Now, I closed the door behind me and remained standing as I slipped my iPhone from the pocket of my hoodie.

Sergeant Mateo De La Cruz and I talked often during the upstate manhunt for Blake Bram. The task force had been led by the FBI, but they'd collaborated with both the Seventh and Ninth Precincts, and that included my old supervisor with the NYPD.

'Mateo,' I said when he answered the phone. 'I need you to tell me I'm crazy.'

'Wouldn't be the first time,' he replied with a laugh.

'Cleo Salazar.' My tone smothered his good humor like a fire blanket. 'There's no doubt about it? She used the same dating app as Blake Bram?'

'Back up,' he said. 'Who used what now?'

'*Cleo Salazar*. That unsolved Jane Doe case Dave Johansson and I worked before my abduction? The fact that they're connected is a lot to process. I'm not saying I doubt what Dave said is true. I just need to hear it from you.'

Silence on the line. At length, De La Cruz said, 'I'm sorry, but you lost me, Shana. That case has been stone cold for years.'

'I know,' I said. 'Which is why I asked Dave to reopen it. I suspected there might be a link to Bram.' Why didn't De La Cruz know all of this? Dave was with the borough homicide squad, but Cleo's body had been found in the Ninth. My former supervisor had to know Dave was working the case again.

'Shana.' Two syllables, like he was learning to speak my name for the first time. Like he thought I might be crazy after all. 'Nobody reopened that case. Dave Johansson hasn't worked for the NYPD in years. Not since you moved up north.'

A chill slid down my back like an icicle tracing my spine.

On the wall above the crib, Tim and I had hung a row of prints. Watercolors of baby animals to go with our theme. The fawn's eyes were closed where it lay curled on a forest floor. The owl and bunny, too. But the wolf cub was awake, its eyes gleaming slits and its mouth open in a howl.

'Why did he leave?' It was all I could do to keep my voice steady. *Please let me be wrong about this. Please.*

De La Cruz said, 'Fucker got canned. Sexual misconduct. He was accused of stalking and sexually harassing the daughter of a homicide victim, if you can believe that shit. Other women came forward after that. I'm surprised you didn't know.'

Though he couldn't see me, I shook my head.

No.

I had no idea.

I'd moved away, eager to leave the city in my rearview. Ready to start fresh in a place where no one but my fiancé knew what I'd been through. Days ago, when I made the decision to revisit Jane Doe, Dave had been my first stop. I hadn't thought to Google him. Why would I, when I could ask him about his life directly? I'd been sympathetic when he explained about his divorce, not prying into the circumstances around the separation. And when Dave told me what I wanted to hear – that he'd help me with Jane – I'd believed him.

I proposed that we meet at the precinct, only agreeing to Dave's suggestion that we grab lunch at the Jamaican place to be polite. With me way up north, busy with Cary's case, Dave had handled everything – including contacting the dating app. Four years ago, Dave had taken the lead too, volunteering to get Jane Doe's image in the news, put in for a reward, set up a Facebook page, none of which had panned out. And the day we'd visited the bar to interview the manager – a witness to Jane Doe's date, a valuable person of interest – Dave had stayed outside.

After the abduction, when I found out it was Dave who convinced my team I was in trouble, I'd felt so indebted to him for his help. How had he known enough about my daily activities to notice I wasn't around? This man, who'd long since moved on to a case with another detective? Whom I hadn't spoken with in weeks?

Downstairs, in my living room with my husband and best friend, sat a person I thought I could trust. A man I'd worked closely with numerous times, who I thought did his job for the same reason as me: to help people in need. People like Cleo. And he'd been lying to me. There was no woman matching Jane Doe's description linked to Bram on the dating app. All of my searching had been for nothing. Her killer was right beside me all along.

'Mateo,' I said firmly, stepping to the nursery window. It overlooked the driveway. Dave's car was still outside. 'I need you to call the State Police barracks in Alexandria Bay. Dave Johansson is here and—'

I caught his reflection in the glass a moment too late. The hand that clamped down on my mouth was clammy, and smelled as rancid as a basement prison cell.

'You should have left it alone.' Dave hissed it, his yeasty breath hot against my ear. 'But you didn't, so here's what's going to happen. Either you go downstairs and act like things are fine while I make up an excuse to leave this Podunk fucking town right now, or I stage a violent home invasion that costs all three of you – I'm sorry, *four* – your sorry little lives.'

As he held his cheek to mine, his groin pressed hard against me, he said, 'It's a real shame. I used to like you, Merchant. Scars and all.'

Dave had underestimated me from the start. Poor country-mouse Shana, imagining the brutal murder of a woman she'd never met could have something to do with her, simply because we'd both felt pain at the hands of a man. Believing I could hold my own against a veteran detective like Dave, who'd maneuvered himself into a place where he could keep tabs on the case and control the investigation. He must have thought he won the lottery when he found out he'd be working with me.

But Dave Johansson didn't know me at all.

His left arm was wrapped around my swollen breasts, his right pinning my head against his cocked neck, but my own arms remained free. It was a common hold, and one I knew well. Three weeks ago, I'd taught Bobby Ott and her classmates how to escape it. *Sink your weight. Hook a leg behind his. Scoop up both his knees.*

Take him down.

Dave hit the floor with a grunt and a ground-shaking thump that I knew would send Tim and Mac running. By the time they arrived in the doorway, I had Dave pinned on his stomach with a knee jabbed in the small of his back.

'Get some troopers over here, will you?' I wheezed as I dug the sharp bone of my elbow deep into his spine. 'We've got a homicide suspect who needs detaining.'

FORTY-EIGHT

Now

Spring arrives like soft mist over water, vegetal and dewdrop-cool. Getting around isn't as easy as it once was, but I'm told movement is good for me. Tim has a hard time with that idea, oscillating between wanting to settle me on the couch and walk me in circles to induce labor. I'm a few days overdue now, which I'm told is normal, but I sense this baby is nearly ready to make its grand entrance.

I know I am.

I'd spent all of breakfast convincing Tim we needed baby books, the child-sized ones with thick, stiff pages that Henrietta used to like. It was in talking with Hen that I discovered she'd been reading them to Hudson. Though he was barely three months old, my nephew loved listening to his big sister's voice, an image that warmed every part of me. Hen would visit – the whole family would – once our own baby arrived, and I wanted to give Hudson a new book when she did. Maybe pick some up for our kiddo at the same time.

Kath knows me as a regular now. In recent months, I've made a point of disconnecting from work, largely by rekindling my love of reading. Thrillers have always been my poison of choice, though I've been known to indulge in nonfiction too. I'm currently working my way through every title on Kath's local author shelf, and she mentioned she was expecting a new release. A saga of the area's shipwrecks, maybe, or the true story of Thousand Island dressing.

When Tim pulls the SUV parallel with the sidewalk and shifts into park, I can see Kath in the window, helping a customer.

'Want me to go?' Tim asks me.

'Nah, I've got it. Back in two.' I bring his fingers to my lips, and heave myself out of the car.

In the shop, I pick out three board books, all with a mix of the textured surfaces babies are supposed to enjoy. Kath has a bag ready for me, the new book about river life nestled inside. I give her a quick hug after I pay, and head back out into the fresh green afternoon.

I suppose situational awareness is a skill I'll never lose, even in a little village by the water. On my way back to the car, I scan the area around me. The pretty street stretching in either direction, and the quaint shops that line it. The river laid out before me. A few people mull around Clayton's municipal dock.

Rich Samson and Jane Budd are among them.

They're loading bags of supplies into a boat. I'd always pictured Rich owning a skiff, something battered and unadorned to get him back and forth to the post office, just two blocks from where I stand. The boat I see now is a twenty-foot Yamaha with a hard-top cabin, and even from a distance, I can tell it's brand new.

We haven't found Tully Lavoy's fortune, though not for lack of trying. When at last the snow started to melt, Tim assembled a team to search every abandoned barn on the island. The old farmhouses, too. He's been in touch with the Ontario Provincial Police, and has agreed to hand over whatever he finds. Tully Lavoy was Canadian, his criminal activity well-documented by the OPP, which conducted the initial raid on his operation. Neither Tim nor I know what will happen if the money is ever recovered.

Something has always bothered me about that photo of Cary in front of the barn, uploaded to Instagram for all the world – including the islanders – to see. By the time he shared it online, he and Sylvie knew the others were looking for the money too. If Cary really found it, if his shiny smile and champagne toast were sincere, he would still need to transport the cash, first to the cabin and then, eventually, back to the mainland. So why tip the islanders off and risk an interception? Tim and his team took the barn from that photo apart, and never found a thing, which makes us think it was a smoke screen. An image intended for a specific audience that Cary needed to divert. In other words, maybe Cary flaunted his success in an effort to lead the islanders astray, while the fortune stayed safely where he left it.

In Jane's book on Prohibition, which I read in double-time, she talks about underground hideouts for concealing booze. Tully Lavoy's operation was underground too, Sol and I learned, beneath the farmhouse the locals burned down. Now, I remember the field watch, the one Sylvie assumed Cary wore on the day of his murder. Sylvie wanted it back to sell in case she struck out with the money, but Tim had found it hanging in the old Lavoy barn. As I picture the barn, I have to wonder if Cary hung the watch on that nail himself.

Keeping it safe while he pried open a near-invisible door in the floor.

Rich Samson has started the engine and is navigating away from the dock, which gives me a clear view of the boat's name. A smile tugs at the corner of my mouth as I get back in the car, where Tim's watching the couple head into the channel.

'Brand new, those things can run close to forty thousand.'

'Huh. See the name?' I ask.

'Sure do. *The Sylvie.*'

For a moment, we're both quiet.

'Hey,' I say after a beat. 'Kath mentioned last week that her daughter's about to graduate from college. She's studying Early Childhood Education.'

'Oh yeah?'

'Yep. She's looking to do some nannying in the fall. Just part-time.'

'Interesting.' Tim's lips twitch. 'You know, a little help could be good for us. Might give you a chance to revisit some of the activities you've always loved.'

He isn't talking about reading.

I tilt my head at him and smile.

There are secrets here, along the river, some of which I know I'll never uncover or understand. Some that might even breed violence. Don't we all have secrets, though? Histories we'd prefer to keep hidden? Despite my best efforts to conceal mine, they're out now. Part of this place. The people I care about accept them, and me.

Things feel different now, Bram's legacy fading like a bruise. The memory of the trauma that caused it may always linger, but every day brings a little less pain. It's easier to focus on the good things now. And I have plenty of those.

In the car, Tim presses his lips to my scar, holding them there until his warmth spreads across my cheek like a North Country sunrise.

'Home?' he asks, turning the key.

'Home,' I reply, patting my belly as I reach for his hand.

ACKNOWLEDGEMENTS

I didn't set out to write a series when, all those years ago, I dreamed up Senior Investigator Shana Merchant. But Shana had other ideas, and I'm so glad she did. Whether this novel represents your first meeting, or you've been following Shana from the start, thank you for choosing to spend a few hours with us in the Thousand Islands.

I am doubly lucky to work with both an outstanding literary agent and a top-notch publishing team. Endless thanks to Chris Bucci at Aevitas Creative Management and to Severn House's Rachel Slatter, Tina Pietron, Martin Brown, Piers Tilbury, Vic Britton, Eleanor Smith, Shayna Holmes, and Joanne Grant. It's a privilege and an honor to work with every one of you.

This book would not exist without Dr. Dick Withington – surgeon, firefighter, and EMT first responder – whose captivating stories about overwintering and river rescues were an endless source of inspiration. Thank you also to Susan Smith and TI Life Magazine (tilife.org), Litz Brown, Jason Allison, former Jefferson County Sheriff Colleen O'Neill, and Jessica Burnie.

The name Jane Budd was the result of the wonderful Eastford Public Library's fundraising auction to name a character in the book. Thank you to Seth Budd, who used the auction to honor his late grandmother, for his generous bid. My gratitude goes out to every library and bookstore that has invited me through their doors, especially the Darien Library, Barrett Bookstore, and The Little Book Store, which inspired the book shop in this story (thanks for everything, Rebecca!). To the bookstagrammers, you add so much joy to the publishing experience. Thank you all.

There's no way to describe the impact that author friends and the mystery and thriller writing community have had on my life. I'm grateful beyond measure to all those who have shared their kindness, enthusiasm, and support, with special thanks to Julia Bartz, Lynne Constantine, Julia Spencer-Fleming, Danielle Girard, Elise Hart Kipness, Vanessa Lillie, Hannah Morrissey, Samantha Skal, Sarah Stewart Taylor, Wendy Walker, Susan Walter, and Greg Wands.

To friends near and far, including the members of the original Supper Club (break out the turkey, Brian, Catherine, Nan, Rob, Jason, and Elsa!), thank you for the many years of encouragement.

As always, I owe the privilege of this author life to my wonderful family: Karl and Leila (my first reader and ice fishing expert, respectively), Karel and Sab, John and Carol, Ethan and Michelle, and my beloved Grant, Remi, and Schafer (Otto too). My love for you is deeper than a river.